C000133798

SUSPEC

Gary Comenas

Jackleton Press, London, 2022

Contents

1. Monday

Blake Webster wished he hadn't done that line of coke before his first day of cop school. He felt great initially, but the drug quickly wore off, leaving him tired and irritable. His black wavy hair was now damp with sweat and clung to his head like melted plastic. His normally bright blue eyes were now dull blue and bored. He wondered if he had made a mistake. All the other rookies in the class looked so normal – like the All-American kids he had avoided in high school.

For most of the recruits it was the first time they had been away from home – the beginning of their adult lives. But Blake had already been to New York the previous year, had already done all the clubs and drugs that his classmates would probably end up doing as part of their apprenticeship to that city. They were about to have the best time of their lives in the most exciting city in the world until it became the worst time of their lives in a living nightmare. Some of them would come out the other side while others would be swallowed up into an abyss of unrelenting fun as the line between cop and criminal became so blurred that there was no reason not to cross it.

He wished he hadn't left the wrap of "Charlie" in his room at The Broadway. There was still enough left for a couple of lines, and it would have helped him get through what looked like was going to be a very boring day. He stared at the teacher, Lieutenant Layton, droning on in front of the class, without taking in much of what he was saying. He wondered why the lieutenant was wearing military fatigues and an NYPD t-shirt which had probably fit once, but now looked uncomfortably tight. Blake and the rest of the students were wearing suits. After all, the class was being held in the force's headquarters in mid-Manhattan, not some African desert, and it was mid-

January, not the middle of summer. Although the heating was on in the training room, Blake still felt chilly and wondered why the lieutenant didn't. Maybe Blake had gotten too used to the climate in the Canary Islands. He had just returned yesterday and the mild winter that New York was having that year seemed freezing to him.

"ESCAPE!" Lieutenant Layton yelled suddenly, as if the rookies were escaping from a rampaging army when all they were really doing was pressing a key on their laptops to go to the next screen on their displays. The software they were using consisted mostly of interactive maps of Manhattan showing the unnamed alleyways that were popular with small-time criminals operating on the fringes of society - mostly thieves selling stolen goods, junkies shooting up dope and prostitutes past their sell-by date servicing low-level businessmen who couldn't afford anything classier. The maps still had last year's date on them – 2019. He wondered if Layton even realised that 2020 had begun. He seemed spaced out, but aggressive, like he was playing a role in an action film.

Blake's mind drifted as Layton's voice droned on and on. He couldn't stop thinking about last year, about Phil and Slick and Blunt. He had been a model, signed to the Slick agency, and hung out where the other models hung out – a club called Blunt. That's where he had met Phil, a dealer who became his best friend until he was killed by a cop.

"ESCAPE!" Layton shouted again as the rookies progressed to the next screen of hidden alleyways. This time they had to deal with "real" criminals in the form of avatars and answer multiple choice questions like, "A woman has reported the theft of a mobile phone on a nearby busy street to a patrol officer. Soon afterwards, a young black man, who fits the description she gave the officer, is seen in the alley exchanging a phone for a pair of new sneakers, still in their box, from another man.

Should you a) pull your gun and shout 'freeze!', b) approach in a friendly manner and engage the men in casual conversation to instil their trust, or c) stay hidden by the alley entrance and call for back-up." Most of the class answered "b," some "c." The correct response was "a." Blake heard one of the students say "wow" when the answer was revealed.

'What a stupid exercise,' Blake thought. The class was beginning to seem more like a training session for gamers than for cops. There was no way that he would pull a gun on somebody trading a phone for a pair of sneakers. What was the world coming to?

Blake comforted himself with the knowledge that he would only have to attend the class until the end of the week - just long enough to be noticed by the other recruits who would have to suffer through it for the rest of the month. Only a few people on the force knew he was working undercover. His main contact was his boss, Lieutenant Warren. Warren's main contact was *his* boss, Captain Seligman.

Warren had supplied Blake with a Beretta, with the warning, "You never know what's behind the next corner," But having a gun on him only made Blake nervous. He hoped that the other students didn't notice the lump under his jacket where the shoulder holster was. He doubted if any of the other recruits were packing.

Lieutenant Layton surprised everyone by ending the class an hour early, at 4 pm. His excuse was that it was the first day of class and he wanted to give the recruits a chance to let everything sink in, but it was really because he and his wife were having a dinner party that evening and he wanted to get home as soon as he could.

None of the students minded that the class was ending early, of course. Groups had already started to form among the rookies who joked around as they left the room, engaging in innocent get-to-know-you chitchat about the towns they came from, where they were staying during training and whether they wanted to meet up later for a drink or a bite to eat. Blake kept to himself. As an undercover cop he didn't want to get too close to anyone, didn't want to answer too many questions.

Being undercover came easy to Blake. He felt like he had been undercover most of his life. His mother left home when he was six years old, and his father never took much interest in his life when he was growing up - he was too busy counting his money. Blake had grown up mostly a loner - he just didn't fit in with the other kids in the small town of Ridgecrest where he came from in California. A Naval Air Weapons Station was based there and most of the other kids came from conservative military families. He got a lot of ridicule for his long hair and slim build. He was almost 6 foot tall by the time he was fourteen and "as skinny as a beanpole." His best friend in Middle School was his skateboard. His favourite author was Stan Lee while the other kids were reading young adult versions of Ernst Hemingway.

As Blake got up to leave at the end of class, Lieutenant Layton called out his name.

"Hey, you, Blake Webster, can I have a word with you?" he asked. When Blake turned, Layton added sarcastically "if it's not too much trouble, of course."

Blake approached the front desk.

"Yes, Mr Layton?" he asked without enthusiasm.

"*Lieutenant* Layton," the teacher said, stressing his superior rank.

Blake dutifully apologised: "Sorry. *Lieutenant* Layton."

"Lieutenant Warren would like to see you," Layton said, his steely grey eyes boring into Blake's forehead like he was trying to read his mind. Blake already knew that Warren wanted to see him – they had travelled back from the Canaries together and had arranged to hold regular meetings after class – but he wasn't about to tell Layton that. Blake didn't know who knew about his status as an undercover cop – he assumed that Layton didn't.

"Yes sir," Blake said and headed toward the door.

"Hold on, Webster. Don't you want to know his office number?" Layton asked.

"Whose?" Blake asked.

"Lieutenant Warren's!"

"It's 63. Warren's office is number 63."

Layton's narrow eyes narrowed even further. The rookie cop had again forgotten to use Warren's title. 'What right did a rookie have to refer to a superior in that way?' Layton asked himself. 'Unless, of course, he wasn't being honest about who he was…'

Layton walked around his desk and sat on the front edge.

"Come here, Mr. Webster."

Blake returned to the desk.

"Who are you?" Layton asked.

Blake shrugged his shoulders.

"I'm nobody," he said.

"Nobody is nobody," Layton countered, angrily slamming his fist on his metal desk.

"I better hurry up before Warren leaves…" Blake mumbled quickly, as he turned and headed for the door.

"Smartass," Layton grumbled after he left.

"Asshole," Blake muttered in the hallway.

Layton couldn't help being suspicious about Blake. He doubted that the rookie cop was as stupid as he acted. 'Oh well, what did it matter?' he said to himself. Layton had done his eight hours and looked forward to going home to see his wife and kids. Their dinner guest was another officer from the force named Dominic – Dom for short - and his current girlfriend Shamrock.

As he drove home to Queens, Layton thought back on how eager he had been when he first joined the force in his early twenties. He could see that same eagerness in the faces of the new recruits that he was teaching, except for Webster who looked distinctly bored – like he had heard it all before. Layton wondered what was up. He hoped that Blake wasn't some sort of plant.

Layton had been adding to his cop salary by taking some of the evidence collected during drug busts and selling it on to a contact outside the force – an old Italian named Luigi who owned a small diner in Hell's Kitchen called Gigi's. Although Layton had stopped being a street cop a long time ago – he was in his late fifties now – he had a few younger colleagues on the force working for him. Whenever they made a substantial coke bust, they gave him a cut of the evidence. He cut their cut and sold it on to Luigi who distributed it to a network of young small-time dealers who got rid of it at New York's nightclubs. It wasn't Luigi's only source of cocaine of course, but it helped. Layton laughed when he thought about all the "cool" clubbers telling their friends they had some "really good stuff" - even after it had been cut by their connection, who had probably got it from another connection who cut it after picking it up from Luigi.

Although Layton knew he was breaking the law, he didn't see how it hurt anyone. The criminals still got caught with more than enough evidence to get convicted - they weren't about to complain that they were being done for three kilos instead of five – and the money he made off the two missing kilos was just a perk of the job. It helped to pay for his four-bedroom house in Queens, his swimming pool, his two-family cars and other essentials. After so many years on the force, he felt he deserved a few extras. The pay was good but not that good for a job that entailed risking your life every day, even if he had never actually risked his life during his long career. He was a traffic cop initially and then spent most of his time training new recruits. He was proud to be a New York cop though; he had no qualms about flashing his badge at New York's *maître d*'s in order to get a good table for himself and the missus, or whoever he was dating, on a particular night.

When he arrived home, Layton parked his Mercedes next to his wife's BMG in their four-car driveway as the family dog, a friendly German Shepherd named Frisky, ran out to greet him from the backyard. He loved that dog, but he had told the kids time and time again to keep the gate closed. He had a dog as a kid who got hit by a car and he didn't want the same thing happening to Frisky.

Layton expected to see his kids, Sally and George, playing in the backyard as he approached the house, but they weren't there. Despite the cold weather, he thought they'd be playing in the elaborate outdoor kid's gym he had bought with some of his cocaine money, but it was empty. Part of the set-up was a heated child-sized shed. He bent down slightly and peered in the window, but no kids there, either. One of the two swings that hung from the swing set was moving back and forth. He couldn't tell if the kids had just used it or whether the movement was caused by a winter breeze. What really made him angry was that they had not only left the gate open, they had also left the sliding glass door open that led from the living room to the yard.

'I'm gonna kill those kids when I see them,' Layton mumbled to himself before he checked his anger. His wife was always warning him about jumping off the handle. Her pet name for him was "Mr. Grumpy." But what did she know? She wasn't even thirty yet and hadn't worked a day in her life. He didn't dare say that to her, though. It would have only brought attention to their age gap. He didn't want her thinking there might be greener (and younger) pastures elsewhere. Still, as a cop, he was used to people following his rules and hated it when they didn't.

He walked through the open sliding glass door into the empty living room and shouted "Hey, what's going on with the sliding glass door? And you left the gate open too.

Frisky was outside when I drove up."

The lack of response only made him angrier. After closing the doors, he went into the kitchen thinking his wife would be preparing dinner, but nobody was there. He got angrier. Dom and his girlfriend were due in less than hour. He was an important guest - one of the street-cops who skimmed off evidence from his busts to give to Layton. He had met his girlfriend, Shamrock, during one of the busts. She got off easy. Instead of going to jail, she ended up in Dom's bedroom. They had been together ever since.

'The kids must be upstairs,' Layton thought. He yelled their names as he walked to the first floor, trying to sound more playful than angry: "Sally, Georgie, 'wheeere' are you? Daddy's here..."

The kids' bedrooms were empty, so he continued to the bedroom he shared with his wife. Maybe they were all in there. The door was open.

"Honey? Are you in there? Where are the kids?"

No response. He looked into the room, expecting it to be empty, and saw his wife's dead body tied to a chair next to their bed, naked with a ball in her mouth held in place by grey gaffer tape that had been wound so tightly around her head that small pricks of blood were noticeable where a few strands of her bleached-blonde hair had been pulled out of their follicles. Her eyes were closed and one of her false eyelashes was drooping on one side as if it was going to fall off. A set of steak knives protruded from her stomach like she had been used for target practice by a circus knife-thrower. She looked more like a discarded mannequin from an S & M shop than a wife.

As he moved closer to the bed, his foot landed on something that made a crunching noise when he stepped on it. He looked down and saw the broken hand of his five-year-old son, his lifeless body lying in a puddle of blood, his clear green eyes still open, staring straight at him. Behind him was the body of his four-year-old daughter, propped up against the wall in a seated position with her dress pulled up over her face. Blood was dripping from between her legs. Someone had used the blood to write the word "witchy" on the wall behind her. The letters were still dripping.

He froze. As a cop he knew what he should do. Call back-up and not touch anything. But as a father, he froze, trying to comprehend the horror in front of him. He didn't stay frozen for long though - just long enough for a man in a black latex mask to leap out from behind the bedroom door and split the back of his head open with an axe. He didn't even have time to grieve.

2. Generic Guru

Lieutenant Warren sat at his desk turning the pages of the morning's *New York Post,* while his drowsy brown eyes tried to follow the text. He had found the newspaper on the bench in the communal hallway outside his office, left there by nobody in particular, and had adopted it to keep himself busy until Blake arrived for the first of their daily meetings. Fortunately, his antiquated wooden desk creaked whenever he leaned too hard on it, helping to keep him awake. His boss, Captain Seligman, had been hassling him for years to get a modern metal desk but Warren liked his old desk. He liked the fact that so many people had used it before him, that if it could talk it would have so many stories to tell, including his own. 'Creeak,' it went as he started to dose off again.

Warren had been out late with his boss the night before and was suffering for it now. He was usually careful about his drinking because of his heart condition – he'd had a heart attack a few years ago – but when he tried to remember how many drinks he had at Seligman's favourite hangout – Oscar's Bar and Grill - he couldn't even remember how long they had been there. Oscar's was Seligman's favourite place for picking up girls. As a balding, overweight sixty-year-old, who clocked every female arrival with his lecherous bloodshot eyes and a chauvinistic scowl that he mistook for masculinity, Seligman had little chance of attracting any of the young women he tried to pick up, without his younger, attractive friend, Lieutenant Warren, by his side, acting as bait.

Warren was in his forties but looked younger. His heart problem hadn't affected his looks. With his thick brown hair pushed back from his forehead, he looked like a movie-star cop. He came in handy when the force needed a good-looking cop to make a statement about a potentially controversial case. The press loved Harry Warren.

Although Seligman often hassled his colleague to take an early retirement because of his heart disease – full pension paid - it was different when they were out drinking. "C'mon, drink up... don't be such a lightweight," Seligman would say.

As Warren sat as his desk waiting for Blake, his hangover getting worse by the minute, he swore he would never fall for it again. Maybe he did have to go out with his boss sometimes, but next time he would be careful not to drink so much. He didn't know what was worse – the headache that was taking over his brain or the irregular palpations that were taking over his heart. He wished Blake would hurry up. Where was he anyway? His class had ended half an hour ago and it should only take him a few minutes to get to the sixth floor from the first.

'At least it will be a slow week,' Warren comforted himself. Blake would be busy with his class during the daytime, which would give Warren time to firm up a plan. The general idea was that Blake would infiltrate the dope scene that he used to belong to as a customer. What happened after that depended on what happened after that...

"Does that guy even know I'm undercover?"

Warren looked up from his paper. Blake was standing in front of him.

"Don't you believe in knocking?"

Blake shrugged and sat down.

"The door was half-open, and I could see you were alone through the window. Late night?"

Warren gave him a dirty look. "When you refer to 'that guy,' do you mean the teacher of your class, Lieutenant Layton?"

"Yeah. Layton."

"Blake, you've got to get used to calling people by

their titles. Lieutenant Layton is a lieutenant, not a 'guy.' It's okay to address me informally but other officers will expect you to use their correct title. We're not in the Canaries anymore."

"Okay, then, does the *lieutenant* know I'm undercover?

"No. Only the people who need to know, know. For the moment, that's me, you, Captain Seligman, Senior Detective Locke and Officer Norris. Maybe a few others."

"Who's Locke and Norris?"

Warren's jaw tightened. Blake was doing it again - leaving out the officers' titles. "Detective Locke and his team supervise the target practice at our uptown arsenal and oversee what you might call the force's 'gadgets.'"

"Gadgets?"

"Detective Locke will fill you in on those on Sunday, if you're available."

"Sunday?"

"At the arsenal. We'll send a car for you at 8 am, if that's okay."

"I guess so," Blake said grudgingly. Why did everything have to start so early?

"Do you still have the Beretta I issued to you?"

"Yeah. Of course. I was worried that somebody would notice it in class."

"It's probably better not to wear it in class."

"You said to always be armed."

"Put it in your locker before class. It's only for a week. You can pick it up after class. Just make sure that nobody sees you."

"Sure. Who's the other guy you mentioned - Officer Norris?"

"You've already met her."

"Her?"

"Yes. You know her as "Amanda." You met her in the Canaries last year when you helped us bust Ginger's gang."

"Amanda! Wow! You mean the nurse?"

"Yes, Amanda, the nurse."

Blake had escaped to the Canary Islands last year, after being accused of two murders he didn't commit. He was followed by Lieutenant Warren who had thought he was chasing a murderer until the real murderer's girlfriend in New York confessed that it was her boyfriend, and Blake's dealer friend, Phil, who was real the culprit.

While he was in the Canaries, Blake fell in love with a woman named Candy who worked for a gang headed by a dealer named Ginger, who ran a gay nightclub in the Yumbo Centre. Blake helped Warren bust Ginger's operation and ended up in the hospital with a bullet in the back of his head. Amanda was the nurse sent over by the NYPD to help him recover – both from the bullet wound and from an addiction to narcotics that he had developed along the way.

Blake did such a great job helping to bust Ginger's operation, that Warren asked him to return to New York and do the same there. He was the perfect choice to infiltrate the New York dope scene because he had once been a part of it.

"You'll see Amanda - Officer Norris, that is - again on Sunday," Warren said.

"One thing I wanted to ask. If anyone recognises me from the work I used to do at Slick, should I tell them I used to be a model or pretend it wasn't me?

Lieutenant Warren shrugged. "Play it by ear. It's okay to tell people you're a model, just don't tell them you're undercover. If they think you're a model, they won't think you're a cop."

"You mean an ex-model."

"Yeah, well, that's something we have to talk about."

"Huh?"

"We might need you to go back into the business."

"No, please, anything but that!" Blake pleaded

dramatically. He hated modelling. Everyone was so phoney. They couldn't wait to become your friend while you were a success but deserted you the minute you were dropped from the agency.

"I'd rather be a criminal than a model," he said.

"Ava, your old boss at Slick, does coke and she could lead us to her supplier who could lead us to the big bosses," Warren explained.

"But she dropped me from the agency for doing drugs."

"Of course, she did. She couldn't risk having the cops snooping around. They might have found out about *her*."

"Where is the arsenal?"

"East 123rd between second and third. Harlem. But don't worry, the driver will know. Have you ever handled an automatic rifle?"

"You mean like a machine gun?"

"Not exactly. I'll meet you at the arsenal on Sunday morning. Don't tell the desk clerk at the Broadway about the car."

Blake wished he could stay somewhere besides that dump, the Broadway Hotel, but that's where he had stayed last year before the Canaries, and the desk clerk, Carlotta (née Carl), was the girlfriend of a Turkish criminal who was part of the syndicate that was flooding Manhattan's clubs with cocaine. He had paid for 'Carl's' operation but was busted during a 'smash and grab' a few months ago.

"The Turk has been singing up a storm," Warren said. "Carlotta could be a good source of information too. We think there's a new gang in town now that the Turk's not around. That's the way it usually works."

Warren wiped his forehead with a weary hand. Sometimes he wondered if it was all worth it. He had joined the police to fight 'the forces of evil,' but whenever they busted one gang, another took its place, until the next gang came along. At what point could you get off the merry-go-round and declare yourself the winner?

"Maybe the new boys are in touch with Carlotta. It wouldn't be the first time that hotel was used as a hideout," Warren continued.

"I was told that by Cameron last year – that the hotel was full of gangsters. Gangsters and methadone addicts on welfare because of that clinic on the corner."

"Yeah, well, the two go together sometimes. Re-establish contact with Cameron. He probably hears a lot of gossip at Blunt, but don't tell him you're undercover."

Cameron was the bartender in the V.I.P. room at the club.

"Don't worry about going back to the club." Warren reassured him. You'll be shadowed wherever you go – for you own protection."

"What do you mean?"

"We'll have a plainclothes cop following you, for your own protection."

"Who?

"Could be anyone. You may never know"

Blake didn't like the idea of being secretly followed. He hadn't realised that was part of the deal. Still, if it was for his protection...

"One other thing Blake. I haven't forgotten my promise to find your mother. We're checking just about every database we have access to."

"Thanks."

Warren had promised Blake last year that he would try to find his mother, Brooke, who had left home when he was a kid. Blake grew up wishing he could hate her, but he couldn't help missing her. He wondered what had happened to her, what she was like now, or even if she was still alive. The last record that Warren found on her was an arrest for solicitation, but that was about five years ago. Nothing since. No address. No social security activity. No body in the morgue.

"Are you going to quit if we can't find her, and you end

up a millionaire?" Warren asked.

When Blake's father died last year, Brooke became the main beneficiary of his will. If she wasn't found, his dad's money would go to Blake. It was a lot of money. John Webster had started out as an avocado farmer and ended up a millionaire after the trees on his farm were replaced by oil derricks. Quite a few farmers in the area found oil on their property back then. John wasn't the only millionaire farmer in Kern County.

Lieutenant Warren sat back and looked at Blake on the other side of the desk.

"What's wrong?" Blake asked.

I don't know. It's weird to think that you're just starting out as a cop. I envy you in a way. Just be careful. Don't have any heart attacks."

"I'll try not to include it on my bucket list. Warren, can I ask you a personal question?"

"Sure."

"Why did you become a cop?"

"I don't know. I grew up the Bronx. I didn't have very many friends. My dad wasn't around. A neighbourhood cop named Mannie became a sort of surrogate father, I guess. He used to tell me not to worry about my dad, that he still loved me, that he just had a disease. The 'disease of addiction' he called it. When Mannie got stabbed by a junkie in the back, I decided to become a cop." He shrugged like it wasn't a big deal.

"I'm sorry to hear that."

"Don't worry. He survived."

"Do you still see him?"

"Not much. He retired after that. He's in prison now – he got busted working for a protection racket after he retired."

Blake wondered whether there were any good guys left in the world.

"Anything else?" Warren asked him.

"Not unless you have anything," Blake replied.

"Don't forget to stop by here after class tomorrow," Warren reminded him. "And every day this week. It should be a slow week. It'll give us time to plan exactly what we're going to do. One more thing. The password is generic guru."

"What's a generic guru?"

"It's not a person, it's a password. Only a few people will know it – if someone says it to you, it means they're okay."

Blake liked the idea of a password. It made him feel like he was in a secret society.

"And Blake, thanks again for doing this."

"No problem. It will be fun."

Just as Blake stood up to leave, a ruckus broke out in the hallway. Warren looked beyond Blake, out the office window, and watched as officers rushed from one office to another accompanied by a symphony of ringtones that didn't stop. A beefy guy drenched with sweat, his pinstriped shirt barely constraining his bulging pectorals, rushed into Warren's office without bothering to knock. He stopped when he saw Blake.

"Don't worry. He's okay," Warren reassured him.

The muscular intruder whispered into Warren's ear. The news of Layton's death had reached headquarters. After Dom and Shamrock arrived at the house, nobody answered the door. It was open. They went in. They eventually found the family together in the master bedroom.

"Gross!" Shamrock shouted when she saw the dead bodies. Dom quickly gave her the wrap of cocaine he had in his pocket, told her to hide it up whatever orifice was handy and rang the police headquarters. It wasn't long before the house was surrounded with cop cars and ambulances. After giving a statement to one of his friends from the force, Dom and his girlfriend faded slowly away from the scene and drove back to their apartment in Manhattan. They didn't want to get too involved. God forbid if their Porsche Cayman became part of the crime scene. Dom had skimmed off a lot of evidence to get that car.

Word spread quickly at headquarters that one of their own had been "Massacred in Queens" (as the *Post* would later headline it). After being given some of the details by Mr. Muscle, Warren stood up and grabbed his grey overcoat from the stand in the corner of his office.

"Blake, I'm sorry. Something's happened. I'm going to have to leave now. I'll see you tomorrow."

"What's up?" Blake asked as he followed Warren to the elevator.

Warren gave him a 'don't ask any questions' look as they were joined by two officers with automatic weapons. A police car was waiting for them outside. Blake barely had time to say good-bye as he watched them speed off, glad he wasn't involved. He was exhausted from yesterday's plane trip and just wanted to collapse in his room at the Broadway.

It didn't take him long to find out what all the hoopla was about. The details were being blasted out on the news crawl at Times Square which he passed on his way back to the hotel. There had been a "mass murder" in Queens involving a member of the NYPD and his family. Then he saw the name of the cop. Lieutenant William Layton - his teacher from the training class.

'How strange,' he thought. 'Who would want to kill *him*?'

Blake began to have second thoughts about his choice of a profession. If a teacher as insignificant as Layton could be a target – he wasn't even out there busting criminals – maybe Blake didn't want to join the force after all. He thought playing cops and robbers would be fun. He wasn't prepared for random murders like this. Sure,

Layton was an asshole, but if all the assholes in the world were killed, nobody would be left.

He passed a newsstand. It hadn't taken long for the press to get hold of the story. The gory details of Layton's murder were plastered all over the front pages. He couldn't resist buying a couple of the papers. One evening edition attributed the killings to a cult: "Cop-Killing Cult Causes Carnage." It didn't have photographs of the actual murder scene – just an artist's rendition of the word "witchy" written on the bedroom wall "with the blood of a child." The murder was described as "ritualistic." Comparisons were made to the Manson murders. Apparently, he had instructed his followers to "leave something witchy" when they murdered their victims. The *Post* had a full-page article about how one follower, Squeaky Fromme, had been paroled in 2009 and was still alive now, living in a New York suburb.

Blake's heart was racing – could there really be a cop-killing-cult making the rounds? Who would be next? He looked around him, trying to detect the "shadow" that Warren had promised him, but everyone just looked like everyone else.

He needed a drink. He hadn't been to Sluggo's since he got back – a run-down watering hole near the Broadway where you could get a drink at most hours. He looked forward to seeing his old friend again. Sluggo was a good listener. And a good pourer.

Maybe Johnny would be there too. Johnny was the resident junkie. Sluggo was old school – past retirement age – he didn't allow drugs to be used on the premises – so Johnny would have a hit outside and spend the rest of the day nodding off in a shadowy corner of the bar. Sluggo didn't mind, as long as he didn't use while he was in the bar. He wasn't against drugs morally; he just didn't want the place to get busted. Johnny might have been an addict, but he was a good guy – trustworthy. Except, maybe, when he was clucking and needed a hit.

Blake felt comfortable with the down-and-outs who hung out at Sluggos. He didn't have to pretend to be anything he wasn't. He missed the 'good old days' at the bar and then remembered that the 'good old days' were only last year. So much had happened since then. Who would have thought that he'd become a cop? It was strange how when you thought about the past you tended to mostly remember the good times.

3. Pinky's

As Blake approached Sluggo's, he felt comforted by the fact that the same neon sign that had been there last year was still there. He remembered the bar as being closer to the Broadway - next door. But now there were a few buildings between it and the hotel. He wondered if it was gentrification rearing its ugly head again or if he had just never noticed the grey, nondescript office buildings before. But the sign was definitely the same sign as last year. The letters, dulled from decades of grime, were still flickering like they were about to run out of energy - the "S" at the end still looked like it was going to drop off at any minute. The single, unmarked, black door that served as the entrance was also the same as before - pushing it was such a struggle that you never knew if the place was open or closed.

Blake entered the bar and was instantly engulfed by darkness. The bright lights of Manhattan didn't affect the windowless interior of Sluggo's where it always seemed like midnight. As his eyes attempted to adjust to the few lights behind the bar, he made out a figure facing the wall, oblivious to the presence of a customer. That was so typical of Sluggo. The only customers he cared about were the ones he already knew.

Or was it Sluggo? As he got closer, Blake realised that it wasn't him at all. It wasn't even a man. It was a slim young woman with long brown hair tied back in a ponytail. She was dressed in tight black jeans and a tight black t-shirt that exposed the pale small of her back as she reached up the wall to get to the control panel of a 50's style neon clock that hadn't been there last year. Her waist looked tiny enough to wrap a finger around.

Sensing a customer, she turned around and met Blake's blue eyes with her milky-brown ones. They 'clicked' instantly, both overcome by the beauty of the person standing in front of them. She looked like a folksinger from the 1960s that his mother used to like - someone named Janie or Judy or something.

The heavenly suspension of time that occurs when two people 'click' instantly, was broken, however, as soon as she opened her mouth, exposing a crooked smile full of tobacco-stained teeth. A couple were the wrong colour of gold – like she had painted them with gold paint. When she talked, she sounded more like a juvenile delinquent than a sensitive folk singer.

"Whaddya want?" she asked in a heavy Brooklyn accent.

He looked down at her chest, which seemed artificially large for a girl her age, whatever that was, and saw the word "Pinky's" appliquéd on the upper left side of her black t-shirt in pink and blue graffiti-style writing. Blake would learn later that the blue had been an afterthought - the girl's boyfriend who ran the bar and designed the logo thought that the male customers might be put off by too much pink. His intention was to create a logo that was both classy and had street-cred, but the ultimate result was an amateurish mess.

"This fuckin' clock is drivin' me nuts," the girl complained to Blake. "The Champagne bottle behind the dial is supposed to pop when the hands reach midnight, but they never do. They get stuck at twelve to twelve."

She took a drag from a cigarette hidden on a plate under the bar and added, "Stupid fuckin' retro bullshit."

"Can I try?" Blake asked as he started to walk around the bar.

"No!" she shouted, holding up her hand like a traffic cop. Bobby would kill me if I let someone behind the bar. Especially a stranger."

"Who's Bobby?"

"Bobby Bosun. My boyfriend. He's the manager."

"Where's Sluggo?" Blake asked.

"Sluggo? You mean that old man who used to own the place?" she asked as she discretely pressed a button under the bar thinking that Blake hadn't noticed. "He left a couple of weeks ago. Were you a friend of his?"

Before he could answer, a pair of dilated pupils entered from the storage room door behind the bar. Like his girlfriend, Bobby Bosun also had long, brown hair, but *his* ponytail was tied to the top of his head and contained shades of grey mixed in with the brown. Blake concluded, from the size of his pupils, that he was either on crystal meth or going through heroin withdrawals.

Bobby was holding onto the necks of three unopened beer bottles as though he was restocking the bar and his sudden appearance had nothing to do with the button that the girl behind the bar had pressed. But who stocks a bar with only three bottles of beer?

"Honey," the girl said, "this guy is asking about Sluggo."

"Oh hi!" Bosun said cheerfully, setting the beers down on the bar and extending his hand to shake Blake's, who neglected to take up the offer.

"Are you a friend of Sluggo?" Bobby asked.

"Yeah, where is he?" Blake asked.

"He's gone. We're managing the place now. I'm Bobby and this is my girlfriend, Sarah."

Bobby wiggled the fingers of his hand which was still hanging in mid-air. Blake shook it this time. Despite his bony fingers Bobby had a strong grip. Blake noticed that he had an infinity symbol tattooed on his wrist.

"Nice tattoo," Blake said.

"Gee, thanks," Bobby said. "It means I'm going to live forever."

Blake had his doubts.

"We're not called Sluggo's anymore," Bobby explained. "We're called Pinky's. "We're still waiting for the new sign."

He pointed to the 'Pinky's' logos on his and Sarah's matching t-shirts. "What do you think?"

"Nice," Blake lied. He hated the new name. It sounded like a gangster's hangout or a children's TV show. Sluggo would have hated it as well.

"Can I get you a drink?" Bobby asked. "The Coors is probably the coldest, but it's still from the old refrigerator. We haven't got the new system yet."

"What about a draught beer?" Blake asked, pointing to the wooden hand pulls on the bar.

"We don't do draught anymore. Those are just for show. Bottles only. It's easier that way. The clientele we get is a lot younger than Sluggo's customers. They usually just drink out of the bottle. It saves Sarah from having to do a lot of dishes."

Sarah gave a tobacco-stained grin.

"I'll have a bottle of Coors," Blake said.

Bobby picked up one of the bottles he had set down on the bar and grabbed an opener that hung with his keys off a clunky chain attached to his snakeskin belt. He opened one of the bottles and handed it to Blake.

"Ten dollars," he said.

"Ten dollars? For a bottle of beer? Sluggo was lucky to get five."

"Times change."

Bobby took Blake's money and deposited it into the bar's new "retro" cash register, without bothering to ring up the sale.

"So, what happened to Sluggo?" Blake asked. "Do you have an address for him?"

"He's at Holly..." Sarah started to say before she was quickly interrupted by her boyfriend:

"We don't know where he is," Bobby said. "He's retired."

"Retired?" That didn't sound like Sluggo. He was always complaining about how he didn't have enough money to retire.

"Well, not exactly retired." Bobby said. "They came and got him or something. He's in a nursing home." Sarah shot her boyfriend a 'that's what I was gonna say' expression.

Blake knew something was up. Sluggo would have hated being relegated to a nursing home.

"You look familiar," Sarah said to Blake. "Are you famous or something?"

Blake remembered what Warren had told him at their meeting – if they thought he was a model, they wouldn't suspect him of being a cop.

"I used to be a model," he explained. "The Style Raven guy."

Sarah's boyfriend perked up when he heard Blake was 'famous.' He used Style Raven products - his aftershave was Style Raven Eau de something or other. Fortunately, it was more "eau" than scent so that the advertised "masculine" battery acid smell didn't last very long. The bottle looked nice though. It was shaped like a black raven, ready to attack. It looked more like a small eagle, but nobody complained.

"You should bring your model friends here," he said. "The space over there – he pointed to a small area in front of the bathrooms - is going to be our dance floor. How about some music?" Bobby suggested, now that they had a celebrity in their midst. "Let's get the party started."

He walked over to a 50s style jukebox next to the entrance – another new addition – and brought out his clunky chain again. One of the implements attached to it was a skeleton key that overrode the need for money to play music on the machine.

"We picked it up in Metro Retro on Canal Street," Bobby said, as he inserted the key. "Along with that clock behind the bar. And the cash register. We're going for the fifties look. It's all part of the gentrification of the area.

We're getting a new sign for outside too."

"But wasn't the original stuff from the 1950s?" Blake asked.

"Yeah, but that was the real 1950's. The new stuff is more realistic – like what you see in the movies."

Bobby turned the key, and the jukebox came to life.

"There's only old music on the jukebox now but it's digital so we'll change it eventually. Whoever owned it before must have been into the '60s. He pressed a couple of buttons on the front and watched through a window as a fake vinyl single made its way to a fake needle cartridge.

"If you look through the window, it looks like it's really playing a record," Bobby explained as if he was describing the Theory of Relativity to a young child. "But it's really just playing the same record each time. A different song comes out of the speakers, but the fake needle always plays the same fake record. Customers don't usually notice. They don't really care, as long as their song plays."

The Buffalo Springfield starting singing, "There's somethin' happenin' here - what it is ain't exactly clear – there's a man with a gun over there – telling me I got to beware – I think it's time we stop, children, what's that sound – Everybody look what's going down…"

"I love this old hippie stuff," Bobby said, as he undid his ponytail and shook his head, letting his hair cascade over his shoulders like he was trying to impress someone, as he returned to the bar.

"Hey, did you hear about the cop thing?" he asked.

Blake pretended not to know what he was talking about.

"What cop thing?"

"A cop and his family got murdered in the suburbs."

"Really?"

"Yeah," Bobby said. "It's all over the news."

"Oh yeah, I think there was something about it on the news crawl in Times Square."

The cops bring it on themselves."

"What? Getting murdered?"

"Yeah. If they weren't so busy busting people for drugs, maybe they could bust some real criminals, like all the rapists and child molesters out there."

I guess so," Blake said, wanting his new friend to think he was on his side.

"Do you ever get high?" Bobby asked.

"Doesn't everyone?" Blake laughed.

Sarah looked uncomfortable. She went back to her clock.

"Do you need anything?" Bobby asked.

"Huh?"

"I've got a friend who sells stuff - coke mostly. I don't do it myself, of course."

"Well, tell your friend I'm definitely interested," Blake said. "Does he do quarters?"

"No, just halves," Bobby answered on behalf of his imaginary friend.

"How much?"

"I think he normally charges 75 bucks, but only 60 to his friends. That's what I heard anyway. Like I said, it's his thing. I don't get involved."

'Sure you don't,' Blake thought. He asked Bobby if his friend had a name.

"Nah, he goes by a nickname. Something like... Dozer."

"Doser?"

"Something like that."

"It's a shame he isn't here now. I wouldn't mind some Charlie."

"He only deals in cash."

"I've got cash."

One of Bobby's dilated eyes winked, and his chin jerked upward to confirm that a deal was about to be made. He fiddled with the front pocket of his favourite jeans which he was wearing at the time - thin blue denim that hugged his ass. When his hand came out of his pocket, he flashed a wrap of cocaine in his palm which he hid underneath a napkin on the bar. Blake reached into his trousers and managed to extract three twenty-dollar bills from his wallet under the bar. He casually rested his closed hand on the bar.

"Hey Sarah," Bobby said. "Stop messing around with that clock and pay attention to the customers."

Sarah returned to the bar and casually wrapped her hand around Blake's.

"So nice to welcome a new customer to the bar," she said, as she extracted the cash from Blake's fist. She took it straight to the locked metal box in the back room that kept the dope money separate from the bar money. When the bar closed in the evening, they would reconcile the money with the wraps that Bobby had left, so to make sure nothing went missing. They noted everything in a small order book which they would show to the guy who provided the stuff when they handed over the week's proceeds – an English guy named Jasper who owned the bar now.

In the front room, Blake took his time picking up the napkin and what was underneath it as he and Bobby continued their casual, repetitive, conversation. The deal had been completed without either of them making physical contact. If anyone else had been in the bar at the time, all they would have noticed was a friendly conversation, a gentle greeting by the bar owner's girlfriend and a napkin pocketed in case it was needed in the future.

Given that Blake was their only customer when they made the exchange, Bobby and Sarah were probably being overly cautious, but Bobby knew that if you always acted like you were being watched, it would become a habit, and the chance of being busted would be minimal. He might not have been so confident if he had known that he had just sold half a gram of coke to an undercover cop. Blake had no intention of doing any of it, of course, he just wanted them to know he was on the same wavelength as them and could be trusted in the future.

Sarah came back into the room and, his sleight of hand completed, Bobby grabbed the blue down jacket he kept stuffed under the bar and put it on.

"I'm going out to get some supplies. I'll be right back."

Sarah and Blake watched his skinny ass go out the door. As soon as he was outside, Sarah leaned over the bar and sneered.

"That's so typical of him. He always makes me take the money. It means if you're a cop, he won't get busted. I will."

Blake reassured her that he wasn't a cop. "You can trust me," he lied. "Before Bobby interrupted, you were going to tell me where Sluggo is."

"Bobby would get pissed off if I told you."

"Fuck Bobby."

"I do," she said. "So could you," she added.

"No thanks."

"Don't lie. I saw you looking at his ass. A three-way would be fun."

Blake had no intention of having a three-way with those two but left the possibility dangling as he asked again about Sluggo. This time he got an answer.

"He's in the Hollywood Fields Retirement Home."

"Hollywood?" Blake asked. "In California?"

"No silly. It's just called that. It's in Jersey. North Bergen."

Blake nodded and made a mental note of the location.

"So, what about it?" she asked.

"What about what?"

"A three-way with Bobby and me."

"I'll think about it."

"I've got big tits."

"I noticed."

Bobby came back in the bar shortly afterward, carrying a box that he delicately placed on the bar and opened. It was a "retro" Miller's Beer sign.

"Look at that beauty," he said.

Picking it up with one hand he took it behind the bar and plugged it in. Was it Blake's imagination or did Bobby's other hand skim Blake's ass as he walked to the wall behind the bar?

Bobby flipped a switch and the fake Miller sign glowed and hummed, just like a real Miller sign from the '50s. He winked at Blake and Sarah smiled.

"He's so good with electronic things," she said to Blake. Bobby leaned the sign against the wall and put his arm around his girlfriend's waist.

"She should know!" he joked, making the burring sound of a vibrator.

"Stop it, Bobby!" she giggled. "You're embarrassing me!"

They pecked at each other lips, each with an eye on Blake. He finished his beer and said his good-byes. As he turned to go out the door, Bobby called after him, "If you need anything else, we'll be here."

"Thanks."

Blake walked out the door, relieved to be away from those weirdos. He breathed in the air of New York like a convict let out of prison, and then had a coughing spell straight afterwards. Despite all the eco-friendly lingo spouted by the millennials, carbon monoxide still permeated the air like it had always done and probably would always do. Trapped among the skyscrapers, New York air would never be clean. But who cared?

Blake took a quick look at the wrap in his pocket. Usually, the colour of a wrap was white, but Bobby's wrap was a gold color. He wondered if the cocaine was gold too but didn't want to open it up on the street. He left it in his coat pocket as he walked to the entrance of the Broadway.

Back in the bar, Bobby and Sarah were discussing their new customer.

"Strange guy," Bobby said.

"Do you think he was a cop?" Sarah asked.

"Don't be stupid. How could the Style Raven guy be a cop? He's exactly the type of customer that Jasper wants us to attract."

"I guess he was too good-looking to be a cop."

"Besides," Bobby continued, "how are we going to get a reputation as a good place to score quality stuff without selling to the odd stranger? After he's had a line of that stuff, he'll be telling all of his fashionable friends where to get it. We'll be millionaires in no time."

"Millionaires?"

"Sure, why not? With Blake as a customer, we could be supplying the entire fashion industry in no time."

"But millionaires?"

"Look," Bobby explained, "We're supposed to get fifty percent of the take. Once our reputation is established, we can start cutting the stuff. Nobody will know the difference. That fifty percent will turn into a hundred percent in no time."

Sarah had never been very good at mathematics. She took his word for it. Bobby had learned most of his math by dealing with grams and ounces. Fractions were particularly easy for him – a tenth, a quarter, a half…

"Maybe with all that money we could get a new retro clock," Sarah said wistfully. "I still can't get the hands to move past twelve to twelve."

"Don't worry baby," Bobby said. "That clock is just for show. Everything is."

4. Blake, Hey Blake!

"Blake, hey Blake!"

As Blake was walking back to the Broadway, a voice that he didn't recognise called out his name behind him. Should he stop and turn or keep on walking? Was it his shadow or a killer?

The footsteps of the person quickened; the voice became more laboured. When Blake got to the corner, the traffic light turned red, and he had no choice but to stop and face his nemesis.

"Blake! How are you, buddy?"

It was Johnny the junkie. What a relief that Johnny was still around.

"Am I glad to see you," he said to Blake. "I was afraid they got you too. Where have you been?"

Seeing Johnny again felt like finding a long-lost friend. Thank God that some things never changed. His cheeks were probably more sunken than they had been last year, his sad grey eyes were probably sadder and his long strings of blonde hair maybe thinner – but it was still Johnny and, boy, was Blake glad to see this blast from the past. Nobody could gentrify Johnny.

"I'm good, Johnny," Blake said. "Glad to see you're still around."

"Cool, man. They performed a complicated young man's handshake, even though Johnny was probably pushing sixty. Heroin kept him young – or old. He had started looking 'close to sixty' at least twenty years ago.

After they shared greetings – lots of 'wows 'and 'cools' and 'greats' – Blake popped the question.

"What did you mean when you said that you were afraid that they got to me too?" he asked. "Who's 'they'?"

"Those guys who took over Sluggo's. The men in the grey suits."

"What men in grey suits?"

"I thought they were cops at first, but their shoes didn't look like cop shoes. They were wearing those boots – Beatle boots they used to call them. Their suits were tailored like rich people wear. They would come in and talk to Sluggo, almost whisper. I couldn't hear what they were saying. I think they were English.

"Did you hear anything?" he asked Johnny. "Anything at all?"

"Not specific words, but they sounded threatening, like 'if you don't do this, we'll do that.' They were angry about something. Then, one night I went into the bar and Sluggo was gone. The new owners, this girl and her boyfriend, kicked me out. They said they didn't want customers like me. They were trying to attract a new crowd. I asked them where Sluggo was, but they wouldn't tell me."

Blake was tempted to mention the conversation with Sarah about Hollywood Fields but held back. It would be better if Johnny didn't know – to see what Johnny came up with on his own. Undercover cops didn't talk. They listened.

Johnny continued: "I told them I'd been going to the bar for years, more than a decade, but they didn't care. I left. Then I saw them again on Canal Street, buying a van load of stuff from Metro Retro. They laughed when they saw me. I heard the guy say something like 'Isn't that the junkie who was in the bar...' I heard the girl laugh too. Like they were making fun of me. I didn't want to cause any trouble. It's sad walking past Sluggo's now. It was the only place left where I was welcomed. Until you showed up in New York, Sluggo was sort of my only friend."

"Listen Johnny, is there anywhere I can reach you if I need to? Where do you sleep at night?"

"I don't know. Anywhere. I'm around, I guess. Sometimes I sleep in Bryant Park until the cops move me on. Anyway, the good news is that I'm not banned from the Hole in the Wall anymore."

"Is that place still around? I thought they busted it."

"It was closed for a while, but it reopened under new management." He laughed. "It's open 24/7 now. The cops don't care. At least they know where the junkies are – they're contained. Away from the tourists."

Blake wished that Johnny hadn't mentioned the place. It was where he used to score. Just hearing about it gave him a funny feeling in his stomach. He wondered if they would still know who he was, if he could still score there. It was so easy – just a doorway with a peephole large enough to fit a twenty-dollar glassine bag of smack. If you knocked and they recognised you, two fingers appeared, took your money and passed you the dope. He stopped letting his imagination get the best of him. He never wanted to go back there. He took out his pen – "do you mind?" - and wrote his number on Johnny's arm.

"Listen Johnny, this is important. If you hear anything about Sluggo, can you give me a call? Or anything else about those men in grey suits that were giving him a hard time?"

"Yeah, sure Blake. Are you gonna look for him?"

"I'll find him. But call me if you see those guys again."

"Okay."

Johnny stood there like he was waiting for something.

"Blake, um, you don't have any money you can lend me, do you? Don't worry, I'll pay you back. I, well, you know what the score is."

"Yeah, I know what the score is." He handed Johnny two twenty-dollar bills. "Don't overdose."

"Wow! I love you buddy, I really do."

As Johnny rushed off to score, Blake noticed that he was walking with a limp. That was new. He had never had a limp before. Or had he? Blake tried to remember if he had ever seen him walk before. He only remembered him sitting down - in his dark corner at Sluggo's. The only thing he knew about Johnny's past was that he had partied a lot when he was younger - 'The good old days when people still knew how to have fun,' he used to say about the 1980s. Sluggo had a similar attitude. "Whatever happened to fun?" he'd ask, looking at his empty bar.

Back at the Broadway, Blake flopped down on his bed, fully clothed. Carlotta had been at the front desk, as usual, and he couldn't help asking about Sluggo's. She knew Sluggo. Maybe she had more information.

"Did Sluggo's move?" he asked with a feigned naivety.

She looked at him with a sadness that came as a surprise. Carlotta had always struck him as someone who was hard as nails – having "grown up on the wrong side of the tracks outside of New Orleans," as she often put it, but now she just looked at him, both sad and worried, like she didn't know how to answer the question.

"Sluggo's didn't move," she said. "But Sluggo did."

"Why? What happened."

"Nothing happened Blake. Time just moves on. That's all."

She pretended to be busy with paperwork and he was too tired to pursue the conversation. He had had enough for one evening. As far as he was concerned, Monday was officially over. He walked down the hall to his room. As soon as he got inside, his phone rang. It was Lieutenant Warren.

"Sorry to rush off after the meeting like that, but…"

"Layton?"

"You heard about it?"

"It would be difficult not to. It's all over the news. What happened?"

"We don't know yet, not exactly. I'll keep you posted. Can't say much right now. Seligman thinks it was probably just a robbery gone wrong, that the press is blowing it up too much. I'll probably know more tomorrow when we meet up."

Blake told him about his trip to Sluggo's (now Pinky's), how he had bought a wrap of cocaine in gold coloured paper from Bobby and Sarah, and what Sarah had told him about Hollywood Fields. He also mentioned that he had run into Johnny who told him about some men in grey suits. Most officers in the area knew Johnny. They knew he used, but they tolerated it. What purpose would it serve to bust someone his age? He was only hurting himself.

"Maybe Bobby and Sarah are trying to make their coke seem special by using gold paper for the wrap," Blake suggested.

"Maybe. Maybe not. Did you do any of it?" Warren asked.

"No, of course not. I'm through with all that. I just wanted them to think I was on their side. I've still got it."

"Good boy."

Blake didn't tell him about the line he'd had before class that morning. But it didn't seem relevant anymore. He hadn't mentioned it at their earlier meeting, so why bother now?

"Blake, I have an idea. Cop class doesn't start until two o'clock tomorrow because they need to find a new teacher. Maybe you could visit Sluggo in the morning in that retirement home that Sarah told you about. North Bergen isn't that far."

"Yeah. Sure. I'll be happy to. He must be miserable in that place. A visit might cheer him up."

"And he might have some information about those men in the grey coats that Johnny mentioned."

'If I have time when I get back, I'll stop in at Gigi's for lunch. I haven't seen Luigi since I've been back."

"It might be a good idea to let Luigi get a peek at the gold wrap. I want to see what his reaction is. Don't make a big deal of it, just let it fall 'accidentally' on the floor – or something like that."

"No problem. I'll figure out something.

"Alright - and report to me after the class as usual. It going to end at 8 tomorrow because of the late start, but I'll stay in the office until late."

"Okay. See you tomorrow."

"And Blake, thanks again for helping us out."

"You're welcome. I think I'll take it easy tonight though. I'm going to bed. I'm exhausted."

Blake liked Warren. Being a cop wasn't as difficult as he thought it was going to be. He got undressed and lied back in bed, taking his phone with him. He wanted to find out where Hollywood Fields was before tomorrow morning. Its website wasn't difficult to find. The main page featured a film of an older couple posing in front of a red sports car, waving happily at the camera, with an old Beach Boys song playing in the background: "And she'll have fun fun fun 'til her daddy takes the T-Bird away..."

Presumably the song was referring to the car and not the cheap 17% alcohol wine that was still popular with Skid Row vagrants and under-aged teenagers who congregated outside liquor stores trying to get adults to buy them alcohol.

Scrolling letters at the bottom of the screen described the retirement centre as a place where residents could have the fun they missed out on when they were younger and had to work for a living. You didn't retire at Hollywood Fields, you swam, danced, roller-skated, participated in fashion shows and ate in what looked like one of the swankiest restaurants in New Jersey. Young waiters, looking like they had just stepped out of the pages of GQ magazine, served blue-rinsed grandmothers showing off their wrinkled cleavage in designer dresses that must have cost a mint in the 1980s.

There was a photo gallery of luxurious rooms but no prices. Potential tenants, or their representatives, were asked to enquire by email for the cost of the "private bungalows, apartments and communal living spaces for the "active over 60s."

'How on earth could Sluggo afford that type of five-star luxury?' Blake wondered. 'And why would he want to?' Blake pictured him in the wrinkled, slept-in clothes he usually wore, with constantly bloodshot eyes and greasy grey hair carelessly pushed back from his face by his dirty-nailed fingers. That picture didn't quite mesh with the well-groomed senior citizen swingers that Hollywood Fields catered to. It just didn't make sense.

5. Tuesday

Blake woke up the next morning to a text message telling him that cop class was delayed until two o'clock, which he already knew from his conversation with Warren. The message also reminded the recruits that "under no circumstances should anyone in the force speak to the media about any police matter without prior permission, or your job could be at risk."

While he got dressed, he listened to the news for information about the Layton case. Most of the stations were broadcasting stories about a new virus in China. He had first heard about it on the plane from the Canaries. The news agencies were making a big deal out of it, but it sounded like a normal flu. The World Health Organisation had issued a statement that human to human transmission was a "possibility." That was news? That there *might* be human transmission of a virus in China? Layton and his family were definitely dead *now*. Where was the news about them?

Blake put on the same suit he'd worn yesterday, making sure that his shoulder holster didn't create too much of a lump. He would put the gun in his locker before class like Warren suggested, but he wanted to have it with him when he visited Sluggo in the retirement home. Something was fishy about that institution, and he wanted to make sure he had protection. So far, he hadn't noticed the "shadow" that Warren had promised him. He hoped Sluggo wasn't too depressed in the home. The residents on the website looked like they were having so much fun. Sluggo hated fun.

Carlotta was at the front desk again when Blake left - did she ever take a break? This time she was in an argument with some men in suits – grey suits. He wondered if there was a connection between those grey suits and the ones that Johnny had mentioned. He tried to listen in on their conversation but the only thing he heard was her saying, "It's not about the money." When they saw him, they stopped talking until he got to the front door. As he left, he thought he heard one of the grey suits say, "Is that him?" Maybe he was just hearing things, he thought, as he escaped into the chaos of New York.

A cab was parked outside the hotel as though it had been waiting for him. It seemed too coincidental – empty cabs were so rare in New York. He wondered if the driver was his shadow.

"Where to?" the driver asked.

"Do you know Hollywood Fields Retirement Home in Jersey?"

"Sure. Get in."

Blake got in.

"If it's the place I'm thinking of, it's through the Lincoln Tunnel and turn right. It's on a private street off Bulls Ferry Road. Does that sound right?"

"I think so."

"Got a relative there?"

"Sort of. More of a friend than a relative."

Blake noticed the driver's suspicious eyes checking him out in the rear-view mirror.

"What kind of a friend?"

"What do you mean, what kind of a friend? A friend - an old guy called Sluggo - he used to have a bar in midtown."

"Used to? I know that place. Haven't been there for a while, but he was a nice guy, a little depressing sometimes but a nice guy. What happened to him?"

"They retired him."

"Who did?"

"That's what I'm trying to find out."

"Was he mafia? The Hollywood is full of ex-mafia."

"Not as far as I know."

"Are you a cop?"

"No, of course not, I'm just a friend."

"Then why are you packing?"

Damn. His holster must be showing. He adjusted his coat. "You can never be too careful in New York," he said. "A lot of people have guns nowadays."

"Uh-huh. Especially the fares going to that retirement home. Know any criminals?"

"Sorry buddy, but I've had a rough morning. Can we just drop the conversation and drive to the place? I've got a lot on my mind."

"Sure. No problem. No problem at all. Sick relative?"

Blake didn't bother to answer. He sat back and enjoyed the calm darkness of the Lincoln Tunnel. When they came out of the other side, the cab turned left up a steep hill.

"What a strange place for a retirement home," he said. "How are the old people supposed to go up and down that hill?"

"Maybe they're not supposed to," the driver answered. I've brought quite a few visitors here, but I've never picked up any residents leaving the place. Maybe once they get in, they never get out."

The driver stopped outside a tall chain link fence in front of a crowded mixture of shrubs and trees that made it difficult to see what was beyond them.

"Here we are."

Blake looked at the bushes outside the window.

"Where?" he asked.

"Hollywood Fields."

"No, I meant the Hollywood Fields *Retirement Home*," it's not an actual field."

"That's it. Behind those trees."

Blake looked between the trees and saw a gate and, beyond that, a pathway through a lawn that led to what looked like a large, gabled building, perched on the edge of a cliff that overlooked the river. Not at all what he expected. He realised that the website didn't have a picture of the actual building, just a lot of happy old people, but this building looked more like a haunted mansion than the modern complex that Blake expected. He wondered if there were stilts on the other side – it didn't look like the safest location for residents who might be suffering from dementia. An outdoor porch that wrapped around the building was covered with iron bars – presumably for the safety of the tenants – but the general impression it gave was that the centre was more like a prison than a retirement home.

Blake got out of the cab for a closer look. A woman appeared to be standing on the porch, behind the bars, wearing a large flat hat that sideswiped her face at such a severe angle that you could only see her pale cheekbones and dark red lipstick. Her pencil-thin body was encased in a dress of similar material to the hat in the same mossy brown color. With its tight long sleeves and ankle length hemline, it was difficult to tell if the creature he was looking at was eighteen or eighty. She appeared to be weeping. Was that a tear on her cheek?

The cab driver rolled down his window.

"There sure are some weirdos in that place," he said.

"Is she real?" Blake asked.

The driver laughed. "Who knows? A time traveller maybe," he joked. "I've seen her before. She just stands there."

"How do you get past the gate?"

"There's an entrance over there." He pointed to a metal box. "Just press the red button on the box and someone will answer."

"Ok. Thanks a lot buddy. How much do I owe you?"

"Forget it," he said. "I know you're a cop. Cops are free."

Blake laughed. "Why do you think I'm a cop? Did you notice the bulge under my coat?"

"I didn't see a bulge."

"Then how did you know I had a gun?"

"Lucky guess. Most of the people who visit this place are either cops or criminals. I guessed 'cop.' Guess I was right."

"Guess you were. Thanks for the freebie."

"Don't worry about it." He started up the cab and then had second thoughts.

"Hey buddy," he said to Blake. "That guy you mentioned – Sluggo. He was a good guy. I used to hit that bar when I was in the middle of my divorce, and he really helped me through it. He didn't know me from Adam, but he always had time to listen to my problems. Gave me good advice too. He probably won't remember me but tell him that the divorced cab driver says hello."

"Will do," Blake said and passed a twenty-dollar bill through the window. "It's not for the fare. It's for you."

The driver thanked him, threw the bill on the dashboard, and gave him his card.

"If you need a cab in a hurry, call me."

"Why would I need a cab in a hurry?"

"I don't know. Seems like everybody's in a rush nowadays."

"O.K. Thanks."

Blake watched the taxi drive off and made a mental note of its license plate. He looked at the name on the card. Ed Collins. Sounded fake.

He pressed the red button that the driver had told him about, and a woman's voice answered through a small speaker.

"Good morning, how may I help?"

Sounded like an English accent. He looked at the porch and saw that the apparition he had seen earlier had disappeared. He wondered if the voice on the intercom belonged to the same person. He told her he wanted to visit Sluggo.

"No, I'm sorry, there is no 'Mr. Sluggo' here," she

said, pronouncing his name like it was a disease.

"But I was told he was living here," Blake protested.

She told him to hold on and warned that the CCTV had taken his picture. He could hear muffled voices in the background and then the woman's voice returned.

"Oh!" she said, returning to the intercom. "You mean Mr. Uggiloro. I'm so sorry. I didn't realise he was called that other name too."

She buzzed him in. The pathway to the front entrance wasn't as long as it had looked from behind the trees. The woman he had spoken to on the intercom met him at the door with two security guards. She held out her hand and introduced herself as Miss Williamson.

"I'm Blake. Blake Webster," he said.

"Yes, we know. We matched your CCTV photograph to a database we have access to. Are you still a model?"

"Sort of."

Blake looked at Miss Williamson, trying to remember her features so he could describe her later to Lieutenant Warren, but she was so nondescript that nothing stuck in his mind. He tried to figure out how old she was – late '50's, early '60s maybe? Somebody in a fashion magazine must have told her that blue suited older women because so much of her was blue. Her plump figure was covered with a light blue dress with dark blue pinstripes that faded into the blue striped wallpaper behind her. Her wispy, blue-rinsed hair had been modelled into a perm that looked as irreversible as concrete. Her expression was as welcoming as a bullet. She wasn't grimacing exactly, but neither was she smiling. She gave the impression of someone who had gone through life following other people's instructions.

She guided Blake through a cream-colored fiberglass archway just inside the entrance of the main reception room. Church bells pealed.

"Gun, please," she requested, holding out a gloved

hand.

Blake handed over his gun. The bells were, apparently, some sort of an alarm system that went off if the metal detectors he had just walked through indicated he was armed. She handed the gun to one of the guards who wrapped it up in a white cloth napkin.

"Don't worry," she reassured him. It's just to protect the residents. You'll get it back when you leave. It's not that unusual. Most of our visitors are armed."

Blake wondered how many retirement homes in New Jersey had metal detectors. After handing over his weapon, he had to walk through the archway again. No bells this time.

He followed his hostess up a grand staircase in the centre of the room that wouldn't have looked out of place in a movie star's mansion. At the top of the staircase, they turned left down a spotless, plush carpeted hallway that smelled like the perfume of ghosts.

"Do you live in New Jersey?" Miss Williamson asked.

"No. I live in Manhattan," he answered.

"I don't blame you."

"You?"

"I live here," she said. "These guests are like family. I don't think I could live anywhere else."

That was one thing Blake hadn't seen. Guests. Maybe one. The woman on the porch. Otherwise, the only people he had seen were the security guards who were no longer with them and Miss Williamson who was now leading him down a long empty hallway of closed doors. He felt like he was being watched. Were there CCTV cameras in the hallway too? He couldn't see any, but that didn't mean they weren't there.

They finally passed an open door – one of the resident's rooms – and Blake took a casual look inside to see what the rooms were like. A frightful looking woman, with skin you could almost see through and hair as dry as straw, sat on a folding metal chair at a small vanity staring at herself in the mirror. The room was tiny – not at all like the rooms on the website. A half-empty bottle of bourbon sat on the vanity table next to a tumbler – the kind of glass that Blake kept his toothbrush in at the Broadway. When the resident saw Blake looking at her, she took a swig from the bottle, flipped him off and kicked the door shut.

"Poor dear," Miss Williamson said. "She's not well."

A few doors down, another senior citizen in a skewed blonde wig was sneaking out of one door in a man's robe to another door further down the hall.

"Here we are," Miss Williamson announced cheerfully. "Room 410." She knocked gently on the door. "Mr. Uggiloro, she called out, "you have a visitor from Manhattan!"

Sluggo got out of bed already dressed from the day before and opened the door slightly, worried that it might be a bill collector from the old days. When he saw Blake standing behind Miss Williamson, he threw the door wide open and greeted his friend, with surprise.

"Blake! My god. I was worried about you! How did you find me? Where did you go? Please, please, come in."

He pushed Miss Williamson to one side and pulled Blake into the room.

"I'll leave you two to catch up on old times, shall I?" Miss Williamson said. Sluggo didn't say anything, he just shut the door in her expressionless face. She didn't mind. She was used to having the door slammed in her face by the residents. She hated them really, but the money was good. The bonuses she got for providing information about them and their families to the syndicate that owned the centre were helping to put her nieces and nephews through college. She stood listening at Sluggo's door until the small device she kept on her belt vibrated, which meant she was needed downstairs. It was nearly time for the Sunrise Disco.

Every morning the staff tried to rev up the guests by serving them breakfast to '70's classics like *Hot Stuff, Bad Girls* and *Native New Yorker*. Guests who didn't want to participate – usually the ones who had been up all-night gambling in online casinos - could take breakfast in their rooms.

"What happened to *me*?" Blake asked Sluggo, repeating the question that Sluggo had asked him. "What happened to *you*? Who is that couple running your bar?"

"Oh, those two," he said. "The hippie ghouls. They're friends of the guys who took over the bar. It's their problem now. I am too old and tired to deal with it anymore."

He didn't look too old or too tired to Blake. In fact, he looked younger than he ever had. And happier. Last year's tired green eyes were now wide open and raring to go.

"What guys?" Blake asked.

"Jasper's boys."

"Who's Jasper?"

"An English guy named Jasper."

"But who are they?"

"Jasper's a nice guy. You'd like him. He's young, like you. Long blonde hair. Looks like one of those California surfers, except for the suit. He was always wearing a grey suit. So were his friends. Nothing special. Just ordinary grey suits. Not matching. Not like a pop band. Different shades of grey. I don't know. Maybe there was a navy blue one in there somewhere…"

Blake couldn't believe what he was hearing.

"Are you saying that you sold your bar to a group of English gangsters?"

"No. They weren't gangsters. Just, I don't know, a group of friends, or something. The guy who signed the contract was called Jasper."

"But how did you know these people? Were they customers?"

"No, they just walked in. It was as if God had answered my prayers."

"What do you mean? You loved that bar. You used to say it was the only thing you had in life. And since when did you start believing in God?"

"Blake, look at this place. I'd never be able to afford a place like this. Okay, it's only one room, but I'm having fun for the first time in a long time. All those customers who came into the bar over the years. What were they looking for? Fun. Now it's my time to have some fun. How about a drink?"

"It's nine o'clock in the morning!"

"9:30."

"It's still too early for me. I'll make you one if you want."

"Time is different for us old folk, Blake. We get up early and go to bed early – so the party starts early. Instead of breakfast we have a Sunrise Disco. It's fun. And there are always some rich widows looking for a good time…"

He'd never seen Sluggo so excited and talkative. Usually, he was trying to shut people up.

"Where's your booze?" Blake asked.

"There's a fifth of Jack in the top drawer of that table by the bed."

When Blake reached into the back of the drawer to get Sluggo's bottle of Jack Daniels, he felt a small, folded paper envelope – like a coke wrap. He set the bottle on top of the table and showed Sluggo the wrap. It was gold-coloured, like the one Bobby and Sarah had sold to him.

"What the hell is this?" Blake asked.

"It's a fucking wrap. What do you think it is?"

"What is going on in this place?"

"I don't know. Do you want a line? I usually do one before the disco. Everybody does it here."

"I don't believe this. You kicked me out of your bar once for doing coke in the bathroom."

"Yeah, well, whatever. You can have a line if you want. Where's my drink? I'm ready to party!"

He did a little dance to prove his point – more of a jig than a dance. "Hurry up or I'll miss the martini man."

"Martinis at breakfast?" Blake asked.

"Why not? You only live once."

"And Jasper is paying for all this? The coke too?"

"Yeah, in exchange for taking over the bar. It was the only way they could get rid of me!" Sluggo said, laughing.

Blake didn't laugh. He figured that wasn't the only way that Jasper could get rid of him if he really wanted to. "For how long?"

"How long?"

"Yeah, how long is he paying your bill? And what happens afterwards?

"I dunno. Forever, I guess. It's probably in the contract."

"Contract?"

"Yeah. I'll send you a copy if you want. What's your address?"

"The Broadway."

"No, your email address."

"Email?" He was surprised that Sluggo even knew how to use email.

"Sure, what's your email address?" he asked. He picked up an iPad that was lying in the folds of the quilt on his bed. Blake thought he saw a pair of naked breasts on the screen before Sluggo quickly clicked on his email program. "I'll forward you the email with his contract attached to it that he sent me."

"Thanks."

He clicked a few clicks and Blake had the contract on his phone.

"I'll have a look at it later."

"Amazing, isn't it? It's like having a computer on a piece of paper," Sluggo said about the iPad.

"Yeah. Amazing."

"Where's that wrap?"

"I put it back in the drawer."

"Let's do a couple of lines before breakfast," Sluggo said, wiping his hands together.

"Before breakfast? Won't you lose your appetite?"

"Breakfast is mostly about the disco."

"I'm afraid I won't be able to join you at breakfast, it's a quick stop. Just wanted to make sure you were okay."

"I'm great." He was putting on a tie now, over the shirt he had slept in last night.

"Well, you can make me a line, can't you?" He said as he checked out his appearance in the full-length mirror attached to his clothes closet, like a teenager getting ready for his first date.

"Sure," Blake said, and rolled him a line. He watched in amazement as Sluggo snorted it all in one nostril. He sniffed in afterwards to make sure he got everything and even dabbed the end of his nose with his finger. When he noticed Blake looking at him, he said, "Things change, man. You gotta change with the times, go with the flow. Get with it." He danced another jig. Then he sat on his bed looking like he was going to have a heart attack. There was a knock on the door.

"Yeah?" he shouted.

"It's me, Daddy."

Sluggo looked at Blake, embarrassed, and opened the door.

"Hi baby, you ready to disco?" his visitor asked, as she let herself into the room. When she saw Blake, she apologised.

"Oh, I didn't realise you had company. Hi!"

"Hi," Blake said.

"Are you coming to the disco?" she asked Sluggo, who walked her to the door as quickly as he could.

"Yes, I'll see you there!" he said.

"Bring *him*," Blake heard her say, as she left. "He's hot!"

As soon as she was out of the room, Blake and Sluggo looked at each other and laughed. "Well, you've made it with the geriatric crowd!" Sluggo joked.

"This place is bad for your health," Blake said. "They should have a warning sign on the door."

"People do die here, Blake. There have been two deaths since I arrived. But it wasn't from old age. I could hear the bullet shots from my room." His eyes widened. Instead of being frightened, he looked excited.

Blake was surprised anyone had managed to get a gun in with all that security. Unless, of course, they only checked certain people. Jasper and his boys probably didn't need to go through that archway. Neither did Miss Williamson. But it was difficult to imagine her pulling a gun on anyone. Or was it?

"Sluggo, are you sure that you are safe here?" Blake asked.

"Yeah, don't worry about me. When they fill out my death certificate they'll probably put "death by martini," on it. I'd better go. I'm late. The Sunrise Disco has already started. Listen."

Blake could hear Donna Summer singing *Bad Girls* somewhere in the distance.

Sluggo sprayed himself a generous amount of cheap cologne and asked Blake if he was ready to leave.

As they walked together down the hallway, Blake reassured his friend that he would be back. He left Sluggo at the disco – a medium sized room with a concrete floor that looked more like a small gymnasium than a disco. Coloured lights were projected against the walls and there was a bar to the left. A small group of residents had already congregated there with their complimentary martinis. He heard one old man say, "no olive, and no vermouth."

Blake continued walking down the hall and eventually found the main staircase. Miss Williamson seemed to appear out of nowhere once he got to the bottom. A guard handed him his gun still wrapped in the white cloth napkin.

"We don't get many cops in here," the kindly Miss. Williamson said.

"What makes you think I'm a cop?" Blake asked.

"We always check the serial numbers of guns in our database. A cop who used to be a model? Interesting."

"I'd appreciate it if you wouldn't tell Sluggo. He doesn't know."

"I would gain no advantage by doing so," she said like a motherly robot.

"Thank you." He handed her a twenty-dollar bill. She kept her hand open, and he gave her another one. She crumpled them up and stuck them in a pocket in her dress.

"Go around the archway, this time," she said.

Blake walked around the archway and headed for the front door. Mrs. Williamson stopped him before he left. She looked worried, almost sad - the nearest thing to an expression he had seen on her face. She kissed him on both sides of his face - not real kisses - her lips never touched his skin. Instead, she used the action to whisper two words into one of his ears without moving her lips, so the guard wouldn't notice. "Be careful," she warned.

It was so unexpected that Blake wondered if he had imagined it. Miss Williamson returned to her position next to the guard and Blake left the building. Outside, on the porch, he noticed a new addition. A large notice board had been erected inviting the residents and their guests to "Disco Bingo."

'Everything is a disco in that place,' he mumbled to himself. 'Maybe those old people think that if they keep on dancing, they won't die.'

There was a large photograph on the board of a drag

queen with frizzy hair turning a bingo barrel with a wacky smile on her face. Underneath the photo were the words, "Her Royal Highest presents Ruby Royal, the Queen of Disco Bingo."

It was the 'time traveller' that Blake had seen from outside the cab. Her make-up was deliberately applied in an exaggerated fashion – her lipstick not only covered her lips, but circled them, and her eyeliner dripped from under her eyes. It was why he thought she was crying. It was all part of her act.

He looked down the path and saw that there was already a cab waiting for him at the end of it.

6. Gigi's

A light snow had fallen while Blake was visiting Sluggo – not much for the middle of January – hopefully he had missed most of the winter while he was sunbathing in the Canaries in December. Looking back at the retirement centre, he noticed that some of the snow had landed haphazardly on the gabled rooftop, making the place look almost magical; but he wondered what was going on behind that fairy tale façade. Miss Williamson had told him to "be careful," but careful of what?

The passenger door was already opened by the time he got to the taxi.

"To Gigi's," he said to the driver as he buckled up in the back seat.

"The Italian place?" the driver asked.

"Yeah. Midtown. Do you know it?"

"Yeah, I know it all right." I live in Manhattan. The diner been there for years. How the owner has managed to stay out of prison all that time is beyond me."

"What do you mean?"

"Well, you know all those Mafia busts in the 1980's? He was involved in all that. Feeding information to the cops is my guess. I wouldn't trust him past my pinkie. My grandpa is still in jail because of those busts."

"Your grandfather was in the Mafia?"

"Isn't everyone's? The Mafia is everywhere, buddy. You're not from here, are you?"

"No, I grew up in California."

"That explains it."

Not wanting to get into an extended conversation about Luigi's possible connections to the mafia with a complete stranger, Blake got his phone out and opened the contract that Sluggo had emailed him. He quickly scrolled to the last page and saw it was signed by someone named "Jasper Devonshire." He gave his address as 12 Henry Mews in

London.

Blake looked the address up on Google maps and saw a small street of quaint, candy-coloured buildings that looked more like country cottages than urban apartments. They were in an area of London called Fitzrovia, which was like a small village inside of a city. Apparently, Dylan Thomas used to drink at a pub there.

No. 12 Henry Mews had recently been purchased by Jasper for £10 million. That seemed like a lot of money for such a small building, especially when he clicked around and found out that the same property had been bought for £2 million a year and a half ago. He looked up the companies involved in that sale and couldn't figure out where the addition £8 million went. It looked like Jasper had sold the property to himself at a handsome profit through a series of nebulous names and short-lived businesses. Whoever Jasper was, he was very rich and very good at moving money around.

"Is this the place you mean?" the cabbie asked, as he pulled up to Gigi's.

"Oh, yeah, thanks," Blake said. He had been so wrapped up in the net that he hadn't noticed they had reached their destination. Luigi was, as usual, behind the main glass counter chatting with customers, many of whom had been going there for years, some for a generation or more – the sons and daughters of the fathers who were busted during the Mafia Committee Trials of the '80s.

"Blake!" Luigi shouted when he saw him walk into the diner. He rushed out from behind the counter (as fast as a 73-year-old can rush) and hugged his old friend with Mediterranean warmth as the calculating wheels in his brain turned, trying to figure out the best approach to take. 'Just how much did Blake know about the death of his nephew, Phil?' And how much did he know about Phil's business? Had he just been Phil's friend, and customer, or had Phil told him that it was Luigi who had provided the coke that Phil used to sell at Blunt?

As they hugged, Blake clocked Luigi's staff of Italian studs standing at attention behind the counter, watching their boss like hawks, in case their assistance was needed. The only thing that happened, though, was that Luigi took Blake straight into his office which doubled as a stock room.

Boxes of panettone were stacked up against the walls. Gigi's was famous for its panettone. In Italy the bread-like cake was eaten mostly during the Christmas holidays, but at Gigi's it was one of the "authentic Italian delicacies" that you could get year-round. Luigi received regular shipments of it from his suppliers in Italy. Hidden in many of the cakes were bags of uncut cocaine which he sold through a network of small-time dealers. His nephew, Phil, had been one of his dealers before he was killed by the NYPD.

Most of the cops in New York suspected that Luigi was a supplier, but they could never pin anything on him. Whenever his name came up, Captain Seligman would argue that he was more useful as an informer than a felon. "For God's sake, he's an old man," Seligman would say. "He probably wouldn't last a whole trial."

Although Luigi got some of his stuff from crooked cops like Layton, most of his supply came directly from his extended family in Italy. Through diversification he had managed to keep his operation going through all sorts of police crackdowns. Although Layton's death was worrying, it didn't interrupt the supply of the white fuel that kept the city that never slept at night, awake.

"Please, have a seat," Luigi said, motioning to a white plastic chair in front of a folding Formica table – the type of thing you might see in kitchens in the 1950s. It had probably been in that room since then. Luigi sat on a folding metal chair behind the table.

"I heard about Phil," Blake said. "I'm really sorry. What was it all about?"

"How?"

"How what?"

"How did you hear about it?"

Blake shrugged. "People talk. He had a lot of customers at Blunt."

"But you had already left New York by the time the cops got to him. Where did you go, Blake?"

"The Canaries. I needed some sunshine."

He regretted it as soon as he said it. He had told Carlotta he had been to Vegas when he had arrived back in New York – and Carlotta was friends with Luigi. She had probably already mentioned that Blake was back from "Vegas." It didn't matter much to Luigi. He was used to liars.

"I guess the police finally caught up with Phil," Luigi said. "Unless you know something that I don't."

He paused to give Blake a chance to say his spiel, but there wasn't one. Blake just sat there without saying anything.

"Why did you go to the Canaries, Blake? Did someone warn you that the cops were onto Phil, tell you to make yourself scarce?"

"No. They were after me too."

Luigi didn't know whether to believe him or not, but he didn't want to get too involved in the past. Whatever had happened, Blake could still be useful to him. Now that Phil was gone, Luigi needed another dealer. Blake was already in with that crowd at Blunt. But he had to be careful. What if Blake had been a cop as well as a customer? What if he had turned Phil in? But then, why would he have gone to the Canaries? He was running away from something, presumably the police.

"Phil's mistake was that he got into those crappy designer drugs and silly stuff like crystal meth," Luigi said. "I always told him to stick to the classics – cocaine, marijuana, pharmaceuticals – but he never listened to me, he had to get involved with crystal and - what are those other crap drugs that young people do nowadays – Mephedrone? And that one that starts with a G – GHP or something."

Blake thought it was strange advice for an uncle in his '70s to give to his thirty-year-old nephew about drugs – "stick to the classics."

"I wonder who Phil's supplier was, who gave him the coke to sell?" Blake asked, fairly certain that it was the person he was speaking to.

"I've asked myself that time and time again," Luigi said, rubbing his forehead theatrically as if it would help him to come up with an answer.

"Where do people get this rubbish?" he continued. "I've never been involved with stuff like that. Why do they call it experimenting with drugs? It's just experimenting with bad health."

Blake shrugged.

Then Luigi took a chance: "I had a friend from the old days. I think he might have helped Phil out. Maybe I'll ask him what happened. I was never that friendly with him. I've heard he's looking for someone else to help him out now that Phil is gone, but I wouldn't know anyone like that – I've never been involved with the stuff. It's a young person's game."

Blake tried to remember how many times Luigi had said he wasn't involved.

"It's sort of a shame that you're not involved, Luigi, because I'm looking for a job," Blake said.

"You shouldn't say things like that unless you mean it."

"I do mean it. I need a job and I don't care what I do. I'm still young. I don't do drugs anymore, but I don't have anything against people who do."

"I hardly see this guy, I think he likes to keep the

business in the family, *capisce*?

"Well, if you see your friend, tell him I'd love to be part of the family, if they'll have me."

"Okay, okay. Enough. Like I say, I don't get involved in these things. Not anymore." Blake seemed too eager. Like an undercover cop.

"Are you hungry?" Luigi asked. Let me get you a panini and coffee to go." He stood up. It was time to leave.

"Okay, sure."

Blake followed the boss back into the restaurant area. Again, the all-male staff snapped to attention. They were looking more and more like an army of thugs. Luigi instructed them to give Blake a ham and cheese panini and a double macchiato to go – with extra foam. He remembered how Blake liked his coffee from last year.

"I'll walk out with you," Luigi said. He wanted to see what direction Blake went.

Blake acted like he forgot something, tapping his pockets. He took out his wallet.

"I forgot to pay," he said. When he opened the wallet, he made sure the gold wrap fell out. He quickly picked it up and put it back in his wallet, pretending that he didn't want Luigi to see it.

"Where did you get that?" Luigi asked, his old-man's eyes suddenly as alert as a teenager's.

Blake shrugged. "Someone in Bryant Park sold it to me."

"Sure they did."

Blake tried to hand a ten-dollar bill to Luigi for the sandwich and coffee, but he wouldn't take it.

"I told you, it's on the house."

Blake put his wallet back into his trouser pocket, said his good-byes and left, walking in the same direction as he would if he was returning to the Broadway. The NYPD headquarters was in the same direction.

Luigi went back into the restaurant and continued to

watch Blake through the window. He saw Blake get on his phone. Who was he calling?

"What's up boss?" his head of staff asked.

"Not sure yet."

"Luigi!" a woman shouted.

"Mrs. Lubinski! How are you? I didn't see you."

Mrs. Lubinski had been one of Luigi's beloved regulars for nearly two decades. She had passed him at the door, and it wasn't until she got to the counter that she turned back and saw him. She immediately started filling him in on the exciting life she had led since the last time she was there, about a week ago. He tried to pay attention while she went through a litany of aches and pains, relatives who had just left and relatives who were just arriving.

"Everybody wants to visit New York, even in the wintertime!" she exclaimed proudly, like she owned the city.

Although Mrs. Lubinski thought that Luigi liked her, he actually thought she was a pain in the ass, like most of his regulars.

While Luigi talked to Mrs. Lubinski, Blake was down the street talking to Warren on his phone, filling him in on his morning. Warren wasn't in a good mood. Seligman had put him in charge of a memorial event for Lieutenant Layton – but told him not to make a big thing about it.

"There are rumours going around that he was a crooked cop." Warren said.

"Crooked? What do you mean?"

"That's what they're trying to find out. Got any news on your end?"

Blake told Warren about the "weird" retirement home and Sluggo's contract with Jasper.

"Can you send me a copy?"

"Sure. I'll do it now. One other thing you should know. Sluggo had a gold wrap in his drawer like the one that Bobby sold to me."

"A gold wrap? But I've been to Sluggo's bar – when it was his bar. He's ancient. What's he doing with a wrap of cocaine?"

"He didn't seem so ancient anymore. He was having a whale of a time. That place is more like a pick-up joint for senior citizens than a retirement home. They serve martinis at breakfast."

Warren laughed. "Maybe I should go for early retirement after all."

"It's probably more Seligman's speed. I can imagine him and his paunchy stomach dancing with the blue-rinse brigade."

"Blake. Be careful about comments like that. Seligman could have you fired."

"It was a joke."

"Yeah, I know, and it won't go any further, but Seligman has a lot of power."

"Okay, okay, forget I said it."

"Forgotten. I wonder where all these gold wraps are coming from. There must be some new boys in town. Did you go to Gigi's?"

"Yeah. I dropped the gold wrap I got from Pinky's in front of the old man. You should have seen his face. It was like I had dropped an A-bomb."

"Which probably means there's competition in town. Did he offer you a job?"

"Not yet, but I'm working on it."

Warren's desk phone rang – his direct line to Seligman.

"I'm sorry Blake, I'm going to have to take this call. Is there anything else we need to talk about?"

The hold button on the phone flashed annoyingly.

"I'll catch up with you after class," Blake said.

"Okay, see you after class. Be careful. We've got you covered but still be careful."

"I meant to bring that up. I keep looking for this shadow, but he doesn't seem to exist."

"If you could see it, it wouldn't be a shadow."

They ended their call and Blake hurried to class, checking out the people around him, trying to figure out whether Warren was telling the truth. Any of the passers-by could be his shadow, or none of them could. That tramp over there was looking at him suspiciously as he went through the trash. There was a power-dressed woman behind him with a shoulder purse large enough to hold a Beretta. A man to the right was staring into a store window, but why would a man be looking at a window display of women's dresses?

7. O Soto Gari

The door to the classroom was still open when Blake arrived. A woman in sweatpants was talking to a blonde guy by the entrance. Blake had no problem sliding into his seat without anyone noticing. He looked up at the clock and saw it was after two, but the new teacher wasn't there yet and some of his classmates had started goofing around with each other – sheets of paper became crumpled up grenades thrown at other students when they weren't looking. One of them almost hit the woman in sweatpants as she entered the room and walked to the front of the class followed by thirty sets of male eyes staring at her shapely curves. Somebody made the mistake of whistling. Another grunted like a caveman.

"Cut the crap, assholes," she said after setting her laptop down on the front desk. "I'm the new instructor. Lieutenant Jackie Foster - but you can call me Lieutenant Foster."

Blake was in such a rush to get to his seat that he had hardly noticed the lieutenant when he first arrived. Now he found it difficult to look anywhere else. Her dark red hair fell loosely in front of her basket-ball sized breasts which were made even more noticeable by the outline of a sports bra under her Lycra fitness top. The only make-up she wore was black eyeliner enhancing her piercing green eyes. Her thick lips didn't need lipstick to look inviting. Her dark eyelashes may have been fake but everything else looked real. Quite a change from Lieutenant Layton.

A skinny young man in a polyester suit with out-of-date lapels raised his hand nervously.

"Yes?" Lieutenant Foster shouted at him, as friendly as a cougar about to strike. 'How dare he ask a question before I've even said anything,' she thought.

The student stood up bravely behind his desk, "I, I just wanted to say how sorry I am for Mr. Layton and his family. I'm sure the rest of us feel the same and, well, I know how difficult it must be for them..."

There was an audible moan from some of his classmates. Lieutenant Foster looked shocked that he had dared to make any sort of comment about a superior. What made him think that she cared about his opinions? He hadn't even finished training.

"Shut up and sit down," she said. "I really don't care about your feelings. You're not here to feel. You're here to be a cop. Got that?"

The student sat down. His classmates sniggered. One said something about 'trying to be a teacher's pet.'

Lieutenant Foster addressed the class in general: "I realise that quite a few of you liked Lieutenant Layton, and I sympathise with you although, to be honest, I always thought he was kind of a jerk. Anyway, different strokes for different folks."

The faces of some of the students dropped. Did she really say that?

Jackie explained: "The point I am making is that to become a good cop you cannot be guided by your feelings. It's okay to feel – it's human – but you're here to learn how to uphold the law and the law is the law. It's about right and wrong and not about feelings."

She pointed to a random boy in the class and said, "You, with the crewcut – would you kill your best friend in order to uphold the law?" The student sat there dumbfounded, trying to figure out if it was a trick question.

"I'm waiting," Lieutenant Foster said, her arms folded.

"Is murder ever a valid response to a question?" he asked. (He had taken a philosophy class in his last year of high school). Seeing Jackie's expression which hovered somewhere between puzzlement and disbelief, he quickly tried to cover up any mistake he might have made:

"I mean if you could just taser him or something like

that, it would be better," he said. "Or maybe hit him with a truncheon."

No reaction from Jackie, her arms still folded.

The student again (nervously): "Wouldn't it depend on the circumstances?"

"Fuck the circumstances." Jackie replied, banging her desk with her fist. "If you are not willing to kill your best friend for the good of humanity than you're in the wrong place."

The students glanced at each other uncomfortably. Blake heard one of them say 'whoa."

Blake laughed. He liked the new teacher. She seemed almost crazy. Who in their right mind would kill – or even taser – their best friend? The other students felt anxious. They were used to sending their BFFs emojis of hearts and hugs. There wasn't an emoji for murder. A dagger maybe, but that could mean anything. Some of the more intellectually inclined students considered the moral dilemma silently, in their heads. At what point did a 'wrong' – killing someone – become a 'right?'

Jackie pointed to a poster on the wall behind her, next to a large blackboard. It featured a handsome cop handing out candy to the neighbourhood kids. "You see that poster," she asked. What do you see?" The students looked at each other, too scared to answer.

"You!" she said snapping her fingers at a spaced-out kid who had managed to acquire a black eye between the end of yesterday's class and the beginning of this one.

He grudgingly gave her the answer he thought she was expecting: "I see a cop trying to help out some kids in the hood, to make friends in the community."

"Really," she said? "*Really*? I see a potential child molester. Cops aren't allowed to hand out candy. Those chocolate bars are probably filled with sewing needles. And he's probably not a cop. Things aren't always what they appear to be."

Apart from Blake, who was trying not to laugh, the students looked horrified.

"My method of teaching is slightly different than Lieutenant Layton's," Jackie continued. "First, I want you to put those god-damn laptops away and clear the room - desks and chairs to the walls. NOW!"

The students pushed the chairs and desks against the walls with varying degrees of enthusiasm, depending on how much they had had to drink the night before.

"Being a cop isn't about sitting in front of computers." She explained. "It's about catching criminals and for that you're going to need protection - your own two hands to begin with."

"You!" she yelled out to a young man who was still dragging his desk across the room, "when did I say to move in slow motion?'

Everyone laughed.

"And You! in the Armani suit."

Blake wondered how she knew it was Armani.

"Take that jacket off before you ruin it."

Fortunately, Blake had put his Beretta in his locker before the class. Unfortunately, his wallet, which was in the inside pocket of the jacket, fell on the floor when he folded the jacket over his chair. When it hit the floor, it opened, and Jackie saw his NYPD I.D. The other students wouldn't be issued one until after they finished training. None of them saw it – they were too busy with their desks. But Jackie did. Her suspicious eyes honed in on it like magnets.

Blake quickly picked up the wallet and looked straight at her with an intensity that said, 'yes, I'm a cop.'

'Later,' her eyes responded.

She looked away quickly and continued to address the class:

"Now that we have some space, I have an announcement to make. In addition to being a proud

Lieutenant in the best police force in the country, I'm also a black belt, second degree, in Judo. Get ready to take some falls, fellas!"

She stuck one arm forward and one leg backward with lightning speed and shouted "*KIAI*!" at the top of her lungs.

The students stood transfixed. She withdrew to a normal standing position and bowed quickly.

"The bow is to show humility," she explained. Do you know what humility is?" she asked the class.

"Yeah, um sort of, I guess so…" they answered.

"Now, you see those mats over there?' There was a stack of thin rubber mats rolled up in the corner of the room. Roll them out. They're our practice mats. You'll be in the gym next week where they have higher density mats, but these will do for now.

This is just a tester session; in case you decide you want to quit now. The most important move in Judo is the fall. Until you learn to fall, you're useless."

She took her place on one of the mats and without warning, she suddenly fell back, shouting *KIAI*! again. She had, effectively, performed a Judo 'throw' on her herself.

"Did you see what I did there?" she said as she stood up. "You allow your body to fall and let your arm slap the mat at the same time. Do not try to break your fall with your arm. It has to meet the mat at the same time as your back. And don't forget to shout *KIAI* – pronounced 'key eye' – as soon as you hit the mat. You won't feel a thing. Now it's your turn."

Another random student was chosen and told to come to the front of the class. She didn't bother to get his name. She saw him more as a demonstration tool than a human being.

The young man looked petrified. Without warning she grabbed his shirt on the upper right side and pulled him toward her. She pushed the left side with her other hand

and swept her right foot under his left. He fell backwards onto the mat and stared up at her helplessly.

"You didn't say '*KIAI*!' she shouted into his face. Then she faced the class again, a sea of frightened faces worried that they would be next.

Another student rose his hand.

"Yes?" Jackie asked sternly.

"Um, Lieutenant Foster…."

"Yessss?"

"What does '*Kiai*' mean?"

Jackie didn't know. She might have been told when she first started taking Judo, but she had forgotten. Maybe it was something religious or maybe it was just a distraction from the pain of the fall. She rolled her eyes as if it was the dumbest question in the world and turned to the rest of the class. "NEXT QUESTION?" she asked.

There weren't any. She explained that the Judo flip she had just performed was called *O Soto Gari*. She wrote it phonetically on the blackboard - 'Oh-So-Toe-Gah-Ree.

She then pulled the student up from the mat and demonstrated the throw in slow motion. When she was finished throwing him backwards again, she told each student to grab the person next to them and practice the throw a few times. She walked amongst them, coaching their movements and reminding them to "*Kiai*." After each couple had "*O Soto Gari'd*" each other a few times, she told them to roll up the mats and get back on their laptops.

"Make sure you bring some sweats with you next week," she reminded them. "Now, where did Layton leave off?"

They returned to studying the seedy alleyways of Manhattan and solving the multiple-choice moral dilemmas that went with them. When the class ended at 8, she called Blake to the front desk.

"Who's your contact?"

"Lieutenant Warren."

"Leave the ID in your locker next time. You wouldn't want any of the other students to see it. They won't get theirs until they finish training."

That was all she said. No questions asked. Blake wondered if she had already been told that he was undercover.

"Sure. See you tomorrow."

Jackie was packing up her laptop by that time and didn't bother to say good-bye.

Lieutenant Warren sat at his wooden desk, watching for Blake out of the long window opposite him which looked out on the communal hallway. He had just returned from a meeting with Captain Seligman upstairs about the memorial service for Lieutenant Layton.

"We need to make the memorial low-key," Seligman had said during the meeting. "We still don't know what Layton was involved in."

"What about the press?" Warren asked.

"Charm them like you always do. Tell them you can't tell them anything because there's an investigation going on. They'll get bored of the story eventually."

"Some of the papers are saying it was a cult."

"Doubtful. Whoever did this was probably trying to make it *seem* like a cult murder, to throw us off the real reason. So far, it's still a robbery interruptus..."

Warren was still thinking about the meeting with Seligman when he noticed Blake walking toward his office. After a brief knock, his protégée poked his head in.

"Anybody home?"

"How was class?"

"Hey, does that Jackie woman know about me?" Blake asked, as he sat down in front of Warren's desk.

"What Jackie woman?"

"Lieutenant Foster. The cop who took over for Layton.

I dropped my ID in class, but she didn't seem surprised I had one."

"Did anybody else see it?"

"I don't think so."

"What did Lieutenant Foster say?"

"Not much. Just told me put it into my locker before class."

"Good idea. But no, I didn't tell her. Maybe Seligman did. Anyway, she's trustworthy. I wouldn't worry about it. I'll talk to her later. How was the class?"

"Okay. If you like Judo."

"Judo? She loves telling people she's a black belt. Excuse me - black belt *second degree* that is. Did it impress anyone?"

"I don't know. I liked her but the rest of the class seemed a little dazed."

"I had a look at that contract you sent me. I also did some research into Jasper Devonshire. His last name isn't really Devonshire – or at least he wasn't born with that name. In England it's easy to change your name – you just fill out a form – you can do it online. He changed it by depot about ten years ago. His real name is Jasper Richardson."

"Why change it?"

"Have you ever heard of the Krays?"

"People on Twitch mention them sometimes. I think there's a game about them. Or they're characters in a game."

"They were old-time gangsters in England. Before my time, but they're famous. They still make movies about them. They were from the East End of London. London isn't like New York – it's got areas called the East End and West End except the West End is sort of in the middle. Then there's North and South London. It's not called Uptown or Downtown like here."

"Sounds confusing."

"It is. They don't have intersections either, they have 'roundabouts.' It's impossible to know which traffic light to follow."

"How come you know so much about London?"

"I had to visit it a couple of times to liaise with the MI6 – now called S.I.S. or the Secret Intelligence Service. They've got agents working in New York and vice-versa."

"Cops?"

"Sometimes. The cops over there are called 'bobbies' – I kid you not."

"If someone called a cop over here a bobby, they'd probably get tasered," Blake said.

"Anyway, the Krays ran a gang that were like a mini-mafia – into everything - protection rackets, kidnap, murder – but they were sort of glamorous too – they had a night club called Esmeralda's. The English version of the rat pack hung out there."

"What's a rat pack?"

"Dean Martin, Frank Sinatra – entertainers who were thought to have a connection to the mob."

"There's a picture of Dean Martin on the wall at Gigi's."

"I'm not surprised. Anyway, as bad as the Krays were, there was a group of criminals who were even more ruthless - The Torture Gang, headed by Charlie and Eddie Richardson. One of their favourite activities was nailing their victims to the floor and pulling their teeth out with pliers, one by one, until they got the information they wanted."

"What happened to them?"

"The Krays are dead of course, but I think one of the Richardson brothers might still be alive. I remember something in the press about how he got out of prison and started life coaching, or something like that. Inspirational speeches for businessmen."

"You think Jasper Richardson – Sluggo's Jasper – is

part of that family?"

"Who knows? The last name could be a coincidence, but I do think there's a turf war going on between the old mob and this English gang – Jasper and his mates. They say 'mates' in England instead of 'buddies.'"

"No way."

"Way."

"Straight guys do?"

"Yep. Try to find out as much as you can about this Jasper guy."

"Is it okay to mention him to Luigi?"

"You might drop his name, but don't get too specific. He already knows you have a gold wrap – and we know the gold wraps are connected to Jasper because of Sluggo. Keep up the good work, by the way."

"It's not like I know what I'm doing."

"You've got a good instinct. That's the best thing to have for a cop. At least in my books. One other thing Blake - about your mother. We haven't stopped looking for her. We have a few leads. I'm in touch with the lawyers for your father's estate. I know they're in touch with you too. They were asking about the contents of a safe in the attic..."

"That was his private stash of jewellery and whatever. I remember the safe. And the attic. It wasn't a nice place."

He didn't mention that his father had purchased the jewellery from crooked pawnbrokers to hide some of his oil money from the IRS.

"I don't know why old people squirrel away stuff like that." Warren said. "In your dad's case, a lot of the stuff was stolen."

"Who knows where he got it? I remember he was always bringing stuff back from pawn shops. I went to a few with him."

"Do you remember their names?"

"I was only a kid. If I remember any names, you'll be

the first to know."

The names were already popping up in Blake's head, but why complicate things?

"Thanks. And I'll let you know anything we find out about your mom. The only thing I should warn you about, is that we're checking the deceased records as well."

Blake felt like he had been stabbed in the heart. He never thought for an instant that his mom might be dead. She was so young. His father had married her when she was young – late teens or early twenties. She would have been in her late forties by now, maybe fifty.

"What are you doing tonight?" Warren asked.

"I'm not sure," Blake said. "I'm tired. I need to get some sleep."

"Have you been to Blunt yet?"

"No, I should be able to do that next week. This week has been busier than I expected."

"You can say that again. I'll see you tomorrow after class."

Blake walked back to the Broadway feeling deflated, thinking about his mother, wondering whether she had survived the city that he was now walking through. He looked at everyone rushing around. What was the point? Where was everyone going? What was the purpose of life? Money? Success? Love? He had already been in love once and doubted that it would happen again. His girlfriend, Candy, had been something special. Now she was dead. Blake had experienced too much death in his life for someone in his twenties. He hoped that Warren would find his mother alive.

Again, Blake checked out the people on the street, wondering if any of them were shadowing him, like Warren had said. A man in an overcoat on the other side of the street seemed to be walking the same pace as him. An old man on the street corner looked at him sheepishly and didn't cross the street when the colour of the traffic light changed. That homeless person over there looked too clean to be a beggar.

He had to stop being so suspicious of everyone. It was starting to drive him crazy.

When he arrived outside the Broadway, his phone rang. It was his dead father's lawyer.

"Hi Blake, this is Simmons. How are you?"

"I'm okay. Have you found my mother yet?"

"No. We're still working on it."

Simmons started giving him the same information he had just got from Warren. Blake knew he charged by the minute and cut him off.

"That's all I need to know."

"Huh?"

"Whether you've found my mother. You haven't. Thanks for calling."

Blake hung up and walked up the short set of steps to the entrance of the hotel. The string of bells that hung from the handle of the door jingled like they always did, and he walked into the lobby. He was shocked by what he saw.

8. The Broadway

The reception desk was empty. No Carlotta. It was the first time that Blake could remember where she hadn't been at the desk. It gave him the creeps. She never left that desk. Even if she was in the back office, she came out as soon as she heard someone come into the hotel. A string with bells hung from the inside handle of the door which alerted her to a potential customer. The door had been left unlocked. If she had gone anywhere, she would have locked it.

Blake waited at the empty counter. Where was she? He noticed that a light was on in the back office and the door was partially open. He had always assumed that it's where she slept, but it wasn't even 10 pm – she never went to bed that early. As he stood there, trying to figure out what was going on, a can of Style Raven shaving cream rolled on the floor and stopped in the middle of the opening of the office door. He wondered if it was the can that he had given to Carlotta last year when he was signed to Style Raven by Slick. He looked at his image on the can which looked back at him. Then he heard what sounded like moaning.

He didn't know what to do. What were his multiple-choice options, now? He was a cop. Did that mean he needed a warrant to go into the back office or could he intervene as a friend? Being undercover meant that he was always undercover, but did that mean he was always a cop? He shouted Carlotta's name. Again, he thought he heard someone moaning. He jumped onto the counter with his long legs and dropped himself on the other side, feeling like his favourite comic book hero, Spider-Man, coming to the rescue.

Carlotta was sitting in a chair; grey gaffer tape had been wound around her large body, binding her to it. A ball had been placed in her mouth, and more gaffer tape had been wound around her head to keep the ball in place.

She had tried to shout out when she heard Blake come into the hotel but could only produce a muffled moan. Her chair was next to a small shelf on the wall where she kept her toiletries, including the can of shaving cream; she'd managed to push it onto the floor with her chin and watched it roll slowly toward the opening in the door. When she heard her super-hero jumping onto the counter, she knew she was saved. There was always a chance it was one of the men who attached her to the chair in the first place but thought it unlikely that they would have jumped over the counter.

Blake quickly ran to her and undid the tape around her mouth.

"HURRY UP!" she whisper-squealed. "They're in your room!"

"Who is?" he asked as he got out his pocketknife and sliced through the gaffer tape that held her to the chair.

"The men in the grey suits."

"Why?"

"They mentioned Phil," Carlotta continued as she tried to catch her breath, "that you'd been a friend of Phil. Or maybe I told them. They forced me to give them your room number. We gotta get out of here NOW!"

Unwrapped, she stood up and squeezed her plus-sized feet into a pair of small black stilettos. Strips of grey tape were still hanging from her dress as she grabbed her purse from the same shelf as her toiletries and made a run for the front door, with Blake following. They quickly waved down a cab and jumped in.

"GO! QUICK!" she told the driver.

"Where to?" he asked.

"Anywhere!"

As the cab joined the slow-moving traffic on Central Park West, Carlotta looked back at the hotel.

"Look, it's them!" she said.

Two men in grey suits had just come out of the hotel

entrance and were looking in all directions, searching for
their missing prey. Blake made sure he got a good look at
them. They were slim, their suits tailored – one light grey,
one dark. They both had brown hair that hung over the top
of their ears. They were young, probably around Blake's
age – in their twenties.

"Any particular address?" the driver asked.

"West 131st Street and Frederick Douglas Boulevard,"
Carlotta said. "I've got an apartment in that building," she
explained to Blake.

"You do?" Blake asked. I thought you lived in that
office at the hotel."

"I do. The building we're going to is my official
address – a housing project I used to live in before I was
discovered by the Turk who helped me transition."

"He paid for the whole shebang?"

"Nah. Just my boobs. My cunt is courtesy of the state."

"Where's the Turk now?" Blake asked, knowing full
well where he was.

"In jail. He got caught during a smash and grab."

"But if you live in the office at the hotel, who lives on
131st?"

"My children."

"You have children?"

"Yes, darling. And test tubes were not involved. I used
to be part of the Ball scene. The House of Carlotta. The
kids who live in the apartment aren't mine by birth.
They're by street. Waifs that nobody wants. Black folk
don't always take kindly to their family members being
gay, even nowadays. Can you imagine being in a gang and
having a sister for a brother?"

"What address do you want on 131st Street?" the cab
driver asked.

"Fuck!" Carlotta said, looking out the window. "They
beat us to it."

The same two men they had seen outside the Broadway

were getting out of a cab in front of Carlotta's building.

"We got to get out of here. Now!" she shouted to the driver.

"You know I've got to keep the fare running."

"Yes! Just get out of here! Quick!"

The driver passed the building and continued down the street. Carlotta looked back at the men.

"Now, how did they find my address?" She wondered out loud.

"Is it listed?"

"Maybe somewhere. It's where they send my SSI."

"Where to now?" the driver asked.

"Downtown."

Going the wrong way on W. 131st, they turned right at Adam Clayton Boulevard and headed back downtown.

"What should we do?" Carlotta asked. "We can't go back to the hotel. Are you okay to pay for all this driving around, honey? I'm *skint*."

"Skint?"

"I picked it up from the grey-suits. They're English. It means you ain't got no money."

"Yeah. Don't worry. I'll pick up the tab. I should call my boss, though, to ask what we should do."

"Your what? What boss? How's he going to know what to do?"

"He's a cop."

"He's a *what*?" Carlotta screeched. "But if *he's* a cop, what are you?"

"I'm a cop too, Carlotta. Sorry about that."

"What the hell is going on! After everything I told you and now, you're telling me you're a cop! How long have you been a cop? You used to be a junkie."

The cab driver clocked them in the rear-view mirror. Their conversation just got better and better. 'What a great job,' he thought. A cabbie in New York. After his shift he would meet up with other drivers at a bar near Times

Square and share their stories. He'd been at the bar most of last night telling stories about all the crackheads he had picked up – some in the middle of the afternoon. But this was even better. A low-speed, getaway to nowhere in particular with a gangster's moll and a junkie cop. He couldn't wait to tell his colleagues when he had a drink with them later. There was always an adventure waiting around the corner when you lived in New York. He wouldn't live anywhere else.

He got back on Central Park West again, but this time he headed toward downtown. The traffic was so slow that driving hardly required his attention. Instead, he listened to the podcast in the backseat.

"Yeah," Blake said, "I used to be a junkie. Then I lost my job. Then the cops accused me of killing another junkie – a model at Slick - and my own father. So, I escaped to the Canaries. The guy who is now my boss traced me down after a shootout with my dealer. You remember Phil, don't you? The guy who the grey suits mentioned."

"Of course, I remember Phil. He's Luigi's nephew - a dealer. And I also remember him going in and out of your room. He never spent the night though. I wouldn't have allowed that. No overnight visitors, except for our gay clientele, of course. It would be useless trying to keep out their trade."

"Well, last year the cops busted Phil. His girlfriend confessed everything."

"Susan. I remember her too. What a mess."

"Yeah, well, Phil tried to shoot the cops that busted him, and he got shot instead. Both him and Susan. When Susan was dying, she confessed that Phil killed the model I had been accused of killing. But I was in the Canaries by then getting involved with Ginger who controlled the dope scene at the gay clubs in the Yumbo Centre. Lieutenant Warren traced me down and I helped him bust Ginger and her mob. Now I'm undercover, trying to do the same in New York – helping the cops to bust the dealers who used to sell to me."

Carlotta looked at Blake's clear blue eyes and knew he was telling the truth, but wished he wasn't. Blake was supposed to be one of the *normal* residents.

"I don't know how I do it. I really don't," Carlotta said. "A friend used to tell me that if there is trouble in the room, it will head straight in your direction. She was right. If you're a cop, where does that leave me?"

"Don't worry, Carlotta, you're not in trouble. You're a friend. If you can provide us with any information, it would be appreciated, but if you can't, you can't. I'm not going to pressure you. Apparently, your Turkish boyfriend is singing up a storm in prison – my boss and his boss are grateful for that."

"He *would* squeal, the cheat. Well, honey, I'm happy to help out. I've always been one of those 'hear no evil, speak no evil, see no evil' types, but not anymore. I'm on your side now.

"Glad to hear it. Now tell me about those men in the grey suits."

As their cab ambled slowly along Central Park West, Carlotta spilled as many beans as she dared to. What did she have to lose? She was in her fifties now and fed up with the criminals she had to deal with at the Broadway. If she had a choice she'd probably move back home – back to the suburbs of New Orleans where she had been brought up – but she felt glued to Manhattan. People who left were considered cowards by people who stayed. If she was going to stay, she might as well cooperate with the police. She might need them someday.

"The men in the grey suits didn't have anything to do with the hotel," she began. "It was run by a different gang – I mean - a different Board of Directors. The grey-suits seemed to come out of nowhere."

Staring into nowhere, she added "And now they're trying to take over the city."

"Does 'they' include a guy named Jasper?"

"You know Jasper?" Carlotta asked. "He's a dreamboat. I *love* his accent. They all have English accents. Jasper oversees everything. I've only met him a couple of times. Him and his boys want the hotel, but the 'Board' doesn't want to give it up and I'm stuck in the middle."

"Buy why? Why do they want it so badly – a seedy dive like that?

"*Excuse me?*"

"Well, um, you know what I mean. It's not exactly the Ritz."

I've worked at worse. A lot worse. Let's just say it has a history."

"Okay, so it has a history. Why does Jasper want it?"

"Blake, I'll tell you what's going on, but please don't drag me into anything. This is between me and you. And *you*," she added to the two bloodshot eyes staring at them in the rear-view mirror. The driver smiled.

"Don't worry, Carlotta, I won't. You were practically my first friend in New York. I remember when I first arrived. I thought you were great. We don't have people like you in Crumville."

She laughed. "I never did find out about Crumville. Where is it?"

"Well, it's called Ridgecrest now, but it used to be called Crumville after the farming family that started a homestead there back in the cowboy days. Do you know Kern County?"

She looked at him as though he was asking about an unknown crater on Mars.

"No, Blake. Can't say I do. Look, Jasper and his boys aren't just after the hotel, they're after the whole city. There's a war going on. I can feel it. It used to be the mob that had control of the city, but after the Mafia Trials in the '80s, the Turk and Albanians got involved, along with the relatives that didn't get busted at the Trials. And now the English gang – Jasper and his boys – are trying to take over from them. That's what it seems like to me."

"Where to now?" the bloodshot eyes in the rear-view mirror asked when they reached Washington Square.

"Can you drive around the park a couple of times? I need to call my boss," Blake answered.

"As long as you pay, buddy, I'll go anywhere you want."

Blake called Warren and explained what happened at the Broadway.

"Did the guys in the grey suits mention you by name?"

"No. They just described me." He looked at Carlotta to make sure he got it right. She was nodding. "They knew I was a friend of Phil."

"Stay in the cab. I'm going to call Seligman. Give me five minutes."

Blake hung up and asked the driver to keep going round the park. He explained to Carlotta that his boss was calling *his* boss. Carlotta started having second thoughts.

"Blake, maybe I should just get out now."

"In Washington Square? Too dangerous." Blake said. It wasn't long before Warren rang him back.

"Blake, listen, I spoke to Seligman. Can you get to Blunt? It's a public club, they know you there, they have security there. I'll meet you in the VIP bar in about an hour and a half. Seligman is sending some plainclothes officers to watch the hotel. If the door's still open, I'll get a locksmith to lock it shut. It's a crime scene now. Attempted kidnapping. Did Carlotta leave keys in the office?"

Blake asked Carlotta where the keys were to the front door.

"Locked in a drawer under the main reception counter."

"Whose got the key to that drawer?"

"Me, but they could bust in easy. It's a small lock."

"Did you hear that?" Blake asked Warren.

"Yeah, Blake," the lieutenant continued. "We'll get you a safe apartment to stay in, but for now is there any chance that you and Carlotta could stay with Cameron?"

"Maybe. I'll ask him."

"Let me know when you get to the club."

"Okay. No problem."

"Does Carlotta know you're a cop?"

"I sort of had to tell her."

"O.K. don't worry about it. We'll talk later."

Blake hung up his phone and told the driver to take them to Blunt.

"Blunt! I can't go to Blunt. Look at me!"

"What do you mean? Because you're black?"

"No! Because I'm ugly! And fat. It's easy for you. You're gorgeous. You used to be a model. Look at what I'm wearing! You look good in everything. I look like I've just been on a shoplifting spree at that Salvation Army store on 46th Street."

Blake looked at her in her springtime flowery dress (in the middle of winter) covered by an aubergine-coloured polyester overcoat pretending to be wool. She fumbled around in her bag, looking dejected, hoping to find some make-up. "We left in such a rush."

"Don't worry. You look great. I was practically famous at that place. They'll let anyone in who's with me."

"Thanks!"

"Just keep your coat closed," he joked.

"But that would be hiding my best assets. My boyfriend used to love my boobs. Turks like their women large."

"Don't worry, you'll get in."

"I hope so, baby, because normally I wouldn't have a chance at getting into a place like that, dressed like this. I wouldn't even be able to get into the Balls dressed like this

– *especially* the Balls..."

The cab dropped them off behind a large crowd that had already formed in front of the club. Howie was still on his soapbox, like last year, and Eloise stood with her clipboard at the entry rope.

"Blake, Blake!" Howie screamed when he saw them getting out of the cab. "You're back! Get your ass up here, honey!"

Blake reached his hand out to Carlotta who was having difficulty manoeuvring herself out of the taxi.

"DO NOT let go of my hand Carlotta. No matter who says what, you are mine now, do you understand?"

"Yeah, Superman, I understand."

"Spider-Man," he joked.

By the time they got to Howie, they had already heard a few disparaging "what is its" by members of the crowd who couldn't believe that they were letting Carlotta in and not them. Even Howie stopped her after letting Blake through.

"I'm with him," she said.

"*Really?*" Howie asked. He looked at Blake.

"Of course she is. Why not?"

Howie turned to Carlotta: "Have you been eatin' blueberry pie, girlfriend?" he asked.

Carlotta had managed to find a lipstick in the cab but some of it had missed her lips.

"That's it," she said to Blake. I'm out of here." She started to leave.

"Oh my god! Carlotta!"

Howie had recognised her voice from the old days.

"Were you The House of Carlotta?" he asked.

"Well, I wasn't exactly the whole house," she answered.

"Don't you remember me? I used to go there to score some smoke."

"For fuck's sake. Of course I remember you. I thought

you was Puerto Rican!"

"I was. I mean, I am. You go right in girl. And here are some drink tickets."

He handed a batch of tickets to both her and Blake and waived them into the magic of Blunt. That's how the club was described on the internet – "magical."

"You see, I told you I was famous," Blake said, as they walked up the stairs to the V.I.P. room.

"Uh huh," Carlotta answered, using her drink tickets as a fan.

Rita, who did the door at the V.I.P. room, hugged Blake as soon as she saw him – "You're back!" And gave him a theatrical kiss on the lips.

Who's this?" she asked about Carlotta.

"She's with me."

"No problem."

Rita undid the rope and as soon as they walked into the room, Cameron shouted out from the bar.

"Hey Blake!"

Carlotta plopped herself down on the first empty bar stool she could find, accidentally knocking over the drink of a glammed-up girl on the next stool.

"I'm so sorry honey! Let me get you a drink!" Carlotta said.

The girl got up, gave her a dirty look: "no thanks" and went to complain to Rita. Rita kicked her out. She loved watching the girl's shocked face make its way down the stairs: "I'm going to tell Howie!" she threatened.

Rita flipped her off and turned to Carlotta. "Don't worry girl, I've got your back!"

"I'm beginning to like this place," she said to Blake.

"Haven't you been here before?"

"It had just opened during my 'going out' days. I had stopped clubbing by then. Too old. Then the Turk came along and the job at the hotel…"

Cameron wiped down the bar in front of them and

asked Blake where he had been "man."

"I, I've been away. I took a break."

"Uh huh," Cameron said. "You can tell me later. And who is this lovely woman?" he asked.

Blake introduced Carlotta.

"What are you drinking? Vodka and air?" It was a joke from last year – what Cameron called a vodka straight. Blake had graduated to whisky since then – a result of Phil's influence – but for old times' sake, he had a vodka.

"I'll have a rum and air, if there's one going," Carlotta added.

"No problem. When he brought their drinks, he refused to take their drink tickets – "next time," he said. Then, after Cameron took out his own vodka and air from under the counter, the held up their drinks and toasted "to the future!"

After a few long sips, Cameron leaned over to Blake and, not knowing where Carlotta fit in the scheme of things, half-whispered, "I heard about Phil. I'm sorry. But I did warn you about him."

"I know. I know. But it turned out all right. His girlfriend told the cops what really happened. And forensics backed up her story."

"Susan. What a handful she was. I hated Phil for getting you hooked on that stuff but looks like you're okay now. Have you been in treatment?"

"Uh. Not really. Maybe. Sort of. I went to the Canaries for a while and cleaned up. I just got back."

"Glad the nightmare is over. Hey, just to be good sports, let's toast to Phil. He wasn't a bad guy, he just had bad habits."

Blake raised his glass: "To Phil!"

"To Phil!" Cameron said.

Carlotta held up her drink slightly, without saying anything, and then downed most of it. She never liked Phil and wasn't going to start liking him now that he was dead.

"It's so good to see you, again, Cameron. Are you still living locally?"

"Yeah, I'm one of the few that haven't moved to Brooklyn - the cowards."

Blake and Carlotta laughed.

"Business good?" Blake asked.

"It's not as crowded as it used to be. Not as many people are coming out because of that virus thing. You know what people are like. Everyone suspects everyone else of having it."

"But it's in China!" Blake said.

"I know but it's moving around the world. I'm not sure if there have been any cases here or not. Some people think it's a fake – a way of keeping the population under control. A friend of mine says that they don't want people to have fun. They just want them to work and shop."

"Who's they?"

"I don't know. Everybody talks about 'they', but nobody says who 'they' are."

Blake noticed that Cameron's glass was empty. "Hey Cameron, can I get you another drink? I can pay for it with drink tickets. You won't have to wait for someone to leave without finishing theirs."

"Wow. A legitimate drink. Thanks. Don't tell Howie."

"Of course not."

Idle chit chat started and stopped as Cameron took care of his other customers. By the time he got back to Blake and Carlotta, they were ready for another round. As Cameron replenished their drinks, Blake leaned forward: "Listen Cameron, I have a favour to ask you."

"What's that?"

"Is there any way that Carlotta and I could hole up with you tonight? It would just be for one night."

"Huh? Why? What's going on? Are you in trouble?"

"Nothing that exciting. I only got back on Sunday, and I've been couch surfing since then. Carlotta just needs a place to stay for a night. We'll be gone tomorrow."

"I don't know Blake. It's just a studio." Cameron hated saying no to anyone. People had helped him out in the past, so he felt obligated to help other people out. But something seemed fishy.

"I can sleep on the floor." Blake continued. "I'm sure Carlotta won't mind taking the couch."

As he talked, Blake took out ten twenty-dollar bills from his wallet. "We're willing to pay for our stay of course."

"Is that for one night?"

"Yeah."

"Two hundred dollars for one night?"

"It's cheap by Manhattan standards. How about it?"

Phil looked down at the money. He could use it. He got good tips at Blunt but living in New York was so expensive. He still owed his landlord part of last month's rent.

"Don't you have anyplace else to stay?"

"I've got an apartment lined up for tomorrow, but we don't have anything for tonight, and I really don't want to stay up all night."

"Okay, if it's only for one night – I mean what could happen in one night?" He took a set of keys out of his pocket and took two off the ring.

"Here, I keep another set in my locker in the office."

"Thanks."

"No funny business."

"Of course not. Really, Cameron, you can trust me. I don't do drugs anymore. I'm really boring, now."

"Okay. Would you mind picking up a couple of bottles of wine on your way home? I like having a drink after work but I'm not sure how much booze I have at home."

"Red or white?"

"Yeah."

Blake laughed. "No problem. I'll let Carlotta choose."

He looked around the room to see if Warren had arrived yet. Maybe he was downstairs. But he said he would meet them at the V.I.P. bar. Carlotta saw him looking and asked if "his friend" had arrived.

"Friend?" Cameron said. "I don't want anyone else at the apartment – just you and Carlotta."

"Yeah, of course," Blake said. "Don't worry. A friend of Carlotta's was going to meet us here for a drink, but he hasn't arrived yet."

"What's his or her name? I probably know them."

Blake was digging a hole he might not get out of. He didn't want Cameron to know he was a cop. Fortunately, a new group of customers arrived at the bar.

"Hold on," Cameron said. As he left to take the orders of the newly arrived, there was a series of loud bangs downstairs, like fireworks.

"Gunshots." Carlotta said, looking worriedly at Blake.

He didn't know whether to believe her or not. 'Why would Blunt be under attack?' he asked himself.

Then all hell broke loose as people started screaming and running upstairs. Howie rushed into the room in front of a panic-stricken group of customers and saw Blake and Carlotta sitting at the bar.

"Blake! Blake! Run. Take the fire exit. Cameron, show them!"

There was blood on Howie's shirt, and it sounded like he was gasping for breath between sentences.

"Men in grey suits... looking for Carlotta... I asked them who they were... they wouldn't tell me... I wouldn't let them in and then they started shooting."

"Are you okay?" Blake asked.

"Yeah. Run. Cameron. NOW!"

Cameron took Blake and Carlotta to a section of the club's black wall that Blake could now see was a door. He pushed it open, and they were suddenly on an outdoor fire escape. Blake and Carlotta ran down it, hunched down, not daring to look back. They ended up on First Avenue. Blake knew the area. They had studied it in class. He took Carlotta to an alley near east 6th Street. A small group of junkies were shooting up in the shadows. "Hey man! What's going on? Terrorism? It wasn't us!"

Blake and Carlotta took a circuitous route through the unknown alleys of lower Manhattan. Cop school had been more useful than expected. When they reached Washington Square, the world seemed completely normal. Cars circled the square as usual and remnants from the conversations of the people who passed filled the air – the excited voices of tourists looking for a place to have a drink.

Carlotta and Blake looked behind them to see how far away Cameron was. When they couldn't see him, they ran as quickly as they could to Cameron's apartment on 17th Street and 9th Avenue – a small apartment on street level with its own entrance. Blake used the keys that his friend had given him to open the door. The living room was empty. No Cameron. He went into the bedroom. No Cameron. He called out Cameron's name but there wasn't a response. He hadn't made it home.

Carlotta collapsed on the couch in the living room.

"Water! Water!" she gasped, holding her throat.

"I've got to go back," Blake said. "I need to find Cameron."

"Are you fucking crazy? We're home now. You ain't going nowhere."

Blake rinsed out two tumblers from the side of the sink, filled them with water from the faucet and handed one to Carlotta.

"I've got to go back," he repeated. When he was finished with his water, Carlotta took his empty tumbler and filled it from a one litre bottle of Svedka vodka that was sitting on a coffee table in front of the couch. He drank it. She refilled it. He drank it again.

"Relax baby, don't be stupid," she said. "You ain't going anywhere. Cameron will show up. Trust me."

Blake sat down next to Carlotta in a daze. He tried Cameron on his mobile, but it went straight to voicemail. He rang Warren, but his phone went straight to voicemail too. In both instances, he didn't leave a message. The fact that he had rung was enough of a message.

"What do we do now?" he asked Carlotta, feeling defeated and confused.

"We wait," she answered.

They waited.

9. Wednesday

Cameron had still not shown up by the next morning. Carlotta was asleep in Cameron's bed and Blake had crashed out on the couch – not the most comfortable arrangement for him, given his height. His feet kept waking him up as his long legs pressed against the arms of the couch. Rather than helping him sleep, the vodka he had drunk seemed to increase rather than decrease his heartbeat. He lay half awake, half asleep and any noise he heard made him scream out his friend's name, only to realise that it wasn't Cameron making the noise, it was just the sound of the refrigerator or the wind rattling the windows. His phone techno-bleeped at 6 in the morning – goddamn that ringtone! - and he grabbed it like he was grabbing a life preserver.

It was Warren.

"Blake, are you okay?"

"Yeah, I'm okay."

"Thank God you weren't at Blunt's last night. It was a stupid idea."

"I *was* there."

"You were?"

"Yeah, both of us were – Carlotta and me. Who said it was supposed to be safe?"

"I'm so sorry. Seligman thought that because it was such a public place, with its own security, that you guys would be okay."

"What happened to Howie and Cameron? Are they okay?"

Warren didn't answer. He could sense the panic in Blake's voice. He didn't know how to break the news.

Blake asked again: "*Are they okay?*"

"I'm sorry to have to tell you this, Blake."

"Give it to me."

"Howie didn't make it. He's dead."

Blake paused, afraid to ask the next question. "What about Cameron? What happened to Cameron?"

"We don't know yet. They're still trying to identify the bodies. It was carnage."

"What about the hospitals?"

"There were a few of them. We're still checking the lists. They change every minute."

"Who was behind it?"

"We're not sure. A couple of guys in grey suits shot their way into the club with automatic weapons. Seligman thought it might have been a botched robbery attempt – there's a lot of expensive jewellery floating around in that place."

"Bullshit," Blake added. "They were after Carlotta – or me. What happened to my supposed shadow?"

"There was someone shadowing you, Blake."

"So, what happened to him? Why wasn't he around?"

"He's dead Blake."

Silence was followed by doubt. Blake was beginning to have second thoughts about joining the force. Maybe he should quit now while he was still alive. When he had first signed up to infiltrate a drug ring, it sounded almost fun – like one of those old detective shows he used to watch when he was a kid. He hadn't been expecting dead cops or nightclub massacres.

Warren asked him what had happened at Blunt: "Try not to leave anything out. It's important."

"Carlotta and I were in the V.I.P. room. Howie ran up the stairs and warned us about the men; that they had come to the entrance of the club and asked if Carlotta was there. Howie pretended not to know who she was. He wouldn't let them in. They started shooting."

"Blake, that changes things. Let me call Seligman and I'll call you back."

"Changes what?"

Warren had already hung up.

"Was that your boss?" Carlotta's sleepy voice asked from the bedroom door, Cameron's robe tied loosely at her waist.

"Yeah."

"Blake, I don't know about all this cop stuff," she said, walking into the living room. "Do I really want to get involved with the law?"

"You already are."

The phone techno-bleeped again. He picked it up and vowed to change it as soon as the call ended, No messing around anymore...

"I spoke to Seligman," Warren said. "There's an investigation going on in regard to Blunt. Can you keep what Howie told you to yourself for the time being? We don't want to blow your cover and we don't want to get Carlotta in trouble. Her boyfriend, the Turk, is being very cooperative with the cops and until we can figure out what's going on, it's better that we keep all this to ourselves."

"Look, I really don't give a shit. Play it any way you want, but I need to know what happened to Cameron. I'm one step away from quitting the force entirely."

Warren paused. "You can't do that Blake."

"Do what?"

"Quit the force."

"Why not?"

"Do you think it's that easy? They wouldn't let you go, Blake. Seligman would get suspicious. He would think you changed sides."

"So what. What could he do?"

"Don't ask me that question Blake. Remember, the force is working for the common good, it's not about individuals."

"Find out if Cameron is still alive."

"I'm working on it, Blake. I really am. There were three hospitals involved. The bodies are still being identified."

"I'm hanging up now."

"Blake, don't hang up. Not yet. It's important that you do what you would normally do today. Get your coffee at Gigi's. Then go to class. Try and find out if Luigi knows anything but don't put yourself in danger. Tell Carlotta not to leave the apartment."

"In another words, do whatever I would normally do, so I can get shot."

"No, do what you would normally do, so they don't suspect anything."

"Who's 'they?'"

"That's what we're trying to figure out. Don't worry, you'll still be shadowed."

"Great job it did before."

"Don't tell Carlotta this, but we've got some people watching Cameron's apartment too. Two 'innocent bystanders' will be hanging around outside the apartment with PDW's under their coats. If…"

"What's a PDW?"

"Didn't they teach you anything in that class? Personal Defence Weapons - basically compact machine guns. You'll probably be issued one at some point."

Blake didn't want a PDW. He wanted out. Once he got his inheritance, he could leave the force, maybe even leave the country. Maybe go back to the Canaries. He thought back on how nice it was lying on the beach with Candy in their favourite spot. Then he remembered that she was dead.

"Hello… Blake are you still there?" Warren asked.

"I'm still here," Blake said. "Just pondering my future. And my past."

"Well, about your past, there's something I should mention. I think we found your mother…"

Blake did what Warren told him to do. He stopped at Luigi's for his morning coffee. Luigi grabbed him as soon as he arrived and dragged him into the back office.

"Thank god you're okay," he said, standing behind his desk. "I heard about what happened at Blunt. It's all over the news. I was afraid you were there."

"I was."

Luigi paused. Was it Blake that the gunmen were after?

"I'm glad that you didn't get hurt," Luigi said. "I wish Phil had been so lucky when the cops came after him."

Blake didn't see the connection between the two events, except that it gave Luigi a chance to express his resentment that Blake was still alive, but his nephew wasn't. Luigi didn't look "glad," he looked worried. The lines of his furrowed brow were V-shaped, his eyes looked like cracked glass, like he had been up all-night waiting for something to happen. He sat down behind his 'desk' and motioned for Blake to sit in the plastic chair on the other side.

"Something's going on Blake. There's a war going on. I'm an old man Blake, I can't take all this anymore. One gang fighting for another gang's territory. Again, and again and again. How long can it go on?"

He almost sounded sincere.

"To be honest, Blake," he continued, "I pretend that it doesn't matter but Phil's death really took it out of me. He was a pain the ass, but I miss him. I really do. He doesn't come for dinner on Sunday's anymore with that cockamamie girlfriend of his. I even miss her. I'm finished, Blake. Finished."

Blake almost felt sorry for him.

"What do you mean, 'a war'?" he asked. "Who are the good guys and who is the enemy?"

Luigi looked straight into Blake's eyes, like a human lie detector, and asked: *"Who are you?"*

"Huh?"

"The last time you were here you dropped a gold wrap of cocaine. Where did you get it? Whose side are you on, Blake?"

"I don't know what you're talking about."

"Where's Carlotta?"

"How should I know?"

"I'm next Blake. I can feel it. If you can save me, save me. Who gave you that gold wrap? Tell me."

Blake didn't like the direction that the conversation was taking. What did Luigi expect? Sympathy? It wasn't in the plan. He had gone into the office thinking that Luigi was going to offer him a job as a dealer. Blunt might be out of action but that wasn't the only club that Luigi covered. And how did Luigi know that Carlotta was missing, anyway?

Blake stood up and left the restaurant, passing Luigi's flunkies behind the counter. He could feel their eyes in his back. When he was gone, Luigi walked out of his office and joined them.

"I wouldn't trust him as far as I could throw him," he said to his staff about Blake. Then, "Mr. Schmidt, how are you! A flat white with an extra shot as usual? No problem. How is the family…"

Blake walked quickly to his morning class, trying to be invisible. Where the fuck was his damn shadow? What was to prevent Jasper or his gang from drilling him down from the open window of a slow-moving car? They knew about him now. They had been to his old room at the Broadway.

"Hey mister!" someone yelled out from a car filled with kids. He walked faster. It was probably just someone asking for directions, but he couldn't take the chance. There was no way that he was going to stay in New York. It was making him too paranoid. Even if he didn't get his inheritance, he could still quit the force and move somewhere else. Not the Canaries, but somewhere. He wouldn't need to tell anyone where he was going. He could just disappear somewhere peaceful. Everyone acted like New York was such a great city, but that was movie stuff. He could move back to California, where he came from. That's what he could do. He could buy a trailer and live in the desert. Nobody would find him there.

Blake arrived late to his class, grasping onto a coffee from the vending machine in the hallway like his life depended on it. Jackie gave him a strange look but didn't say anything. He tried to concentrate on her lecture, but his brain kept on thinking about California, about that trailer in the dessert. What was she saying? Something about the history of the organised crime in New York, how it had been exaggerated by Hollywood and what it was really like dealing with criminals on a day-by-day basis – all the paperwork you had to fill out and how only about a third of the criminals went to prison...

He couldn't stop thinking about Cameron. He tried to call him during the break, but this time Cameron's phone didn't even go onto voicemail. It didn't connect at all. It was dead. All he heard was silence.

By the time the class ended that day, Blake had decided he wouldn't be coming back tomorrow. He'd had enough of the force. He was tired of looking for his shadow. Despite Warren's earlier comments, there was nothing they could do legally to stop him from leaving. It was a job, not a prison sentence.

When he got out of the elevator on the sixth floor, he walked stridently to Warren's office, his eyes staring straight ahead like pointers on a map. The cops he passed in the hallway might as well have been invisible. When he got to the office, he walked in without knocking.

"Blake!" Warren stood up, surprised. He looked down at the head of the person seated in front of the desk. He had a visitor.

"I, I'm sorry," Blake said. "I didn't realise you had a visitor. I should have knocked." He started to back out of the office but was stopped by Warren's apology:

"Blake, I'm sorry too. I didn't realise it was so late, I didn't want it to be like this."

Blake stopped and asked, "Be like what?"

"I might as well introduce you," Warren said. "Blake, this is your mother, Brooke."

Brooke Webster turned in her chair and faced her son for the first time in more than two decades. She was almost fifty now but looked a lot older. The lines on her ravaged face mapped out a life of suffering. Her hair was dirty, a dull mustard colour that should have been blond. The cheap grease she had applied to it the day before to add some shine had dried out after a night in the cells and was flaking onto the black halter-top that criss-crossed her sagging breasts. Her eyes were half closed She had to lean forward to get a good look at her son. She was still wearing the same dark red lipstick he remembered as a child, but now it looked too dark, too desperate, and her lips too thin. There was nothing attractive about her.

Blake stood in silence looking at the stranger in front of him. Brooke thought about standing up, maybe shaking his hand, but she was tired and pissed off that she had been left in a cell all night. She couldn't be bothered to get off her chair. Even for her son.

"I'll leave you two to get to know each other," Warren said, falsely cheerful. Mumbling something about how he "needed a coffee," he told Blake he could have his seat at the desk, leaving the remainder of his morning coffee in a half-empty Styrofoam cup on the desk.

Blake took Warren's seat and stared out the side window to avoid his mother's gaze. She didn't notice that he was watching her reflection in the dirty window as she unclasped a black padded purse on her lap with an overlapping C on its buckle. He knew that buckle. Some of the models at Slick - the successful ones - had that purse. He wondered if it was fake. He watched her take a pack of cigarettes out of the purse, pull Warren's coffee cup toward her to use as an ashtray, and light up a Marlboro.

"Mom!" he shouted. "You can't smoke in here! It's a police station."

"Fuck the police," she said as she blew a cloud of smoke defiantly into the air and flicked her ash into Warren's cup. Her shoulders started to shake. She stared into the coffee so Blake couldn't see her face.

"Are you okay?" he asked.

She straightened up. Of course she was okay. She was always okay.

"What's the matter?" Blake asked.

She shrugged silently. She looked sideways and then down at her lap, silently.

Then she said: "You called me mom."

The tears came streaming down. She couldn't hold them back anymore.

Blake watched her from the other side of the desk, not knowing what to do. He wondered if the tears were for real. Last year, when the force had suspected him of murder, they sent a female undercover agent to his hotel, pretending to be his mother, in order to get a confession out of him. How could he be sure they weren't up to their old tricks?

"How do I know that you are who you say you are?" he asked as sternly as his gentle nature allowed.

She looked at him as though she was seeing him for the first time. The tears dried up quickly. "You're worse than me," she said. "I don't trust anyone either. Hold on, hon..."

Blake watched her rummage through a purse full of used tissues, receipts she no longer needed, and had never needed in the first place, and old notes reminding her to do things that she forgot about as soon as she stuffed them in her bag. Eventually she found a creased, faded photograph of a little boy, about six years old, standing between two adults who were each holding one of his hands. He recognised his father instantly, and then he recognised the other adult, barely an adult then, as the woman who was sitting across from him. His mother.

"My god, it really is you!"

"Oh, it's me all right," she said, taking another drag from her cigarette before dumping it into the coffee. One of the things she had taken out of her bag was a silver compact. She examined her face from different angles in the compact's mirror, using the round make-up sponge to touch up her blotchy skin.

"I don't usually look this bad," she said. "I'm older now, of course, but you can still see the resemblance."

He laughed and brought his chair around to her side of the desk and held out his hand to shake.

"Well mom, it's very nice to meet you after all these years," he said with a feigned formality.

"Fuck it," she replied, as she stood up and hugged him.

"Aargh! You're choking me!" he joked.

They both laughed and sat down. She held his hands in his lap.

"Blake, I'm so sorry I left. I thought so much about you. Every day, I've looked at that picture. Every day for – what - two decades?"

"Not quite, but it'll do."

They laughed again.

"Hey," he said "don't give yourself a hard time for leaving. I left too, you know. As soon as I could. I never blamed you for leaving. Dad was a monster."

"You can say that again," she said, as she rolled her eyes upward. "You don't know the half of it."

"Neither do you."

"Oh Blake, I'm so sorry. Damn. Damn. Damn."

"The best memories I have of my childhood are of you. How you used to do the vacuuming in that glamorous Hollywood gown. Do you remember?"

She laughed. "Do you mean that green thing? Advertised as 'emerald-green?' I thought they meant that the sequins were real emeralds when I ordered it. I probably still have it."

"You knew all the songs from the old musicals by heart. You used to sing them when Dad wasn't around."

"What was your favourite?"

He paused. "Well, I guess it would have to be 'Candy.' Do you remember it?"

"I can't believe you do! That was from a live Ella Fitzgerald album. I used to picture myself onstage talking to the audience like she did."

"I met a girl named Candy in the Canaries last year. She was a singer – she sang that song in her act."

"Girlfriend?"

"Yeah. Sort of my fiancé, I guess."

"Will I get to meet her?"

"I doubt it. She's dead."

"Oh my god! What happened?"

Blake told her about how he used to be a model and how he had met Phil, the coke dealer who became his best friend, and how he had escaped to the Canary Islands after he was accused of a murder that Phil had committed. That was where he met Candy.

"Phil? I knew a Phil," his mom said. "His uncle, Luigi, runs a diner in mid-town – it's been there for years – a *family* operation, as they say. I stay away from it, but the gang I pay for protection have something to do with it, I think, or used to. They're supposed to be protecting my place from the police too, but it certainly didn't happen last night. I was in the middle of a private party when the cops arrested me. That should never have happened. I can't figure it out, but something is going on. I tried to call one of the guys I pay protection to – they're supposed to provide bail. But the number wasn't working anymore."

"Do you mean lawyers?"

"Something like that."

"You know, when I came to this office tonight," Blake said, "I was determined to quit the force. I'd had enough. Now, I'm not so sure. Warren kept his word. He said he was going to find you and he did."

"So, you really are a cop?"

"Undercover. But don't tell anyone."

"See no evil, hear no evil, speak no evil."

You know you're a millionaire, don't you?" he said.

"Apparently. The lieutenant was telling me they were looking for me – that I would inherit John's money. We never got divorced."

"Has the lawyer been in touch with you?"

"They've only just found me. The weird thing is that the cops already knew about me. But I go under a different name now – Blanche instead of Brooke. Blanche Westwood."

"You know, Dad had a lot of money by the time he died. He got a percentage of whatever that oil company made from those drills on his land."

"I hated the sound of those derricks."

"Me too, but at least it means you'll be able to stop what you're doing and move to someplace nice. Get out of the city."

"Are you nuts? I hate the suburbs."

Blake laughed. "I thought everyone wanted a house in the country with a white picket fence. That's what Candy wanted."

"Fuck white picket fences. I couldn't think of anything worse. Besides, why would I want to stop working?"

"I, I'm sorry, Blake stuttered. "It's just that, well, what you said earlier. I thought they had arrested you."

"They did. At my place of business."

"What sort of business?"

She remembered she was talking to a cop. "I suppose you could say we're a service provider."

He laughed. Blake liked his mother. She was 'cool.'

She leaned closer. "Listen, this is between mother and son, yeah? Not mother and cop."

"Don't worry. You can trust me."

"When I left your dad, I helped myself to some of the stuff he kept in the attic safe – some of the jewellery and cash he was hiding from the tax man. As much as I could take. I sold it to whoever I could in New York. It wasn't difficult. With the cash I bought an apartment in a run-down building on the Lower East Side. It was so cheap back then. I divided it up with hanging blankets and started my business. I shared it with a few girls and eventually bought the whole building. I don't work anymore except for a few clients left over from the old days. Usually, I just give other girls a place where they can operate safely, away from the pimps. I guess you could call me an entrepreneur."

"But if the police have known about the house for ages, why did they arrest you?"

"Fuck knows. Something is up."

"We need to talk," Blake said. "What about Monday? I'm in training until then. Dinner?"

"Sounds like fun. But I should warn you, I don't come cheap," she joked.

"Only the best for mom," he said. "Don't worry. I'll get us a table someplace fancy." They traded numbers by text and Blanche got up to leave. She held her arms out for another hug.

"I love you, Blake."

"I love you mom."

She turned to walk out of the office. Then she stopped, turned around, and sat back down on the chair she had just left.

"What's the matter?" Blake asked.

"I forgot. I'm under arrest."

Blake could see Warren in the hallway outside the office, talking to some of his colleagues around the water cooler.

"Hold on," he said to his mother. He went over to Warren and thanked him for "giving us some privacy."

Warren came back into the office.

"Everything okay?" he asked Blanche.

She nodded. Blake joked, "Do you think it would be okay to let this reprobate go?"

"Reprobate!" Blake's mother pretended to be outraged.

Warren smiled. "Yeah. I guess it's okay. We'll call it a release for compassionate reasons."

"Well then, Gentlemen, I shall be on my way." Blanche said, as she got up walked out the office. Blake and Warren watched her weave her way down the hall in her black stilettos.

"Everything okay?" Warren asked.

"Couldn't be better."

Warren dragged his chair back to its position behind the desk and Blake sat on the chair his mother had used. He could still smell her perfume.

"How did you find her?" he asked Warren.

"Initially we looked for her under her real name, Brooke, but that didn't get me very far. We eventually tracked her down by her DNA; or rather yours."

"Mine?"

"We got it from the hospital in the Canaries. We checked it against our database. Your mother had been to one of those ancestry sites where the customer sends in a sample of hair or saliva and they trace their DNA – tell them what percentage of them is Norwegian, that sort of thing. We have access to most of those databases."

"But what about the privacy laws?"

"Privacy? What's that? It doesn't exist anymore. They get around the laws by assigning the DNA results to a number. But it doesn't take much sleuthing to match the number with other information already held by other companies – social media mostly. It's part of your 'digital footprint.' Did you know that every time you use your browser, your computer takes a picture of you?"

"Not mine. I taped a piece of paper over the camera."

"What about your phone?"

"I see what you mean."

"I was surprised when we found out who your mother was," Warren continued, "because the place she runs is almost a New York institution. It's on 8th Street and D. We turn a blind eye to it most of the time. It keeps the girls off the street and at least she pays her taxes – lots of taxes – which we wouldn't get from streetwalkers."

"She said she pays a gang for protection and one of the things they protect her from is the police."

"I don't get involved with that."

"Involved with what?"

"Malicious gossip to make the force look bad."

Blake looked worried.

"Don't worry," Warren said. "Your mom is okay."

"It's not that. I told her I'd take her some place nice for dinner on Monday, but I'm not sure where. Any suggestions? Someplace private. Quiet. But it's got to be nice."

"Let me ask Seligman. He knows all the best places."

Warren called his boss who called back a few minutes later.

"Thanks. I'll tell him."

He hung up and turned to Blake.

"Seligman has got you a table for two at Wang's. It wasn't easy. 8 pm. Use the credit card the force gave you. We'll consider it a business expense. And here, take some petty cash."

He unlocked his bottom desk drawer and took out a large metal box which he opened with a key on his keychain. It was filled with hundred-dollar bills. He gave Blake five of them.

"Get receipts if you can. Otherwise, don't worry about it. I've got a drawer full of receipts if you need any. A lot of places will give you ones that haven't been filled out, once they know you're a cop. It's always good to have a few extras. It's nothing illegal, it's just to satisfy the accounts department. Everyone does it."

The department's complaints about being underfunded didn't apply, apparently, to their abundance of petty cash.

"Would Seligman know if Cameron has been found?"

"I don't know Blake. As soon as I hear something, I'll let you know, okay?"

It didn't sound very reassuring, but there wasn't anything else he could do but wait. Maybe when he got back to the apartment, he would start calling the hospitals himself. He said good-bye to Warren, told him he would see him tomorrow, and used some of the money to take a cab to Cameron's apartment. He sent a text to his mother on the way.

"Hi mom. Blake here. Is Mr. Wang's okay for dinner on Monday night. 8 pm?"

"Wang's? Terrific."

"Great, will pick up at 7:30."

"Can I meet you there, instead? It'll be easier that way. I can just jump in a cab outside."

"Sure. Do you know where it is?"

"Doesn't everyone?"

"Ok. Will see you then."

He added two heart emojis, then replaced one of them with an 'x'.

She responded with three heart emojis, a 'thumbs up," and two Champagne flutes toasting each other.

As the cab approached Cameron's place, Blake looked

out for any lingering bystanders that might be the "protection" that Warren had promised but couldn't see anyone. Most people were rushing by in the cold weather, not 'hanging out,' and there were no noticeable bulges in their overcoats that hinted at automatic weapons.

'What a load of rubbish,' Blake thought. 'Nobody is protecting anybody.'

Blake used the keys that Cameron had given him to get into the apartment. He was surprised by what he saw when he opened the door. Carlotta had a guest.

10. Scoring

Carlotta sat on a couch in yesterday's dress next to a man whose head was bent over the coffee table in front of him, rolling a cup full of dice. They hadn't seen Blake come in.

"Yahtzee!" the man yelled as the dice hit the table.

"Cameron!" Blake shouted.

"Blake!"

Cameron stood up to hug his friend.

Carlotta looked up, pissed off at Cameron's five-of-a-kind, and poured herself another glass of wine from the half-finished bottle of Beaujolais that sat on the table.

"Thank god you're okay," Blake said in mid-hug. "Nobody knew what happened to you."

"When I reached the sidewalk, something fell on my head and knocked me out. It probably saved my life. Whoever the gang was who robbed the place, they probably thought I was already dead. I woke up in Beth Israel without my phone. I didn't have any numbers."

He sat down and offered Blake the armchair at the side of the coffee table. Blake took off his coat and hung it over one of the arms of the chair before settling into it.

Are you playing?" Carlotta asked.

"Huh?"

"Yahtzee."

Yahtzee? Who cared about Yahtzee? Blake was just happy to see that Cameron was okay.

"Yeah," Blake said. "I'm playing."

Cameron threw him a score pad. Carlotta got another glass from the kitchen area. While he was helping himself to some wine, she rolled a full house.

"Mama's lucky tonight!" she said as she wrote down her score. Cameron reached over and put the dice back into the cup, ready to roll, but then stopped:

"Hey Blake, can I borrow your phone? I want to call

Howie. Make sure he's okay. My phone doesn't work."

Blake didn't answer. Carlotta looked at the pained expression on his face and knew what was coming.

"Cameron, I don't know how to say this. I'm so sorry, but Howie didn't make it."

"Didn't make what?" Cameron asked, focused on the dice.

"He's dead," Blake said. "Howie is dead."

Cameron set the cup of dice down slowly.

"What do you mean?"

The last time that Cameron had seen Howie, he had blood on his face, but he was still very much alive.

"I mean that they got him, buddy. They killed him."

Cameron started to say something, but he didn't know what to say. He wanted to argue, but how do you argue with the truth? He sat still, expressionless, in shock. Then he began to talk:

"If it hadn't been for Howie, who knows what would have happened to me... I'd still be on the streets... He was like my family...The nicest fucking person that I ever met in this fucking shithole of a city..."

Silence. Cameron's eyes were dry – there were no tears – but he could feel a pit of sadness forming in his stomach that would never go away. He suddenly felt as lonely as the people who hung out at his bar, telling him their problems because they didn't have any friends they could talk to. New York was full of lonely people. Now, he was one of them. He was glad that Carlotta and Blake were there, but they couldn't replace Howie. They were more like customers than friends. He had never socialised with Blake outside of Blunt, and he hadn't known Carlotta at all before last night.

"I didn't even get to say good-bye." Cameron continued. "If he hadn't run up those stairs to warn us, we'd all be dead."

Blake noticed the dull look in Cameron's eyes as he

spoke. It scared him. No emotion at all.

Carlotta was familiar with death and misery. Probably too familiar. Her life had been full of friends who had died of overdoses, of friends who had been shot by cops for crimes that wouldn't have landed a white person in jail, of friends hit by the crossfire of neighbourhood gangs, and friends who had committed suicide because they felt the world didn't care about them and they were probably right.

Blake felt horrible for being the bearer of bad news. He tried to figure out a way to make it better. He reached into the pocket of his coat and took out the gold wrap he had bought from Bobby and Susan.

"Anybody want a line of coke?"

"Now we're talking," Carlotta answered.

"Thanks Blake. I could use one, if it's okay," Cameron said. His eyes didn't seem so dull anymore.

"What are friends for?" Blake answered, as he rolled out three thick, New York style lines.

11. Thursday

Blake woke up the next morning on Cameron's couch next to a half-finished game of Yahtzee and a half-empty bottle of whiskey. When they finished the bottle of Beaujolais last night, Carlotta brought out a fifth of rum she found in her purse and when they finished that, Cameron brought out his emergency supply of booze – a bottle of whiskey - from the kitchen cupboard.

Blake checked the time on his phone. Cop class was due to start in ten minutes.

"Damn." He wondered why his alarm hadn't gone off. Then he remembered he had forgotten to set it. He would be late for class which meant everyone would be staring at him when he walked in. He quickly got dressed in yesterday's clothes. Cameron, who was sleeping on the floor, woke up for a few seconds and Blake told him he could have the couch now. Blake splashed his face with cold water in the bathroom and took a slug of mouthwash before he grabbed his coat from the back of the armchair and left the apartment.

Outside it was snowing again, and every cab that passed was full. It only took him ten minutes to find an empty one, but it felt like an hour. His head was throbbing. He made himself comfortable in the passenger seat and called his boss.

"Blake?" Warren answered.

"Yeah."

"Everything okay?"

"Yeah."

"I guess you know that Cameron is okay."

"Yeah, he told me. You didn't tell me. He did."

"Where are you now?"

"I'm on my way to class."

He tried to keep his sentences short. It wasn't until he started talking that he realised he was still drunk.

"I've gotta run," Warren said. "Seligman is asking for me. Anything that needs to be reported right now?"

"Not much. Cameron won," Blake slurred.

"Huh?"

"Cameron won Yahtzee."

"Are you sure you're okay, Blake?"

"Yeah. I'll see you after class."

Blake arrived at class late, again. Big deal. Jackie gave him a dirty look. Big deal. The rest of the class sniggered. So what?

A couple of times during the lesson, she passed his desk and knocked on it lightly to wake him up. She needn't have bothered. He already knew most of what she was talking about and had even used one of the guns she described. There were no actual guns yet, just pictures and descriptions, but you could tell that the rookies were desperate to start using the real things. What they wanted most of all was the uniform, with the big belt to hang a holster from. When a student asked if they would be getting their uniforms soon, Jackie told him to slow down, that it wouldn't be until the end of the month when, and *if,* they graduated. That shut them up. Nobody had mentioned that they might not graduate before.

After class, Blake went to his daily meeting with Lieutenant Warren. As he walked down the hall to the office, he tried to wish the wrinkles out of his clothes and the smell of alcohol out of his breath.

The first thing that Warren did was to reassure Blake that they were getting him an apartment to live in.

"No more Broadway, of course," he said.

"What about Carlotta?" Blake asked.

"It's difficult. She doesn't officially work for us. Can she stay with Cameron one more night? I'll contact Housing and see if we can get her an apartment in the projects, but it might take a few days. I'll get a social worker to help her out. If she has any information she wants to share, we might be able to get her police protection, but we can't afford to protect everyone Blake."

"You've got to protect her, Warren. Don't worry, she'll talk. She's probably got plenty of information. She was the desk clerk at that gangster hideaway for years."

"If she's got anything we can use and she's willing to appear in court, I can probably get her into our witness protection scheme."

"Don't go out of your way," Blake said sarcastically. "And speaking of protection, where was my fucking shadow this morning while I was freezing my ass off trying to catch a cab?"

"A shadow is not a warm coat or a ride to work. They're there for your protection...."

"Stop with the bullshit Warren. There is no shadow."

"You're protected Blake. That's all I can say."

"Why am I not convinced?"

Warren moved a meaningless piece of paper from one side of the desk to the other. "So, what did you three get up to last night?" he asked.

"Doesn't the shadow know?"

"He's a shadow, Blake, not the man with the x-ray eyes."

"We got drunk and played Yahtzee. Why?"

"What happened to that wrap you bought at Pinky's? Show it to me."

Blake didn't know what to do. Most of the contents of the wrap had been snorted, and he didn't have it with him anyway. Why would Warren even ask that question? It was like he already knew the answer. How could he?

"I left it at Cameron's. I didn't want to carry it with me on the street."

"I want you to get more. Go to Pinky's after our meeting and score another wrap. You need to establish yourself as a regular customer."

"Yeah. Sure."

"Do you need some cash?" He started to take the metal box of money out of the desk drawer.

"No. I'm okay."

"Just one more question."

"Yeah?"

"Have you still managed to stay clean? You didn't dip into the other wrap, did you?"

"No, of course not."

"I'm trusting you, Blake. Remember, you're a cop now."

"Don't worry, I told you before that you can trust me."

"I hope so Blake. I really do."

Blake walked to Pinky's after the meeting. He felt guilty for lying about the cocaine, and now he was about to get more. But this time it was his duty.

As he approached the bar, he could see that the new Pinky's sign had arrived and was fully installed. The bright pink neon was difficult to ignore. Sluggo's was officially no more. All the lights on the new sign worked perfectly. Blake was disappointed. He preferred the flickering lights of Sluggo's sign. He was even more disappointed when he got inside.

The place was packed with young people who thought it was cool to hang out in a retro 'dive.' It was if the real down-and-outs had been replaced by fake ones. Worn out jeans and plastic loafers had been replaced by ripped jeans with designer labels and Gucci sneakers. 'Slumming it' was 'in.'

Blake thought about Johnny the junkie shivering in some nameless alley, like the ones they had studied in class, instead of his warm corner at Sluggo's - all in the name of gentrification, of progress – the type of progress that didn't care about people who had nothing – useless people like Johnny. Blake couldn't help thinking that someday the useless ones would fight back. What did they have to lose?

"Hey, Blake!"

It was Bobby, pushing his way through the crowd so he could get to his most famous customer – the Style Raven guy. He was wearing darker jeans this time, but they were still faded around his ass.

"I've got some good stuff," he whispered when he reached his famous friend. Bobby slipped a wrap into the front pocket of Blake's jeans, pushing it toward his crotch, and then pushing it some more.

"Okay, okay, I get the message," Blake said.

"When you go to the bar, buy a beer for $60.00," Bobby murmured with a smile and a wink before he went on to his next customer.

Blake walked up to the bar and handed Sarah three twenties. She gave him an empty bottle of Coors. He pretended to take a few gulps and left the rest of the bottle on the bar. He couldn't wait to get out of that claustrophobic space of people pretending to be happy. The noisy traffic outside was a relief after the techno crap they were playing inside. He followed the moon to the end of the road and hailed a cab going south to Cameron's apartment. He looked forward to turning them on again with the stuff he had just bought.

12. Home Sweet Home

Cameron and Carlotta hadn't left the apartment all day. They got up late and started drinking early. After finishing what was left in the bottle on the coffee table, Cameron produced another bottle of whiskey he had stolen from Blunt as an emergency back-up to his emergency supply. He preferred vodka but so did most of his customers. Whiskey was easier to steal. The cheap stuff, of course.

After a frozen pizza for dinner, they brought out the Yahtzee game again. They were still playing it when the front door buzzer went off.

"Blake's back!" Cameron said as he went to open his door. Carlotta was focused on her latest roll of the dice until she heard Cameron's "what the fuck?" and looked up to see two men in black latex masks push him aside and enter the room. Guns pointed; they told Cameron to get back on the couch next to "black mama." Then the gaffer tape came out and one of the intruders wrapped it around Carlotta's mouth. When Cameron protested – "What are you doing?" - he was pistol whipped.

"Don't worry mate." the other intruder said, just follow directions and you'll be okay."

Cameron clocked their English accents.

"Who are you? he asked. "What do you want?"

"The person we want isn't here," he said. "But I'm sure he'll get the message when he sees you two."

Cameron could tell the intruder was sweating. His latex mask was sticking to his face. Both were wearing heavy black overcoats. They took turns taking them off. While Latex 2 pointed his gun at their two victims, Latex 1 too his coat off and hung it over a chair. No. 2 did the same when 1 was finished.

"That's better," Latex 1 said. I can breathe now. While he stood with his gun pointed at Cameron, Latex No. 2 wound the tape around the rest of Carlotta's face, then bound her ankles and calves together so she couldn't stand and taped her wrists behind her back so she couldn't use her arms.

"You're going to love this," Latex No. 1 said to Cameron. Still holding his gun, he broke the bottle of whiskey against the coffee table and poured what was left over Carlotta. Then he handed Cameron a broken piece of glass and told him what to do with it.

"Let's see. Why don't you begin by slicing up her legs and then her cunt?"

"Are you fucking crazy?"

"No, I don't think so," Latex No. 1 said. "I think I'm perfectly sane. Go on. You'll be surprised how enjoyable it is."

Cameron tried to figure out how he could use the broken glass to attack the man in front of him. The problem was that there were two of them. If he attacked one, the other would come to his defence.

"'Ere mate, I'll start," Latex No. 1 said.

He picked up the broken bottle from the table and started cutting one of Carlotta's thighs. Thick, dark blood seeped out of the wound as the tape covering her mouth quickly moved in and out – a silent scream of pain.

"Look at that! He said, pointing to her taped mouth. "I love that. Pure panic. Brilliant." Cameron felt he had to do something quick - he couldn't just sit there, regardless of the risk.

"You're going to love doing this," Latex 1 said. "And I'm going to love watching you do it." That was his thing. Forcing friends to torture each other, as if to prove that friendship didn't exist. Most people would do anything to survive. Even cutting up a friend.

"It's fun, innit?" he said to Latex 2.

In that short moment, when Carlotta's torturer was focused on his partner instead of their victims, Cameron managed to slip his piece of broken glass to Carlotta, who held it in her fingers behind her back. Her hands were taped but not her fingers. She slowly started to cut through the tape behind her back. Cameron tried to keep up the conversation. Having noticed their English accents, he asked them where they were from in England.

"Who said you could talk?" No. 1 said to him.

"Of course, I've done it, loads of times you wanker…"

"Hey, what's going on?" No. 1 asked. He noticed that Carlotta's body was moving. He pulled her forward and saw the broken glass in her hand. He showed his partner.

"Kill her," No. 2 said.

"Really?"

"Really."

No. 1 shot two bullets into her chest. Her head went down. She stopped moving.

Cameron screamed "No!"

"And him," No. 2 said.

It only took one shot in the middle of the face to end Cameron's life. The intruders put on the overcoats they had arrived in and left the apartment. As they walked out, one said to the other, "that's a shame – I thought we could have some fun."

The other said, "It was better to finish it off quickly."

Then they both disappeared into the darkness, like shadows.

13. The End of Night

When Blake arrived at Cameron's apartment, he thought it was strange that the door was unlocked but figured that one of them must have stayed home while the other went out to replenish their booze supply. He didn't expect to see the middle of Cameron's face missing or blood pouring out of Carlotta's thighs. The blood was flowing freely – it looked fresh, new. Whatever had taken place recently. He ran out the door, looking for help – where were the "innocent bystanders" that Warren had promised? The sidewalk was empty. People in cars drove by like any other night, unaware of the blood drenched scene they were passing. Blake screamed out at the darkness: "Where the fuck are you? Help!"

Two men in in black overcoats ran out from the corner of the other side of the street.

"Blake!" One of the men shouted. "Blake Webster!"

They ran toward Blake flashing their NYPD identification cards. He looked at them with suspicion until one whispered the words "generic guru" into his ear. "We're shadowing the apartment."

"Where the fuck were you?" Blake asked, motioning to the open door of the apartment. They looked in and saw the bodies – Cameron had fallen to the floor and Carlotta was still sitting on the couch. One of the cops looked at Blake and said, "We're so sorry buddy. We really are."

The other cop tried to explain what happened: "We got a call from the boss. Someone had reported a robbery in a bar around the corner and he knew we were in the area. We were only gone a few seconds."

Blake was furious. "How could Warren have done that?"

"No, not Lieutenant Warren," one of the men said. "It was his boss, Captain Seligman. Only Captains have the authority to arrange protection. Or withdraw it."

Blake's legs felt weak. He started to drop. The men held him up and guided him into the back seat of an unmarked sedan.

"What about my things?" Blake asked, dazed but not so dazed that he hadn't forgotten about the gold wrap with his fingerprints that he had left in the apartment last night. He wasn't so worried about the one he had just scored at Pinky's – that had been approved by Warren. But the other wrap was almost empty. Maybe his two friends had finished it off while he was at work. But even if they had thrown the wrap away, the police would find it during a search of the apartment. It would show that he was using again. He felt guilty for worrying about it, but his brain was on automatic now.

"I'm sorry, Blake. It's a crime scene. You can't go back there. Don't worry, we'll take you to a hotel. You'll be moved to an apartment after your class tomorrow."

"Class? Do you honestly think I can make it to class tomorrow?"

"Blake, you have to. You don't have a choice. You're a cop now. Bad things happen when you're a cop. We've all been through it. Don't act suspiciously. Don't blow your cover. Stick to your normal schedule. Sometimes you have to fake it to make it."

"I can't."

"Yes, you can. Because if you don't, it means that they've won."

"Who *cares*? Criminals, cops, they're two sides of the same coin."

"Cops didn't kill your friends, Blake."

"So, what happened to the robbers in the bar?" Blake asked. "Did you bust them?"

"Well, that's the weird thing," the cop on the passenger side said. "They weren't there. There was no robbery. At least not one we could find. We thought that maybe we were at the wrong place, so we checked out some of the other bars on the street, but nobody had heard of any robberies. Then we heard you yelling."

"How long were you checking out robberies that didn't exist?"

Guilty glances were exchanged by the cops in the front seat.

"Don't know exactly. Maybe half an hour or so," the driver said. That was in addition to the time it took to drink the free beers that they were treated to.

"Look, we're really sorry," the other cop said. "There really wasn't anything happening at the time. No suspicious characters on the street, nobody sitting in parked cars. Nothing."

Blake felt guilty for blaming the guys who were protecting him. It wasn't their fault. It was just a wrong call by a superior. What if they hadn't checked out the robbery and people had been killed?

"I'm sorry guys, I know it wasn't your fault."

Any thought he had of quitting the force disappeared. He had to get the guys who killed his two friends. He didn't care how he did it. It wasn't about good or bad anymore. It was about revenge.

14. Friday

Blake was early for class the next day – for once. After his colleagues had dropped him off at a hotel near headquarters, Warren had called to make sure he was okay and repeated the advice of his 'protectors.'

"Keep to your regular schedule. "Don't skip class. Come to my office afterwards, as usual. I'll have the keys to your new apartment."

Blake hardly slept that night. He felt like he was floating in a different reality than the rest of world – 'normal' humanity who were part of the world's daily grind – who woke up, went to work and returned home to spend the evening with their family. 'Fake it to make it,' the shadow had said. But when would he be able to stop faking it and join the human race again?

If it hadn't been for the 'shadows' outside the hotel, he probably would have scored. The murder of Carlotta and Cameron fertilized the craving that had been planted by Johnny at the beginning of the week. He wished that Johnny hadn't mentioned that the Hole in the Wall was still open.

Now that he had arrived at class, he was glad that he hadn't scored. He'd probably still be nodding off in bed. Jackie had arrived early too. She was setting up her desk when she saw Blake walk in and motioned for him to come forward. At least she knew he was undercover now. He wouldn't have to pretend to be somebody else.

"Well, well, well, to what do we owe this honour?" she asked. "Early for once. It couldn't be that it's Friday, could it – your last day?"

"Please Jackie. I had a rough night last night."

"*You* had a rough night!" She countered. "Tell me about it! Do you know how hard it is to teach a class with a hangover? My head feels like it's going to explode."

Blake wasn't in the mood for humour.

"I'm not talking about a hangover. Two of my friends got killed last night."

Her demeanour changed instantly: "Oh, Blake I'm so sorry. I heard about it but didn't know you were involved."

"What do you mean you heard about it? How could you have heard about it so soon?"

"Don't be so suspicious. We get a crime report every morning. I have a quick look at it in the morning."

"Yeah, well, I was staying in Cameron's apartment. I knew him from my modelling days."

"Oh yeah. Of course - the bartender at Blunt. What's going on, Blake?"

"You probably know more than I do. You're a Lieutenant. I've heard there is some sort of turf war going on."

"Did Warren tell you that?"

"Yeah, or maybe it was Carlotta. I can't remember."

"Take a seat Blake. I'll get you a coffee."

As he found a seat, students began arriving and asking where the teacher was.

"Maybe she's been massacred," one student conjectured, sounding like a newspaper headline about the Layton murders. Another said something about how "he wouldn't mind massacring her, himself, with those knockers." A few of the students laughed, some moaned.

Jackie arrived back in the class carrying two Styrofoam cups of coffee and set one down on Blake's desk as she made her way to the front of the room. A few of the students noticed Blake's cup and elbowed their neighbour. One stuck a finger down his throat a couple of times to simulate oral sex.

"So," Jackie said, when she reached the front of the class, "it's Friday, the end of your first week of training. I usually begin Fridays with a quiz," she continued, "to test how much you've taken in during the week."

She launched into a series of basic questions with basic

answers that boiled down to 'cops are good, and criminals are bad.' Eventually, the questions became more nuanced - she stressed that "everyone is proven innocent until guilty" and when she used the term "criminal" she meant the "*alleged* criminal," of course.

"Alleged," she repeated. "Remember that word. You'll use it often, even when you know the creep you've arrested is guilty."

Blake was grateful that she didn't ask him anything. The whole class was grateful when the clock reached 12 and it was time for lunch. Usually, there was a fifteen-minute break before then, but she had kept the quiz going through the break. She couldn't ignore lunch, though. Even she was hungry.

"See you in an hour," she said. "Any questions?"

Nobody had any questions because asking them would have taken up some of their lunchtime. The rows in the back of the class were already walking out the door.

Blake sat by himself in the cafeteria during lunch, as usual, munching on a cheese sandwich he had bought from a vending machine and chugging down a double espresso he had got from another machine. He had been toying with the idea of becoming a vegetarian for a while. Maybe now was the time to start. He didn't see the sense in protecting human beings and killing animals, even though he hadn't done much protecting yet. If he had been at Cameron's when the killers arrived, maybe he could have protected him and Carlotta. It would have been two against three and he would've had a gun.

Copies of the latest edition of the *New York Post* were scattered around the cafeteria for the cops to read, supplied by the publisher at no charge and scattered throughout the communal areas of the headquarters by one of their office boys. The newspaper liked to keep on good terms with the cops; it's where they got most of their tips from. Blake picked up an issue and read about the Layton murders. The story that had made the headlines when it happened was now relegated to the third page – "Cop killing was a robbery gone wrong." Apparently the "robbers" didn't know Layton was a cop, although Blake couldn't figure out how the *Post* could know that since no arrests had been made yet.

"Mind if I join you?"

Blake looked up and saw the blonde student that had been talking to Jackie on Tuesday, outside of the classroom.

"Sure," Blake said, even though he would have preferred to be on his own.

The recruit sat down with his roast beef sandwich and large milky coffee. Blake went back to his paper but couldn't help noticing how uncomfortable the student looked – like he wanted someone to talk to. Most of the other recruits had formed small groups of lunch buddies, but this guy didn't fit in. His hair was longer than the other recruits – he looked more like a surfer than a cop. When he bit into his sandwich, he clumsily knocked over his coffee with his elbow. Blake watched one of the drips heading straight for him.

"Fuck! I'm so sorry," the surfer boy apologised. He quickly put a napkin down to sop up the spill. Blake laughed, told him not to worry, and helped him wipe the table.

"I'm so clumsy," the new recruit said. "The last thing I expected to be in my life was a cop!"

"Me too," Blake said. "I'm clumsy too. Always have been. Except on my skateboard! At least most of the time."

The blonde guy laughed. "I was a pretty good skater, too. Where are you from?"

"California."

"Same here! Whereabouts?"

"Ridgecrest. It's a small town. Nobody has heard of it. It used to be called Crumville."

"Crumville? Sounds like a town in the Simpsons.'

Blake laughed. "I loved the Simpsons."

"Me too. I'm Sebastian, by the way," he said, holding out his hand to shake. "My friends call me Seb."

"I'm Blake." They shook hands. Blake had spent all week avoiding the other students – but it was his last day in class and this guy seemed okay.

"What was your favourite episode?" Blake asked his new friend about the Simpsons, struggling to find something to talk about that wasn't too personal. The last thing he wanted to talk about was himself.

Sebastian hesitated. "It's difficult to choose just one. Maybe the monorail one. When they hired Bart to drive a monorail. So funny."

"I like that one too," Blake said. "Did you ever see the one when they try to deport Bart by sending him to France on a student exchange program? The episode was called The Crepes of Wrath which I thought was really clever.'

"No. I missed that one."

"What other episodes did you like?"

Seb shrugged, like he had already become bored with the subject. Blake tried to keep the conversation going by asking him where he was raised in California.

"Even worse than Crumville, probably," Seb said. "Simi Valley. Do you know it?"

"I've heard of it. Didn't it have something to do with that murderer, Charles Manson?"

"Yeah, that's about its only claim to fame. That and the Ronald Reagan Library. Spahn's ranch, where the Manson cult was based, was up in the hills. But that was before my time. Oh yeah, they also had Bottle Village."

"Bottle Village?"

"Yeah. A small group of buildings that a granny had

built out of bottles that people threw away."

"What? Miniature buildings like doll houses?"

"No, they were regular buildings but not very big. She lived in one."

A bell rang signifying that it was time to go back to class. They both stood up at the same time.

Seb: "That was quick."

Blake: "It sure was."

Seb: "Hey, would you like to get a bite to eat later, after class? I don't know many people and, well, do you like burgers?"

Blake thought about his vegetarianism, which he still hadn't started, and decided he could start it another day. The thing about burgers is that as soon as someone mentions one, you want one.

"Yeah, if they're good ones."

"Have you been to Joy Burger in the lower east side yet?"

"No. Do they have cheeseburgers?"

"Yeah. And bacon burgers and lamb burgers and..."

"O.K. Sure."

"Meet me after class?"

Blake remembered that he usually met with Warren after class.

"Would you mind if we meet there? I've got to see someone after class, but it won't take long."

"Cool. I'll meet you there." He gave Blake the address and they agreed to meet at 8.

Blake wished he had met Seb at the beginning of the week. It would have been nice having a friend in class during the week. He seemed different than the other students - more like a friend than a cop. But, at the same time, there was something about their conversation that made Blake feel uneasy, but he couldn't put his finger on it. He had to stop being so suspicious of people. He looked forward to dinner. It might help take his mind off of what happened to Cameron and Carlotta. Whenever he tried to stop thinking about it, he started thinking about it again. How could the force have let it happen?

After class, Blake told Seb he would see him later, at the restaurant, and walked to Warren's office. Although he had promised himself that he would be reasonable when he saw his boss, the first thing that came out of his mouth was, whose fucking idea was it to send those flunkies to a robbery that didn't exist?"

"The robbery did exist, Blake. At least it was reported to 911."

"The 'shadows,' themselves, told me there wasn't a robbery!"

"Blake, let me put it this way. What if there was a robbery, what if innocent people had been killed, and the cops weren't there to save them? They were only gone a short time. There was no way that we could have predicted what would happen."

"But who made the emergency call in the first place?"

"I don't know. I wasn't involved. I only heard about it afterwards. If it had been up to me, I probably would have kept those cops outside Cameron's. DON'T tell my boss that."

"Forget it."

"Blake, I know it's not easy. Hell, even I get depressed by the people who don't make it − criminals or cops. Sometimes I don't even know the difference anymore. I wish I could retire early like Seligman wants me to, I really do. But I can't. Police work is like an addiction. I've seen some horrible things during my career, but I always come back for more."

He threw a set of keys across the desk.

"These are the keys to your new apartment. No more cheap hotels. It's downtown. 20 Thompson Street, Apartment 33. I'll write it down for you but trash the piece of paper once you remember it."

"I'll remember it." He took the paper anyway and pocketed it.

"You'll like the apartment. It's in the village. Near Washington Square. A one bedroom, not a studio. 77-inch TV screen with all the movie stations. Take the weekend off. I'll see you on Sunday at the arsenal."

Blake picked the keys up off the desk and stood to leave.

"And Blake," Warren said, "I just want to reassure you that we've still got your back. Whoever is shadowing you won't be called upon to do anything else. Those guys may have been after Carlotta, maybe Cameron, or they could have been looking for you."

"Is that supposed to be reassuring?"

"I'm sorry about your loss, Blake, I really am."

15. Joy Burger

After his meeting with Warren, Blake wished that he hadn't promised Sebastian that he would meet him for dinner. It seemed like a good idea at first, but he wasn't in the mood anymore. He just wanted to get to his new apartment and rest. His slow week had turned into a fast one, but it was over now, and he just needed a break. Tomorrow was Saturday. A day off. He would get through dinner as quickly as possible, and then his time would be his own - to process what he had been through during the week.

He flagged down a cab and asked the driver if he knew where Joy Burger was.

"Yeah. Of course. It's that gourmet burger place on the lower east side."

"*Gourmet* burgers? They better have regular cheeseburgers." Blake said to the cabbie. "And French fries."

"I think they do those thick fries."

"I hate those."

"So do I."

That was about the extent of the conversation. Blake was relieved. He wasn't in the mood for a long conversation with a New York taxi driver. He wondered whether the driver was plainclothes but thought it unlikely given that the cab wasn't waiting for him outside headquarters - that he had to flag it down from the street. He doubted that the force was 'watching his back' to the extent that Warren had promised. It would be too expensive. They needed their money for 'petty cash.'

When they reached the restaurant, Warren paid the driver and gave him a generous tip.

"Thanks! Do you want a receipt?"

"Oh yeah, I forgot about that." Blake remembered what Warren had said on Wednesday. "How much would you sell me a whole pad of receipts for?" he asked the driver.

"Is twenty too much?

"Deal."

The driver handed over the whole pad. It would come in handy when Blake had to pay cash to people who couldn't provide a receipt. It also confirmed that the driver probably wasn't his 'shadow.' What sort of a plainclothes cop would sell you a pad of receipts so you could cheat on your expenses?

Stuffing the pad in his inside jacket pocket, Blake got out of the taxi and went into the restaurant. He was surprised to see a *maître d'* standing behind a lectern with the reservations list.

"Good evening, sir, your name?"

He didn't know what to say. Was he supposed to give his name or Sebastian's?

"Blake!" Sebastian yelled from a small table where he was already nursing a beer in one of those big glass mugs that looked more like a movie prop than a glass.

"Your party is already waiting for you," the *maître d'* said, like he was reciting something from Shakespeare. He even pulled Blake's chair back for him so he could sit down. Then he set down a large plastic menu of cocktails on the table, along with what appeared to be a handwritten list of burgers on a sheet of parchment paper.

"A *maître d'* at a burger joint?" Blake asked Seb after the guy left.

Seb laughed.

"I guess it's what makes it 'gourmet.' But don't worry, the burgers here are really good. Do you like truffles?"

"No." He wasn't actually sure what a truffle was, but it was bound to taste horrible on a cheeseburger.

Eventually a waiter took their orders – a truffle burger for Seb and a cheeseburger with raw onions for Blake.

"Raw?" Seb asked.

"Yeah. Cooking them takes out all the taste."

Once the waiter left, neither of them knew what to say to each other. After a silence that seemed longer than it was, Seb finally broke the ice by asking Blake about New York. Had he been to many of the clubs?

"No. Maybe Blunt a few times last year."

"There's this new club that some of us have been going to since Blunt closed down. It's called The Coliseum. Have you heard of it?"

Blake assumed that when he said "some of us" he meant some of his classmates. "I've heard of it," he said "but I've never been there. Why?"

"Do you want to go there after dinner?"

"I'm pretty tired. I'll probably just go home."

"No problem. Hold on a sec. I have to go to the men's room."

Sebastian took so long in the men's room that Blake wondered if he was doing a line of coke to get ready for the evening ahead. When he returned to the table, he was putting his phone in his pocket.

"Are you sure you don't want to come to the Coliseum?" he said. "Everyone from the class is going – to celebrate the end of the first week of training."

"I'm sorry Seb. Maybe some other time. I'm really tired. I sort of just want to go home."

"Oh sure. No problem."

When they finished their meal, Seb insisted on paying the bill and told Blake he could give him a ride home.

"You have a car?" Blake asked. "Nobody in New York has a car."

"Oh yes, I definitely have a car. Let's get out of here and I'll show you," he said.

The only car that Blake could see was an expensive Jaguar parked illegally outside the restaurant.

"Where is it?"

"What?"

"Your car."

"You're standing next to it."

Seb pulled out a key chain with a fob imprinted with 'Jaguar' on a silver panel and the sports car came to life.

"This is yours?"

"Yep."

"Good parking space."

"You can get a parking permit while you're in the class, you know."

"What is it?" Blake asked.

"A Jaguar F-type."

"Must have been expensive. How could you afford it on your salary?"

"My dad was posh."

"Posh?"

"Yeah. It's an English expression. British English. My dad came from England. I picked up some of the lingo."

"I thought you came from Simi Valley?"

"I do. I was born there. Went to Bellwood Elementary. My mom was American. They met in the war or something."

Sebastian looked like he was in his early to mid-twenties – around Blake's age. That meant he would have been born in the late 80s to early 90s. Blake tried to think of a war that involved the U.S. or England around that time. There wasn't one.

"Here, get in," Sebastian said as he pressed down on another section of his fob and the passenger door opened. They got in. Yet another section of the fob started the car's engine. The radio came on when the car started. Blake thought there might be something about the murders at Cameron's apartment, but instead there was just news about that Chinese virus. Three cases had been reported in France. 'Three cases of a virus are news?' Blake thought. It was like Cameron and Carlotta had never existed. Seb scrolled through the stations until he stopped on a station playing music.

"Don't forget your seat belt," he said, as he turned on the sat-nav and joined the slow-moving traffic going down 12th Street.

"So, where's home?" Seb asked.

Blake wished he had taken a cab. He couldn't remember the address of his new apartment. He knew it was on Thompson Street but couldn't remember the number. He had to get the small piece of paper that Warren had given him out of his pocket.

"Don't you know where you live?" Sebastian asked.

"I know it's on Thompson Street but I keep forgetting the exact address. It's a friend's apartment." He found the paper. "Number 20."

"You've been staying there all week and you couldn't remember the number 20?"

"Yeah, well, it's been a busy week."

Blake had an idea.

"Hey, do you mind if we go down 8th Street?" he asked.

"Sure. Why?"

Blake wanted to check out his mother's building, but he didn't want to tell Sebastian that. Instead, he said that as a kid he had seen pictures of all the graffiti on 8th Street and he wanted to see it for himself.

"It's probably not there anymore, but, yeah, why not? We can take a graffiti tour. I love that stuff too."

Seb drove down 8th Street, around Tomkins Square Park, and took a left on D. He was right. Most of the graffiti had been removed – just one of the results of gentrification. But Blake did get a good look at his mother's building. He expected something seedy, like a small run-down apartment building with peeling paint. Instead, he saw a modern, black granite, three story structure that looked like expensive offices. The windows were heavily tinted. The occupants could see out, but outsiders couldn't see in, even when the heavy blackout curtains weren't drawn.

"Not much graffiti left," Sebastian observed. "Don't you want to stop for a drink?" he asked. "I'm not meeting the other guys at The Coliseum until 11.00."

Seb took his right hand off the steering wheel and rested it on the edge of Blake's seat. Blake wondered if he was coming onto him.

"I'm kinda tired." Blake said. "I could take a cab the rest of the way if you want."

"Don't be stupid. I'll drop you off and then go for a couple on my own before braving the Coliseum."

Blake laughed. "I know what you mean. When I went to Blunt last year, I usually had to go someplace else first for – what do they call it? Dutch courage."

"Blunt's supposed to be opening again in a few weeks. Maybe we can both go there. I've never been. I read about what happened though. Weird."

"Very weird."

When Sebastian got to 2nd Avenue he turned left toward 6th, when he should have gone in the opposite direction.

"Where are you going?"

"Don't worry, it's a shortcut. It's one of those small roads they mentioned in class. It leads to Cooper Square."

Seb turned down an alley, slowing down the car.

"We have to take it slow, it's such a narrow road."

Blake was confused. Something was wrong but he couldn't figure out what it was. It was the same feeling he got at lunch when him and Seb were talking about skateboards and The Simpsons. What could possibly have been suspicious about something like a cartoon series or a skateboard? He rewound the lunchtime conversation in his head a few times and suddenly realised what the problem was. It wasn't Bart Simpson who drove the monorail in the episode they talked about. It was Homer. No self-respecting Simpsons' fan would make such a stupid mistake. Bart was a kid; Homer was the dad. He was surprised he hadn't picked it up at the time. But did it really matter?

While Blake was pondering the significance of the Simpsons conversation, Sebastian was cursing the driver of a car behind him.

"Stupid idiot," he said. "His headlights are off."

Seb flashed his parking lights twice, but when the driver didn't react, he stopped on the side of the road to let him pass, mumbling something about "women drivers." When he turned off his own car's lights, Blake turned to ask him what was going on and found himself looking straight down the barrel of a Beretta M9.

"I'm sorry matey, but your voyage has come to an end," Sebastian informed him with a fake frown on his face, like he cared.

"This isn't where I live." Blake said.

"I don't mean that voyage, you idiot. I mean your life voyage."

Blake thought about the gun underneath his jacket but knew that if he moved, Sebastian would shoot him.

"Is this a joke? We're both cops for God's sake."

"One of us is, at least."

"But how did you get into the class?" he asked.

"That's for me to know and for you to never find out."

Sebastian was holding the gun with two hands now, aiming carefully at Blake's forehead to make sure he didn't miss.

"Just one other thing you should know, Blakey boy," he said. "I hated the Simpsons. They sucked. And I much preferred playing with guns than playing with skateboards."

All it took was one quick shot and he was dead. The vast amount of blood was hardly noticeable on the red leather upholstery of the Jaguar.

16. The Other Side

Blake woke up the next morning in darkness, surrounded by blazing heat, like he was at a barbecue, or in one. His skin felt like it was on fire and his clothes were soaked with sweat.

'Damn those radiators,' he said to himself. 'You'd think the force would have got me an apartment that actually worked.'

He got up from his bed - making a mental note that he had to stop sleeping in his clothes - and opened the window. A cold wind blew into the room so fiercely that he had to close it immediately. At least the temporary burst of cold air helped to freshen up the room.

Apart from the heating problem, he liked the new apartment. It was in a good location. Downtown, like his mother's place, but on the other side of town, near Washington Square. It was close enough to make meeting up with her easy, but far away enough to lead separate lives. Having a mother who ran a house of ill-repute could get complicated for a cop, but he was looking forward to having dinner with her on Monday.

He couldn't get over how expensive his mother's place looked when Sebastian drove past it. He thought about the inheritance she was due and wondered if she really would split it with him. At least his father's lawyer would stop hassling him now that they had found her. She would have to deal with the all the legalities involving the money. He hated filling out forms.

No matter what happened, he was determined to remain a cop. All previous doubts had disappeared after that incident with Sebastian last night. What a moron! How could anyone not like the Simpsons? Okay, the later episodes weren't so good, but the original reruns were practically masterpieces.

At least he knew that Warren had been telling him the

truth about being shadowed. The plainclothes cop who was trailing him seemed to come out of nowhere. It was only after his shadow shot Sebastian in the back of his head, that Blake realised that a man had been sitting in a darkened car on the other side of the street. When the "woman driver" without headlights passed Seb's car, neither of them noticed that the car stopped further up the alley. And that the "woman driver" – actually a man - had left the car and crawled back to Seb's Jaguar, positioning himself under the driver's window, his Glock semi-automatic ready to go.

The window was closed but the shadow knew that the windows of an F-type Jaguar were bullet "resistant" rather than "bullet proof" and no match for the weapon he used to shoot Seb. If Seb hadn't gone into that spiel about hating the Simpsons, Blake would probably be dead. It gave his shadow just long enough to stand and take aim. The bullet went straight through the window into Sebastian's head. As Blake and his protector sped away in the darkened car, they could hear the sirens of police cars speeding to the scene of the 'crime.'

"Isn't there something you want to say to me?" Blake asked, after getting into the car.

"Huh? Oh yeah. Generic guru."

They both laughed.

"Phew," Blake said, relieved. "I was afraid I was getting out of one situation only to land in another."

"No, buddy. Don't worry. You're safe. Do you still have the keys that Lieutenant Warren gave you?"

"Yeah, I still have the keys."

"Don't leave the apartment until Sunday morning. Someone from the force will pick you up at 8 am for the arsenal. Don't go outside before then." He dropped Blake off at 20 Thompson Street - he didn't need to ask for the address.

"In case we don't meet you again, it was nice working

with you," Blake said.

"Likewise. I'm off in half an hour and somebody else will take my place to keep an eye on the building."

"Thanks. I was starting to wonder whether the shadows were real."

"Oh, we're real all right."

Blake got out of the car and the shadow parked across the street, waiting for his replacement. As Blake opened the door to his new apartment, he felt for the first time since arriving back in New York that he belonged to a family of sorts – a family called the New York Police Department.

Despite what had happened earlier, he slept easily that night – until the heat of the broken radiators woke him up. After blasting the room with cold air from the window, he went back to bed, but it wasn't long before his phone techno-bleeped and he saw that Warren was calling him.

"Just wanted to make sure you were okay after last night," the lieutenant said. "Sorry about all that. You didn't mention you were going on a date after I saw you."

Blake laughed. "I wish."

"I can't believe that with all the legitimate rookies in that class, you chose the one imposter to have dinner with."

"I thought we had stuff in common. He said he was a Simpson's fan."

"Huh?"

"Never mind. How did he get in the class anyway?"

"Who knows? I told Seligman about it and he's having the enrolment register checked by admin. It does confirm one thing. That someone is after you. Probably the same guys who were looking for you at the hotel."

"And who killed Carlotta and Cameron."

"I was trying not to mention that."

"Jasper's boys?" Blake asked.

"I assume so."

"Where do we go from here?"

"Not sure. We can talk about it at the arsenal tomorrow. Take today off. Relax. Is the apartment okay?"

"It seems okay – except for the heating system. It's boiling. How do you turn off the heat?"

"I think it's supposed to be automatic. I've been in that apartment before. Where are you?"

"In the bedroom."

"I think there's a thermostat in the living room that controls the whole apartment. Just to the left of the door."

Blake found it and turned it down to zero.

"If that doesn't work, call the main number at headquarters and ask to speak to housekeeping."

"I'm sure it will be fine."

"Did your shadow tell you a car would pick up tomorrow at 8?"

"Yeah. No problem."

"There should be some food in the fridge – check the freezer too. I think there's some frozen pizzas in it. If you want fresh, get it delivered. It's important that you don't go outside, for your own safety. There'll be protection out there, watching the apartment, but it's safer to stay inside. I'll ring you later if I have any more information – otherwise I'll see you tomorrow."

"Okay. Don't worry. I'll stay inside. The shadow told me about the protection. Thanks."

"I owe it to you. You saved my life in the Canary Islands."

Blake thought back to that moment in the Canaries when he saved Warren's life – how Ginger had a AK47 pointed at Warren and how Blake grabbed a gun that he kept under his pillow and took out Ginger before she took out the lieutenant. Blake had ended up with a bullet in the back of his head from one of Ginger's flunkies, but he survived with the help of Amanda, an NYPD nurse who was flown in to keep him company. Now, here he was, back in New York, helping Warren bust the dealers who had sold to Blake. Except that so far, they hadn't busted anyone. They hadn't expected to walk into a turf war. So far, it felt like Jasper and his boys were running the show.

Still thinking of leaving the force?" Warren asked.

"Nah, I think I'll stick with it for a while."

"Good man."

Blake hung up the phone, found some eggs and cheese in the fridge and mixed them together in a frying pan for breakfast. Afterwards he laid back on the couch and turned on the TV. He flicked through the stations but didn't find anything particularly interesting. He stopped at an old Columbo episode - "It's All in the Game." Although he liked old detective shows, television seemed boring compared to everything he had been through that week. He was glad when his phone went off. He picked it up without bothering to look at the screen. Who else could it be but Warren?

"Hey Blake, it's Johnny. How are ya?"

He tensed up. Why would Johnny be calling him on a Saturday afternoon? He could only think of two things – dope or money.

"Hi Johnny, what's up?" Blake asked brusquely.

Johnny wondered if he had made a mistake by calling. He could tell that Blake wanted to get rid of him.

"Um, you told me to call you if I found out anything about Sluggo," Johnny said.

Blake felt guilty for answering the call so harshly. Johnny was only trying to be helpful, but the minute he heard his voice, Blake thought of heroin. It made him angry at first – until the back of his brain started sending messages to the front of his brain like 'it's Saturday, your day off, who would know? You deserve a fix after everything you've been through. Why not treat yourself just once?'

The tone of Blake's voice changed as though it had a

life of its own. It became mellower, friendlier, as the back
of his brain waited for an opportunity to satiate its craving.

"It's nice to hear from you Johnny. What did you find
out?"

"I think I might have found out where he went."

Blake already knew where Sluggo was, of course, but
he wanted to know what Johnny had heard and, most of
all, he wanted to keep the conversation going until it led to
the inevitable.

"Where?" Blake asked.

"Well, I was panhandling outside his bar – the one
those weirdos took over - and that guy in the tight jeans
came out to shoo me away - they won't let me in the place
and now they won't even let me be outside it - he waved
me away like I was a stray dog. When I told him I had a
right to be on the sidewalk, that it was a public sidewalk,
he said that I better watch what I said, or he was going to
get his friends to take me away like they did with Sluggo. I
think he said, 'to Hollywood,' that they had taken him to
Hollywood. I think Sluggo is in Hollywood, Blake."

Blake tried not to laugh. He had this image in his head
of Sluggo arriving on the red carpet at a Hollywood
premiere and the paparazzi shouting - 'Sluggo, look this
way! Smile! Show us some teeth! Do the snarl!'"

"I don't know Johnny. It doesn't sound right. Keep
your ears open for any other information you come
across."

There was silence from Johnny as he tried to figure out
how to bring up what he really wanted to bring up.

"To tell you the truth, Blake, I've been kinda' sick
lately."

"Sick? You don't have that virus, do you?"

"No, it's not like that, Blake. I mean, sick in the head. I
don't think I can take it anymore. It feels like my life is
over. Nothing's going to change. I can't live without hope
anymore. I'm gonna be sixty next week. Who would have

thought I'd even reach fifty? Maybe it's time to call it a day."

Blake didn't like what he was hearing.

"Can't you get help with a charity or get on methadone or something?" Blake asked.

"I've tried all that. Nothing works. I always go back to dope. Even if I cleaned up permanently, what sort of future would I have? I never got trained for anything. I just went out to nightclubs. You know, Blake, I always thought that tomorrow might be better than yesterday, but I don't feel like that anymore. All my life I've been waiting for tomorrow, like it was going to make any difference. But the future is now, Blake. Today. There is no future, tomorrow. I'm finished Blake."

Of all the people Blake had met in New York last year, the ones he cared most about were the outsiders – people like Sluggo and Johnny – who had either arrived in the world with the cards already stacked against them or had ended up that way. He would never forgive himself if Johnny did something stupid. At the same time, his friend's bleak assessment of his future also gave Blake's craving the opportunity it had been waiting for.

"Hey Johnny," Blake said. "Why don't you stop by here. I can give you some money as an early birthday present. How about that? You won't have to panhandle today."

"Blake, would you really do that? I'd be so grateful, I really would. I'm so dope-sick..."

Blake knew from past experience that only dope could cure a depression like Johnny's. The physical symptoms of withdrawal were nothing compared to the psychological ones. He never wanted to go through that again. He wasn't surprised that Johnny was suicidal.

Johnny was still talking:

"...I could pay you back next week, when I get my food stamps. I know someone who will buy them from me...."

"Don't worry about it, Johnny. Like I said, it's an early birthday present. How much do you need?"

"Anything you can spare Blake. Would $20.00 be too much?"

"20 is no problem at all, my friend. Hey, I just had an idea. If you're going to score with the money, do you think you could get me some too?"

The words came out automatically, without thought, like his mouth had a mind of its own. Johnny got excited at the idea.

"Sure Blake! That would be great."

Johnny was happier than he'd been in a long time – probably since Sluggo left. Not only would he get some dope, he'd also have someone to shoot it up with. They could get stoned and do things that normal people did – like watch TV and talk about the past. Maybe he could even have a shower.

There was only one problem. A shadow was outside watching the apartment. Blake had been told not to go outside and having Johnny in the apartment would be too suspicious.

"I'll be right to pick up the money," Johnny said.

"Wait a second Johnny. I need to think about this." He couldn't exactly tell him he was a cop, and another cop was outside somewhere. When Blake hesitated, Johnny was afraid he was changing his mind.

"Blake, what's the problem? I can get there in twenty minutes and I'll come straight back with the stuff. Or you could come with me if you don't trust me."

"It isn't that Johnny, it's just that I've just moved in, and my neighbours are watching me like hawks and..."

"If they saw me, they'd think you were a drug addict too?" Johnny said.

"Don't take it personally, Johnny, it's just that, well, you know what New York neighbours are like. They have a tenants' committee in the building, and I could get kicked out if they thought I was up to something."

"Do they have that much power?" Johnny asked. "

"Of course they do."

"Maybe it's not so bad living on the street."

"Listen, I've got an idea," Blake said. "Do you think you could get hold of a pizza – or even just an empty pizza box?"

"Sure. There are tons of pizza places around here. I can get a box from the trash. Why?"

"You could pretend you were delivering a pizza and when I paid for the pizza, I could give you the money for the dope."

"But I'd have to come twice – to get the money first and then come back with the stuff."

"We can pretend that you made a mistake, that you gave me the wrong pizza and when you came back with the replacement you could bring the dope. If any of my neighbours notice, I can just say you brought the wrong pizza the first time."

"But why would they even mention it?"

"You don't know what the people are like in this building. They notice everything. They're suspicious of anyone who looks um…"

"Like a homeless drug addict?"

"Well, yeah, you know what I mean. They're not like us. They're middle-class. They're protecting their neighbourhood."

"O.K. I get it."

"Don't worry, I'll give you enough money for the dope and the cabs. Take a cab. Don't bother with the subway."

Now that Blake had made the decision to use, he wanted to get a needle in his arm as soon as possible. He told Johnny he would give him a couple of 'c notes' and that he only wanted four dime bags for himself. The rest of the money was for him.

"What's a c-note?" Johnny asked.

Blake laughed. It's slang for a hundred-dollar bill. I heard it on a Columbo rerun."

"Okay, okay, I'm on my way, buddy. I'll be there in a few minutes."

He didn't want to risk Blake changing his mind. As soon as he hung up, he headed to the trash can behind Bootsy's Midtown Pizza to get an empty box. One of the young guys who worked there opened the back door and asked him if was okay.

"Yeah, yeah, I'm just looking for a box."

He shouted back to the kitchen "Any returns?" Someone in a white uniform peeked out of the door and handed the guy a box.

"Here, friend. We can't resell this. A customer returned it."

Johnny had found an empty box by then but took the one with the pizza in it too.

"Oh, great. Thanks guys."

"No problem. Just don't tell anyone else."

"Thanks."

He heard someone else come to the door to ask what the pizza guys were doing, and some mumbled voices saying things like "he could be my grandfather for God's sake – he's harmless – just an old junkie."

He didn't care what they called him, as long as he got a free pizza. Now he had an empty box and a full one. Perfect. After he scored, he wouldn't have to go back to Bootsy's a second time.

While Johnny sorted out his pizza boxes, Blake's mind went into overdrive. What was he doing? He was a cop! There was a plainclothes shadow outside, watching the apartment, who would be reporting back to Warren. You just had to take a look at Johnny to know he was a junkie.

Blake sat on the couch, stood up, walked nervously around the couch and sat back down on it. All he had to do was to call Johnny and tell him the plan was off. He took his phone from the pocket of his jeans and laid it on the coffee table. He sat there for a few minutes, staring at it. His brain wanted to pick it up, but his hand didn't. He looked at the clock. If Johnny didn't arrive in twenty minutes, he would cancel the whole thing. Twenty minutes went by. No Johnny. That was it. The nightmare was over. Time and chance had made his decision for him. He wasn't going to score.

Ten minutes later there was a knock on the door, and he rushed to answer it. It was Johnny and his two pizza boxes.

"What's with the two boxes?"

"They were really nice at Bootsy's; they gave me a free pizza."

"For fuck's sake, Johnny, the whole idea was that you would arrive with the wrong pizza and go back to the pizza place to get the right one. How are you going to do that when you already have both of them?"

"Oh yeah. I didn't think of that."

"Don't worry about it." Blake wondered if his shadow had seen him with both boxes. He should have cancelled the whole thing right then and there. He could always just give Johnny some money to score for himself so he wouldn't have to come back. Instead, he took one of the boxes and handed over $200.00.

"Get me four bags. The rest is for you and the cab fare. Can you get some syringes too?"

"Yeah, sure. I'll be back in no time."

"O.K. Thanks. Just hurry up."

Blake was now desperate to get a needle in his arm. He wasn't even thinking about the high. He just wanted to get the craving out of his head.

"Take a cab and make it wait!" he shouted at Johnny as he ran down the stairs outside the apartment. Caution had gone out the window. Blake didn't even check to see if there were suspicious characters on the sidewalk, watching his apartment before he slammed the door.

"Fuck it. It's done now."

He went back to the couch to wait. And wait. Every time he looked at the clock on the wall, it seemed to indicate the same time. His phone was the same. He got confused. Surely, more than five minutes had gone by since the last time he looked. He wondered if Johnny would rip him off, just leave him sitting there like a fool, while he did all the stuff himself. Junkies were always talking about the bond they had between themselves, until they got the opportunity to rip each other off.

Blake walked to the sink and filled a glass with water in anticipation of Johnny's return, if he ever did return. He took out a clean spoon from the drawer and took it over to the table with glass. Shit. He would need a filter, and he didn't have any cigarettes. He ransacked the apartment until he found a bag of cotton balls in the bathroom. Perfect. He put one next to the spoon. Then he looked at the clock again. How could it possibly be that only five more minutes had gone by since the previous five minutes ended?

A lighter. He would need a lighter to dissolve the dope in the spoon. He went through all the kitchen drawers until he found a box of matches on the counter. He looked back at the wall. He wished that clock would hurry up.

It took Johnny a little more than an hour to score. He decided not to take a cab like Blake said. He'd have more money for dope that way. It took him about half an hour to walk to the Hole in the Wall. It had started raining by then, so he took the subway back. The Washington Square stop was only a few minutes from Blake's place on the F train.

He felt stupid appearing at the door again with one of the same pizza boxes he had before, but Blake didn't seem to mind. He just took the box and handed him the one he had left earlier and said loudly, "I did say a Vegetarian Supreme when I ordered," to back up his nosy neighbour excuse.

Johnny came into the apartment and headed to the kitchen table where everything had been set up and took out the bags of dope he had bought and the disposable syringes. He started to empty one of the bags into the spoon.

"Whoa – hold on," Blake said. "I'm really sorry but you can't do it here. The neighbours probably saw you come in." He didn't care about the neighbours. He cared about the plainclothes cop outside the building, but he couldn't tell Johnny that.

Johnny looked like he had just been stabbed in the heart by his best friend.

"But I thought we were going to do it together. I thought we could hang out and watch TV or something."

"I'm sorry Johnny. Look, here's another hundred. But you're going to have to leave. You've already stayed here too long. You're supposed to be a pizza boy."

"I see," he said, scooping up the bags of dope, leaving Blake two of them. He walked to the door with Blake behind him apologising, trying to explain, except that he couldn't explain because that would give his cover away.

"Johnny, I'm really sorry, something's going on, please try to understand…"

Johnny turned around. "Don't worry about it, Blake. I'm not upset. It happens all the time."

"Johnny, please, it's not like that. We'll do it another time with each other, but I can't right now."

"I told you not to worry about it. I don't blame you; I blame me. I should have quit a long time ago."

He left.

Blake locked the door and walked to the table to get stoned.

17. Sunday

Blake aimed his AK47 at Ernst Blofeld and let go a volley of shots.

"Not bad for an amateur," Lieutenant Locke commented.

Blake hoped that his eyes weren't still pinned from yesterday. It might have been his imagination, but it seemed like every time Locke spoke to him that he was examining Blake's eyeballs. Blake had taken his last shot of dope at midnight and still felt spaced out – more happy than spaced out – but had no problem concentrating on his targets for the few minutes necessary to fill them with holes.

He liked Lieutenant Locke. With his bald head framed by two grey tufts of hair on the side, he looked more like a mad professor than an arms expert. He was wearing a suit, but the front tail of his shirt was hanging out over his trousers which were slightly too short for his legs. His round wire-rimmed glasses made his greenish-brown eyes look bigger and friendlier than they probably were.

"You know," he said to Blake as he handed him a loaded Colt rifle, "a while back, we used cut-outs of enemy heads of states for target practice, but they kept on changing. Yesterday's villain became tomorrow's hero. It got too confusing. That's when we switched to Bond villains. Why don't you take a swipe at Auric over there?

Blake pointed his semi-automatic rifle at Auric Goldfinger and blasted the top of his head off.

"Try a bit lower next time, but not bad, not bad at all. Are you sure you haven't done this before?"

Blake laughed. "Nah, I had a pistol in the Canaries last year, but no rifles. Aren't you worried that people on the street might hear the bullets?"

"With all the soundproofing in this place, you wouldn't be able to hear a jet if it landed here – not that one could.

There's a heliport in the garden, though."

Warren was watching them from the other side of a bullet-proof window. He pointed to his watch and mouthed the word "lunch."

"I think Lieutenant Warren is trying to tell us something," Blake said.

Locke motioned to a uniformed cop nearby who took the weapons from them and returned them to the storage area, carefully filling out the appropriate forms. Every time a weapon was taken or replaced, a form had to be filled out, and a list of safety precautions ticked.

Blake and Lieutenant Locke walked through a metal detector to join Warren in the observation room which led to the lunchroom. "Lunchroom" was somewhat of a misnomer. It was more like a five-star restaurant with its own bar. Although they were the only diners at the time – it being Sunday – the room was fully dressed. Each table was still covered with a newly starched white tablecloth. The staff were in black tie. It was easy to forget that Harlem was outside. Blake wondered what the people outside thought of the large, windowless structure when they passed it on the street. It looked more like a run-down warehouse than a high-tech arsenal.

Over lunch, Warren asked Locke how the session went.

"He's a natural," Locke said.

"Yeah, I'm thinking of joining the army now," Blake said.

Warren went along with the joke: "You can't do that; we need you in the force. Who's going to do all my running for me?"

Locke asked how he was coping since the Jaguar incident.

"You know about that?" Blake looked at Locke and then at Warren.

"Locke knows just about everything about everyone," Warren answered. "He's our main security guy."

"Do you know what happened to Layton?" Blake asked.

"Ah," Locke said. "Now that is a mystery. I probably know more than you, but it's still a mystery. I will, however, give you one bit of advice in this business, Blake. Everyone learns it eventually. You might have been told already."

Locke was sounding more like a wise grandfather than the head of security.

"What's the advice?"

Locke paused and then leaned forward as if he was revealing the deepest secret of the universe.

"Suspect everyone," he said.

"Huh?"

"That's the advice. Suspect everyone."

"Even you?"

Locke smiled. "Yes, even me."

"Even Warren?" Blake asked Locke.

"Yes, even Lieutenant Warren," Locke answered, smiling. "Even you."

"Me!" Blake said, surprised. "But how could I suspect myself of anything?"

"What was Johnny doing at your apartment yesterday?" Locke asked.

The question seemed to come out of nowhere. He wasn't surprised that Locke knew who Johnny was. He'd been living on the streets so long that most of the cops knew him. Warren knew Blake had been a regular at Sluggo's last year when Johnny also hung out there. The shadow must have told Warren or Seligman about Johnny's visit, who then told Locke. Blake was glad that he hadn't let Johnny shoot up in the apartment with him. He started to stammer a response but was fortunately interrupted by the arrival of three bowls of fish soup – the first course of their four-course meal. Blake hated fish but was grateful for the diversion which gave him time to gather his thoughts. He had learned in high school, when he got caught ditching classes, that the best lie was a variation of the truth.

"Johnny was delivering a pizza," Blake said.

"Why didn't the restaurant deliver it?"

"They did. Johnny works for them sometimes when they need extra help with deliveries."

"But there were frozen pizzas in the freezer," Locke said.

"I hate frozen pizzas."

"Okay Blake, I believe you. Just don't break the rules again. Lieutenant Warren told you not to leave the apartment and not to have any visitors."

"And to call for a pizza if I didn't like frozen."

Locke turned to Warren: "Did you?"

"Well, yeah. I mean I don't like frozen either, but I didn't know Johnny would be delivering it," Warren answered.

"I didn't know I was doing anything wrong," Blake added. He looked at Warren for support, but Warren was staring at the tablecloth. Locke didn't pursue it.

Blake sipped his fish soup. It tasted rancid. Too fishy. He made a face.

"Don't you like the soup?" Locke asked.

"I'm not that crazy about fish soup."

"How do you know we haven't poisoned it? Do you trust us?"

Blake looked at the soup. It did look strange. Too many different colours for one bowl of soup. Not colourful colours. Grimy colours. He wished that the cook hadn't left a fish head in the broth. The sockets of the eyes were staring straight at him. When he moved the liquid with his spoon, he could see tiny dark brown pea-like balls floating among the bits of fish. He managed to get a couple of the balls on his spoon and showed them to Locke and Warren.

"What are *these*?" he asked, feeling nauseous.

Warren and Locke looked at each other, trying not to laugh.

"I don't know Blake," Locke said. "When I said to suspect everyone, I also meant every *thing*. A pea that size could probably contain enough poison to kill the population a small country.

Blake quickly set them aside.

"They're capers you div!" Warren said as he and his co-conspirator broke out laughing. "They come from a plant."

"What's a div?" Blake asked.

"Did I say div?"

"Yeah."

"It's a word I picked up on one of my trips to England. It's slang for 'fool.'"

"Thanks."

"Don't worry, I didn't mean it. A lot of people don't know what capers are."

The discussion about capers had taken the heat off the questionable pizza delivery. When glasses of brandy were produced at the end of the meal, Locke suggested they take them into the "library."

"I've got some gadgets I want to show you," he said to Blake.

The library was a wood-panelled room without a book in sight, only a few overstuffed armchairs and a long table in the centre of the room. Warren sat down in one of the chairs nursing his brandy while Locke gave Blake a tour of a selection of innocuous objects that had been laid out on the table – nothing particularly complicated – recording devices in belt buckles that could record a few hours of conversation on a mini SD card, a small transmitter, in the form of a button, backed with adhesive that could be pulled off the cuff of a sleeve and attached discretely to the underside of a desk, or wherever else it was necessary to pick up a conversation. The receiver – which could pick up the button's signal from almost a mile away - looked like a mobile phone. There was also a small bowl of ice that was sharp enough to cut an enemy's throat, a poisonous lipstick, and a ballpoint pen that turned into a knife with a single click.

Next to the gadgets was a book titled "The Art of Misdirection" that looked more like a magician's manual than the top-secret CIA guide that Locke presented it as. Apparently, it gave instructions on how to redirect someone's attention in order to poison their drink, plant a recording device, or poison their drink with the contents of a pencil with a hollowed-out eraser which lay next to the book.

"All pretty basic stuff," Locke pointed out, "that's been around since the Cold War, but they still come in handy after all these years."

"I feel like I'm in a Bond movie," Blake joked.

"Most of this stuff is from the CIS but they let us borrow it for undercover work," Locke said.

"Do you mean the CIA?"

"No, the CIS is the Criminal Intelligence Section of the NYPD. Some of the older gadgets did come from an old CIA project called MK Ultra during the Cold War period. It was run by a chemist, Sidney Gottlieb. Have you heard of him?

"No."

"His speciality was brainwashing and poison. The project ended after the staff was given LSD secretly at dinner to see how they would react and one of them later committed suicide. Anyway, that's all history now."

"Brainwashing?"

"Oh yes, there were all sorts of experiments. Sometimes the police work with the CIA, but usually they stay out of it. We tend to get their leftover gadgets and are grateful for them, especially in regard to undercover work. I'll put a kit together for you, but please make sure you follow the safety precautions."

"Of course."

"And we'll need to get your measurements too, for bullet-proof vests, and in case you ever need a false passport."

"Do you mean I might have to leave the country?"

"Who knows? I'm not a fortune teller. At the moment it looks like a gang from England is trying to take over turf that was previously controlled by a gang of Italians and Turks."

"Jasper?"

"Yes, well, Jasper does seem to be in charge over here. But who is in charge of him? All you have to worry about now is infiltrating the drug scene in the clubs. There are a lot of clubs in New York besides Blunt."

"But what about Layton and the Broadway and the other killings? Aren't they part of the turf war?"

"Probably. Layton may have worked for Jasper's competition; we know that Carlotta was involved with the Turk and that his gang was involved with the people who sold drugs at Blunt. Now we have to figure out who or what is the next target. Hopefully, it's not you."

"Amanda!"

Blake had noticed that the nurse who had helped him detox in the Canaries had come into the room while Locke was in the middle of his history lesson. Locke scowled and mumbled something about 'history not mattering anymore' before he turned his attention to Amanda who was approaching their table – more specifically, approaching Blake, who stood up to give her a hug.

Blake was accustomed to seeing her in her nurse's uniform, but here she was dressed casually in black jeans and a cream jersey top that barely met the brown Gucci belt on her jeans. Her hair wasn't as blonde as it had been in the Canaries - more brunette than blonde, and more natural. He preferred her that way.

"Blake! You look fantastic. It's so good seeing you look so healthy. I forgot how blue your eyes were."

The comment both reassured and worried him. He liked the "healthy" part but were his eyes looking too blue, his pupils too pinned? A nurse would notice that sort of thing.

Still seated, Locke asked Amanda to take Blake into the examination room.

"Yes, please," Blake joked flirtatiously, wrapping his arm around her slim waist.

"… to measure him for his body armour," Locke continued.

"Follow me, big boy." Amanda took Blake's hand and led him toward an unmarked door. She turned back to Locke.

"The works?" she asked.

"The works," he answered. "Weight, length and width."

Blake tried to remember if he was still wearing the same socks, he had gone to bed in. Would he have to take off his shoes when she weighed him?

While Amanda gave him "the works" in the examination room, Warren and Locke discussed their new recruit.

"What do you think?" Warren asked.

"Oh, I suppose he seems harmless enough." Locke said. It worries me that Johnny visited him. Blake isn't doing drugs again, is he?"

"Well, he didn't exactly have Johnny over. It wasn't a visit. My men said that he left as soon as he delivered the pizza."

"What about the Canaries?" Locke knew about that too. "It was only after you told him that the forensics' report indicated he was innocent of last years' murders that he opened up about working for Ginger and being in love with Candy. What happens the next time he falls in love? Where will his allegiance be? Toward the force or more

Candy?"

"I almost envy him for that."

"For covering up for someone?"

"No, for still being able to fall in love."

"Love. Humph. Doesn't exist. How many married couples do you know who are still in love? Couples learn to tolerate each other, that's all. Love is just a fear of loneliness."

"You're ten years older than me. I'm only in my forties. I still hope that someday, just someday…"

"You'll meet Mrs. Right?"

"Maybe."

"Don't bother. It's a waste of time. Cuddling up to a good book is far better than cuddling up to another human being. Give me a history of World War II anytime. Far more interesting than a wife. For instance, did you know that Hitler's men were fighting on a steady diet of an amphetamine called Pervitin?"

Locke never ceased to astonish Warren by his wealth of World War II trivia. Just as he was about to launch into a lecture about Hitler's drug habits, Blake and Amanda re-entered the room with guilty looks on their faces. Blake was buckling up his belt.

"Well, you did say to measure everything!" Blake joked.

"I'm not complaining," Amanda teased.

Locke turned as far away from the belt buckle as he could manage, as his face went bright red.

"Don't get too excited," Amanda explained. "I had to remove his belt when I weighed him. The buckle was too heavy."

She turned to Blake, "You'll get two vests – a light one for everyday use and a thickly padded one for when things get really exciting."

She sat with the men in the library and a waiter brought them another round of drinks. It was pretty much small talk after that. Locke said the vests would be delivered to his apartment on Monday. Warren knew that Blake was meeting his mother at Wang's that night and told him to take Monday off to make up for spending Sunday at the training centre. He'd meet with him in his office on Tuesday when they could go over the plan."

"What plan?"

"I'll tell you on Tuesday. Right now, I've got to talk to Locke about something. There's a blue sedan outside waiting to take you home."

"Should I go?" Amanda asked, standing up.

"No, you can stay. We might need your expertise."

Warren and Locke stood up and shook Blake's hand.

"Thanks Blake," Locke said. "We do appreciate your help, and please stay away from that crap that Johnny takes. Remember, you're a cop now."

"Of course. It really was just a pizza."

Outside, he had no problem finding the sedan. The driver already knew his address. As they drove toward mid-town, Blake regretted that Johnny had come up in their conversation, but he still looked forward to finishing off the small amount of dope that he had left in his apartment.

18. Live for Life

The next morning, after several strong coffees and a couple of slices of burnt toast, Blake got on the internet and cancelled the reservation that Captain Seligman had made for him and his mother at Mr. Wang's that night. He made another one at a smaller, more intimate restaurant he had noticed in Greenwich Village, not far from where he lived; a quiet place called Hobgoblin on Waverly Place, decorated mostly by potted plants that hid the tables behind them. He thought it would be better to avoid Wang's because he didn't want to run into anyone from his old agency, Slick. Ava, the head of the men's division at the agency, often entertained clients there. She had signed him over lunch at Wang's last year. He had barely glanced at the contract before signing it, and it wasn't until he was dropped that he realised he had been duped. After his expenses had been reconciled – he didn't realise that he was paying for the limousines they hired to transport him to jobs – he was told that he owed them money, but that he shouldn't worry because they would write off his debt "as a gesture of goodwill." He hoped that Warren wasn't serious about him going back into modelling. He even wondered whether Seligman had chosen Wang's knowing that Ava would probably be there, and that it would give Blake and her a chance to re-establish their working relationship, now that he wasn't using anymore – at least not officially.

'Maybe I was being too suspicious,' Blake thought. It was true that Locke had said to "suspect everyone," but how long could you go through life with that attitude before being overwhelmed with paranoia?

When he called his mother and told her about the change, she agreed that it was a good idea. Wang's was too much of a big deal. People went there to be seen and she didn't have anything to wear. It was too loud, too gossipy and too glamourous. Normally she would love a place like that, but this time she just wanted to have a quiet dinner with her son; a private conversation between a mother, who happened to be a prostitute, and her son who happened to be a cop.

Blanche was already at the restaurant when he got there – hidden behind some ferns at a corner table with banquette seating, biting her nails, staring at the double whiskey she had had just ordered. She jumped slightly when her son appeared. She was so focused on rubbing a cuticle into submission that she hadn't noticed him approaching.

"Blake! Hi! I didn't notice you; I mean it's not that you're not noticeable, but I wasn't watching and…"

He laughed at her nervousness, told her not to worry, and sat in the chair opposite her. The *maître d'* asked if he wanted a drink and he saw that his mother already had one – a "double whiskey, straight" she said when she saw him looking at it.

"Sounds good to me" he said.

She looked better than she had in Warren's office. A pair of large, blue-tinted glasses helped to hide her bloodshot eyes and the dark circles under them. Her long, thick hair was now 100% blonde – probably a wig - and cascaded over her left shoulder like a movie-star from one of the old Hollywood films they used to watch together when he was a kid. Her fingers were covered with chunky rings with different coloured stones that glinted when they caught what light there was in the dimly lit restaurant. He noticed the trade name, "Cartier," on the rectangle face of her watch that was outlined in gold and topped with a tiny blue stone. An old black leather biker jacket hung loosely over her shoulders like a mink stole. 'Biker chic,' they used to call it at Slick.

"Ready to order?" a waiter asked.

The menu was a combination of American dishes and

what Americans thought were European dishes. Blanche ordered the 'Poulet Grille' with mixed vegetables and Blake, the Honey Garlic Pork Chops with mash potatoes and gravy.

"Are you on expenses?" his mother asked.

"Yeah, why?"

"And a bottle of Veuve Cliquot," she said to the waiter. She looked at the menu and added "vintage."

"Is that okay?" she asked Blake.

"Go for it," he said.

When the waiter left, Blanche moved forward and almost whispered, "So tell me more about this cop thing. I hope you're not vice!"

Blake laughed. "No. I'm not vice, although I do have a few, if that's any comfort."

She giggled like someone much younger, and suddenly he felt like he was sitting across from Candy. The only thing missing was the beach and a bottle of Cava.

"I'm not sure how much I can say," he said. "I'm not sure how much I even know. You were probably right when you said one gang is trying to take over the territory of another gang, but it's all mixed up. I'm not sure who's on whose side. One of the cops said to suspect everyone."

"Sounds like good advice to me."

"Do you suspect me?"

"Of course," she answered. "You're a cop. Do you suspect me?"

He laughed. "Of course, you're a criminal."

"Tell me more about Candy," she said.

"You know, I was just looking at you, thinking that you sort of look like her."

"I like her already. How did you meet her?"

He laughed as he recalled how he woke up on the beach and saw her standing above him dressed like she had just got offstage, slinging a bottle of Cava around.

"She worked in a show at the Yumbo centre. She sang

a lot of the songs that you used to sing. When she wasn't singing, she helped her boss, Ginger, deal Charlie."

"Who killed her?"

"Ginger and her flunkies in the backstage area of Ginger's club – where they used to cut the stuff during the day. I was on the beach, waiting for Candy, in our usual place. She never showed up. But Warren did. That's when I learned that I had been cleared in the U.S. and we went looking for Candy to tell her. It meant she and I could move there and start up a home – Mr. and Mrs. Average, like she always wanted to be."

"What happened?"

"She was already dead by that point. That morning she had done her usual trade off – a shopping bag of cash for a shopping bag of coke from Ginger's suppliers. Except, this time, the coke turned out to be flour. But Candy didn't know that. They'd been working with the same suppliers for years and there'd never been a fuck-up before. Ginger blamed Candy – she said Candy had probably sold the real stuff to somebody else and that me and her were going to take the money and split."

"Were you?"

"No, we had no idea that it wasn't coke. It turned out that Ginger's usual supplier had been busted and his two flunkies substituted the real stuff for flour. Candy ended up with flour. They sold the real stuff to somebody else and took the first plane back to Italy. Nobody found out about the switch until much later. By that time, Candy was dead. So was Ginger."

"What happened to Ginger?"

"I shot her."

"Good."

"I didn't have a choice. She was pointing an AK47 at Lieutenant Warren at the time. It was either him or her."

The waiter arrived with the Champagne. He poured a small amount in a flute and handed it to Blake's mother to test. She held the glass up and stared at it at all the bubbles like she was looking up at God. Then she tasted it. The coldness of the bubbles burnt her throat as it went down. She loved Champagne, particularly the first, harsh sip.

"Perfect!" she said to the waiter, who proceeded to fill both their glasses.

"Let's toast Candy!" she said, clinking glasses with Blake.

"Listen, darling," she added after the toast, "I might be able to help you in your job, Blake. If you ever need any information, just let me know – between you and me, of course. I don't like all this gang fighting. It's bad for business."

"I might have to take you up on that at some point. Has there been any news about the inheritance?"

"Nothing new. But I'll let you know as soon as I hear something. I've decided that when it arrives, I'm going to buy a penthouse somewhere in the city and retire. Maybe even the Dakota, if there's enough loot. And I was serious about that promise I made – you'll get half of what I get. You can trust me, Blake."

He wished she hadn't said that. It made him automatically suspicious.

Blake's phone rang. He took it out of his pocket and looked at the name on the screen – 'Johnny.' Should he answer it or not? He probably wanted more money to score. One thing might lead to another. But Blake was determined never to use again. He was clean now (again). No more 'one-offs' that became "two-offs" or worse. He let the phone techno-bleep until it went into voicemail, staring at it like it was a bomb about to go off. He could listen to the message later, when his mother wasn't around.

"I hate that ringtone – techno bleep!" she said.

"I know," Blake said. "Me too. I have to change it."

Their food arrived, their Champagne flutes were topped up, and their conversation veered away from cops and robbers to life in general.

She asked him what it had been like being a model – "Do people still recognise you? ("Sometimes.") Had he saved any clippings? ("A few, not many.") He asked her whether she still sung when she did the housework. (She had cleaners now.) What did she do for fun? (Fun? She was "too busy to have fun.")

"I seem to be spending most of my free time on self-maintenance nowadays," she said with a theatrical frown. "I have to at my age. I'll be fifty soon and all the fifty-year-old men want girls in their twenties. But who knows, someday my prince might still come, even at my age. I feel so old, Blake. It's horrible."

"Fifty's not so bad." He tried to change the subject. He felt uncomfortable talking about his mother's love life with her.

"What's your favourite song from the old days?" he asked.

"That's easy. *Down with Love*. Streisand's version."

He laughed.

"I'm not really *that* bitter," she said. "I adore Abbey Lincoln's version of *Live for Life* too. Do you know it?"

She started to sing the lyrics under her breath as she reached for the Champagne bottle: *"Come with me my love and seize the day and live it, live it fully, live it fast, never thinking once about tomorrow till tomorrow's been and gone and past…"*

"You can still sing!" Blake said, thinking of his childhood.

"If you can call it that!" she replied. Then she filled their glasses again and continued the song: *"We'll pour the wine and drink it as if it were the last. Live, just live for life…"*

They clinked their glasses together again "to Candy."

"Oh Blake, I'm so sorry about your Candy. I really am. The first love is always the best," Blanche said.

"You mean you loved Dad?'

"God no. That freak? I guess my first love was in high school. We were both about sixteen – just two years before I met your father, who was already in his fifties. Tommy Parker."

"What happened?"

"We were pretty wild. I guess you could say we came from the wrong side of the tracks. One night we drove to the Pass in his dad's pick-up truck – it was an old road where couples went to make out under the moonlight. Real romantic. I was rearing to go. I wasn't wearing underwear for a reason!"

"Mom!"

Blanche laughed "Sorry, I'm not used to having a son."

"So, what happened?"

"Well, he said he couldn't go through with it. He started crying. I asked him what was wrong. It turned out he was gay."

"What did you do?'

"I asked him if he'd ever been to a gay bar and he said he hadn't, so I told him that the next weekend I'd take him to one. We had to drive for over an hour, but we finally got there and God, did we have a blast. I guess I've always been a bit of a fag hag."

"Mom, you're not supposed to use that term anymore."

"Who's gonna stop me? I'm a fag hag through and through and proud of it. Always will be."

Another toast. "To fag hags!"

"I'll be right back, Blake, I have to use the restroom. Does the budget stretch to another bottle? Just get the cheap stuff this time."

He noticed she had left her purse on the banquette where she had been sitting. He picked it up and started to go after her with it, but then had second thoughts. He opened it and quickly riffled through the contents before setting it back down where it was. She was bound to come back for it. A few seconds later she did, saying something about how she'd forget her head if it wasn't attached to her neck, grabbed her purse and went back to the restroom.

Blake regretted his action. What had he done? She was his mother for God's sake, not a suspect. It was a quick glance but long enough to notice a wrap of gold coloured paper. Suddenly, things seemed a lot more complicated between them. It was one of Jasper's wraps – the same that Bobby and Sarah were selling, and the same that he had found in Sluggo's drawer.

When his mother returned, she was dabbing her nostril with her finger. "Did you order the Champagne she asked?"

"No. I couldn't get a waiter's attention."

"*Garçon, garçon,*" she said, waving her hand at a nearby waiter. "Can we have another bottle of Champagne – non-vintage this time."

"Of course, Madam."

"No," Blake said. "Make it vintage. Same as before."

"Blake, I don't mind, really. Non-vintage is fine." She noticed that he sounded angry and wondered why. She'd only been gone for a few minutes. Had anything happened?

Blake caught the waiter's eyes with his own and said in a serious tone, "vintage."

"Yes sir." He went to retrieve another bottle.

"Blake, is something wrong?" his mother asked.

"No."

"No?"

"There's something I should warn you about," he said. "I probably should have told you earlier, but I'm so used to it, that I don't even think about it anymore."

"What?"

"I'm being shadowed."

"What do you mean?"

A plainclothes cop is trailing me – for protection."

"Where?"

"Anywhere. Everywhere."

Blanche took a quick, shifty look around the room. She was good at recognising cops but didn't see any.

"Why?"

Blake shrugged. "I'm undercover. I need to be protected."

Silence. There was no response from his mother until he said, "someone tried to kill me Friday night."

"What!?"

"A fake recruit from class. We went out to dinner. He pulled a gun out on me. He said his name was Sebastian."

"What did he look like?"

"I don't know. He had longish blonde hair, sort of curly, said he was into the Simpsons, but he was lying. You know that Simpsons' episode where Homer becomes a monorail driver…"

"No Blake, I'm sorry. I don't. I'm afraid my television watching has always been limited to glamour and crime."

He laughed. She reached into her purse and pulled out a pack of Marlboros. "Cigarette?" she asked.

"We can't smoke in here."

"I know. We can take turns."

Although Blake had given up smoking in the Canaries, he accepted the cigarette his mother gave him and put it on the table. She kept an unlit one between her fingers as she sipped her Champagne.

"Tell me more about this Sebastian character," she said.

"He said he was from California but he used an English expression. When I asked him about it, he said his father was English and he had picked up some of the lingo."

"English" set off a warning bell in Blanche's head, but she kept it to herself.

"There is something I want to ask you, mom."

"What's that, darling?" she asked as she leaned forward sympathetically. Blake looked at the size of her pupils and knew she had done a line in the restroom.

"Why do you have a gold wrap in your purse?" he asked.

Blanche leaned back against the banquette. The lines on her face hardened as she tried to figure out what to say...

19. Konnichiwa – Bang!

While Blake was having a meal with his mother downtown, Lt. Warren and Captain Seligman were having drinks at Oscar's uptown, near Mr. Wang's. As usual, Seligman had asked Warren along more as chick bait than anything else. It wasn't just his looks that the girls were attracted to, it was the way he listened to them and seemed genuinely interested in their lives. Seligman's bar chat consisted mostly of chauvinistic jokes that had gone out of style decades ago. The laughter, when it came, was usually uncomfortable.

Although they had a rule about not talking shop during their nights at Oscar's – the staff there didn't know they were cops, they just knew they were good tippers – Warren couldn't help bringing up the Layton case. His memorial was coming up and Warren would be expected to make a speech.

"We've got to be careful with that case," Seligman said. "Layton was a corrupt cop. He was helping himself to a percentage of the evidence from drug busts and selling it on. An internal investigation has been going on to see if anyone else in the force was involved but it looks like it was just him. If the press asks any questions, it was just a robbery gone wrong."

Warren looked surprised. "Why cover it up?"

"We have our reputation to think of. Once people hear about one corrupt officer, they suspect all of us."

"But who killed him?"

"That's what the investigation is trying to find out."

Although Seligman was talking to Warren, his eyes never left the front door. He couldn't help checking out the new arrivals. When two Japanese girls entered, he whisper-whistled to Warren, "Hallelujah, help has arrived."

The girls could have been sisters. They both had long

straight black hair and short skirts, but it was difficult to see their faces because they were both wearing small black masks that covered their noses and mouths – like the blue surgical masks that people wear in Japan, but in black. Seligman assumed it had something to do with the flu that everyone was talking about.

"Those masks are kind of a turn-on," he said.

The girls were met at the door by the *maître d'* and, not being regulars, were guided to the bar until a table became available. They shared the one empty stool at the bar, next to Seligman, while scrutinising the cocktail menu on the bar.

"Oh look, they have retro cocktails," one of the girls said, pointing to a special section of the menu. They ordered a Mai Tai and a Blue Moon.

"Watch and learn." Seligman said to Blake as swung his seat around to face the girls – his stocky legs spread wide, credit card at the ready.

"*Konnichiwa*," he said to the girls, bowing slightly, at least as far as his stomach allowed.

The girls looked at each other and giggled.

"We're Korean, not Japanese, one of them said. Actually, American. Both of us were born here. I've been to South Korea, but my friend hasn't. Neither of us speak Japanese – or Korean for that matter."

"My apologies," Seligman said, bowing again.

Warren knew Seligman was drunk but didn't realise how drunk until he nearly fell off his stool in mid-bow. Waving his credit card in the air he told his "good friend Sal" – the bartender – to start a tab for their group.

"Drinks are on me, ladies."

The girls side-glanced Warren and giggled which caused Warren to laugh which caused Seligman to laugh, not knowing that he was the brunt of the laughter in the first place.

"They know me here," Seligman said to the girls for no

reason. "Can we get us some nibbles as well?" he asked
Sal.

"Sure, what would you like?"

"Any preferences?" he asked the girls.

"It's nice of you to offer but we were going to have
dinner together," one of the girls said.

"Oh, don't worry about that," Seligman said. "There's
nothing like a little group action," he joked. Nobody
laughed. "Anything will do" he said to Sal. As long as it
includes chicken wings."

He turned back to the girls and stuck his hand out. "I'm
Charlie," he said "and this is my friend Harry. Harry
Warren. We usually just call him Warren."

They looked at Seligman's sweaty hand, wondering if
it was safe to shake it with so many germs around, and
decided to throw caution to the wind. Afterwards, they
made sure to use the cleaning gel on the bar.

"I'm Barbara," one of the girls said. "This is my friend
Patricia. We're both students at Columbia."

"What are you studying?" Warren asked.

"I'm an undergraduate in English Lit. and Pat is doing
a masters in architecture."

Seligman was disappointed. He was expecting naive
tourists that he could show around town – or at least his
apartment. These girls were too educated, too intelligent. It
didn't help when Warren asked the 'architecture one' –
Seligman had already forgotten their names - whether she
had ever been to Europe. Warren had been to England
several times and liked the modern architecture over there,
but thought it was sad that so many of the older buildings
were being torn down to make way for it.

"Okay, okay," Seligman said. "We're here to have
some fun, not for a history lesson."

The girls laughed. The 'literature one' asked Warren if
he was familiar with Shakespeare's sonnets – did he have
a favourite? Fortunately, the nibbles arrived, and another

round of drinks were ordered on Seligman's card.

"Wow. This is so great," the girls said, as they dug into a silver platter of chicken wings, breaded mushrooms, small squares of avocado toast and grilled shrimp. "We won't have to have dinner now."

Seligman tried to think of something intelligent to say.

"Columbia! That's where that drunken poet went wasn't it?"

Silence.

"Jack Cataract or something like that?" he said. "I used to read his stuff all the time."

"Do you mean Kerouac?" Warren asked.

"Oh good. A new author to discover," Barbara said enthusiastically. Seligman scowled. She hadn't been so enthusiastic when *he* had mentioned the author's name.

After they had finished the bar snacks, Sal asked if they wanted more. The girls pointed to their stomachs to indicate they were full, and Seligman took over.

"Hey, why don't we have one more drink here and then head over to Pinky's," he said. "It's open late and you can dance there."

The girls looked uncomfortable. Did he say "dance"? They found it difficult to imagine Seligman on a dance floor.

"Are you going too?" they asked Warren, almost at the same time.

"Of course he is." Seligman said. He ordered "one more round" from the bartender. As he was explaining the plan for the rest of the evening to the girls – "one last round here, and then Pinky's, and then who knows" - a series of loud bangs could be heard coming from the street outside.

20. Eighty-sixed

Johnny the junkie had run out of options. The money he had borrowed from Blake was gone and he wasn't answering his phone. Blake wasn't any different than anyone else; he had got what he needed from Johnny, and it wasn't friendship. As the night got darker, Johnny got sicker and colder. In the old days he could have at least found some warmth at Sluggo's, but Sluggo's was gone. And he wasn't welcome at Pinky's or anywhere else. He felt like he had been eighty-sixed from the world.

The depression from withdrawals was unbearable. 'I either need to score or to give up' Johnny said to himself, and he didn't mean giving up dope. He began imagining ways to end his life – all he had to do was jump in front of a subway train and his agony would be over. Nobody would even notice he was gone. He had made no mark on the world. 'Hurrah for me,' he said sarcastically to the cold night air.

He decided to make one last attempt at getting some money together for a hit. It was useless panhandling in the usual places. Too much competition. There was one place where he might have some luck – outside Mr. Wang's. If he could get to the rich people coming out of their cabs for dinner before Charles, the *maître d'* did, he might get enough money to score. The customers got so freaked out by a homeless junkie approaching them that they often gave him the first bill they could find in their wallets just to get rid of him. Hopefully it was a ten or a twenty. But he also risked getting beaten up by security. He didn't care anymore. It was worth the risk. It was either that or the subway. What did he have to lose?

He first positioned himself on the opposite side of the street from the restaurant to check things out. He watched Charles poking his head out the door now and then, looking for arriving customers. He was too busy helping people out of their cabs to notice Johnny. He seemed to know most of the customers by name. When he took one group into the restaurant, Johnny would try to get to next taxi before Charles came back outside.

The first few times he tried, he didn't get any money, but he was determined not to give up. That's when the blasts happened that Seligman and Warren heard from Oscar's down the street. Johnny was killed instantly by the first of two grenades thrown from a passing car. He never had to worry about committing suicide again.

21. Oscar's

Back at Oscar's, the sound of the blasts was followed by an eerie silence. Then the sirens started. The anxious eyes of diners searched out other anxious eyes, wondering whether it was a terrorist attack, As the bartender rushed to lock the door, three young businessmen in blood-splattered suits ran into the restaurant. One of them yelled that Wang's was under attack and the two Korean girls left the bar to help the men to an empty table.

Warren stood up quickly. Wang's was where Blake was supposed to meet his mother. Blake hadn't told him about the change of plans.

"Cool it!" Seligman whispered tensely. "We're off duty. Don't blow our cover."

Warren couldn't believe what he was hearing. "Don't blow our cover!" he shouted. "Our cover for what? For picking up girls? Those girls aren't interested in you. They're only interested in your fucking wallet."

Seligman stood up, weaving slightly from the effects of the alcohol he had drunk. He grabbed the lieutenant by his lapels: "I'm warning you Warren. Sit down and shut up. It's none of your business. Didn't you hear the sirens? Let them deal with it."

Warren showed his ID to the bartender who had replaced Sal a few rounds ago, asked him to unlock the door, and ran out of the restaurant.

Seligman sat hunched over his drink, trying to ignore what was happening around him. It was his night off, for God's sake. Maybe when he was younger, he would have reacted like Warren, but he had lost his idealism a long time ago. Maybe he never had it in the first place.

He thought back to his past, and how his alcoholic father never had the money to send him to a decent college like those businessmen had probably gone to. Seligman went into the force straight after high school. You didn't need good looks or intelligence to work your way up the ranks back then. You just had to keep your head down. He gave up figuring out the difference between 'right' and 'wrong' a long time ago. The important thing was to get ahead, become a success, so that you could treat girls to free drinks at places like Oscar's. It was easy to be virtuous for good-looking guys like Warren.

Hugging his whiskey in his fist, his drunken eyes ogling the legs of the Korean girls who were bending over a table in their short skirts to help the wounded businessmen, Seligman wondered if the girls would have been as eager to come to the aid of an overweight sixty-year-old like himself. He could hear parts of their conversation – the men telling them that a car had passed Mr. Wang's and the person on the passenger side "threw out one or two grenades" – they weren't sure how many – "could have been more" – and the only reason they didn't get hurt was because the *maître d'* didn't know them – they weren't regulars so he sat them at one of the worse tables in the house – under the stairs leading to the main floor.

"We're from Ohio," the other man explained. "We heard that Wang's was where all the celebrities went."

Seligman knew that he didn't have a chance with the girls now. He looked at himself in the mirror behind the bar, trying to figure out if he should go to Pinky's on his own, or maybe somewhere else. He slapped his face a few times to sober up and rearranged the thin strands of hair that made up his receding hairline.

The Korean girls would miss out tonight. 'Their loss, my gain,' he said to himself as he finished his drink. He asked the bartender to let him out.

"Are you sure you'll be safe sir?" Sal's replacement asked. Seligman gave him a dirty look. Did he think he was an old man?

"Just open the fucking door, you asshole," Seligman

said.

The bartender opened the door.

Seligman waived down the first cab he could find and told the driver to take him to Blanche's on the lower east side. He could hear all about the trouble at Wang's tomorrow at work, but tonight he wanted to get his rocks off.

22. Hobgoblin

While Blake and his mother were finishing their deserts at Hobgoblin, they noticed the waiters whispering to each other. He was sure he heard the name "Wang's" mentioned. When the waiter brought the bill, Blake asked if something had happened at Mr. Wang's.

"Do you know Mr. Wang?" the waiter asked, with a worried expression.

"Not personally. But I know the restaurant of course."

"There's been some sort of explosion there. Not sure what happened exactly. It's been on the news. They have a radio in the kitchen. They're saying it might be terrorism."

"Weren't we booked in at Wang's originally?" his mother asked.

"Yeah, yeah, we were."

The waiter looked back at the other diners whose phones were going off. Their friends were calling to make sure the "terrorists" hadn't gotten them.

One diner loudly announced, "I was just at that restaurant last week!"

Another commented, "I like the soft-shell crabs there, but everything is so overpriced. I'm sure the lychees are from cans…"

People began to leave, not knowing whether Hobgoblin was next. Although Hobgoblin's was downtown and Wang's was in midtown, and the two bore no semblance to each other in menu or price range, *you never know what restaurants will be next!*" a diner nearly screamed. A baby could be heard screaming outside – or maybe it was just a cat.

"We better go," Blake said to his mother. "I might be needed."

As Blake put his mother into a cab, she repeated what she had said before, about wanting to be on "his side," now.

"Please, darling, be careful and remember, no matter what happens, I'm on your side. I fucked up once and it's not going to happen again. I'm a 'good guy' now, like you. I love you, Blake."

He told her not to worry and gave the cab driver $30 to take her home. She waved at him through the back window and blew him a kiss as she headed home. He walked home in the opposite direction. As soon as he turned a corner, he called Warren.

"Blake! Thank God you're okay. Where are you? I'm at Wang's."

"We didn't go there – we decided to go to a small restaurant in the Village. I didn't want to run into anybody from Slick. My old boss, Ava goes there."

"I know, Blake," Warren said. "She's dead."

"No!"

"She was killed in the first blast. I'm still getting information about it. Someone threw a grenade at Wang's Lalique doors. Ava was coming out of a cab and Charles was coming out of the restaurant to meet her. Shortly afterward another grenade was thrown, probably from the same car."

"Did the car just drive away or was it a robbery?"

"Still trying to find out. I was with Seligman at a bar down the street when it happened."

"Is Seligman with you?"

"No. I'm not sure where he is. I just tried to call him, but no answer. He was pretty drunk. He might be sleeping it off."

"Do you want some help? I can get a cab up there."

"No. Go home. There are already tons of cops here. I'll talk to you tomorrow when I should know more. Actually, maybe there is something you can do. Can you get to Gigi's? I want to see how Luigi reacts to the news. Ava's purse flew halfway down the street during the blast. A wrap of cocaine fell out."

"A gold wrap?"

"No, that was the strange thing. Just a wrap, a normal white wrap. Not a gold one like they were selling at Pinky's."

"My mom had one of those gold wraps. I went through her purse when she left for the restroom."

"Good man. Now you're beginning to think like a cop."

"When we left each other, she said she wanted to be on our side now, that she wanted to be a 'good guy' like me."

"Sounds suspicious..."

23. The Back Room

As soon as Blake got to Gigi's, Luigi pulled him into the back office.

"Thank god you're okay," he said, looking more worried than relieved.

"Why shouldn't I be?" Blake asked.

"They invaded Wang's."

"Who's 'they'?"

Luigi sat down behind his desk.

"Don't be a smart aleck," he said. "Two cars drove by and the drivers threw grenades at the place. It was on the news."

Blake took the seat in front of the desk, surrounded by boxes of Panettone filled with cocaine.

"Why would you think I'd be at Wang's? Blake asked.

Luigi realised his mistake. Blake had never told him he was going to Wang's in the first place.

"You used to work in the fashion business. A lot of fashion people go there. I thought you might be there."

"I see. Did you know they got Ava?" Blake said.

Luigi's eyes tried not to react. Why would Blake think he had anything to do with Ava? Had Phil told him he was supplying to Ava last year?

"Who's Ava?" he asked.

"The head of the men's division at Slick. The one who scouted me last year."

"Oh yeah, we used to deliver coffee to her. Sorry to hear that. I liked Ava. She always gave a big tip to the delivery boys."

"I bet she did."

Luigi's eyes narrowed.

"What do you mean by that?"

"Weren't you her dealer?" Blake asked.

Luigi's face hardened.

"Who are you, Blake?"

"You asked me that before. I'm nobody." Blake responded.

"Whose side are you on?"

"What's the choice?"

"The cops? The criminals? The old mafia or the new one?"

"Who's the new one?"

"Where did you get that gold wrap, Blake - the one that you conveniently let drop from your wallet the last time you were here?"

"From that couple who took over Sluggo's, why?"

"Why do you kids get so involved with that crap?" Luigi lamented as though he meant it. "Why do you risk your money and your lives to get high when you know you're just going to have to come down again?"

"It was just one wrap."

"Yeah, just one wrap. And how many deaths have been caused by those gold wraps? The gang behind them are trying to take over my friend's business. Remember that friend I mentioned who sells the same thing? First, they killed that cop because he wouldn't change sides and then Carlotta when her bosses wouldn't give up the hotel."

"The new gang killed Layton and Carlotta?"

"How should I know!" Luigi shouted. "*I'm not involved*. Get it? I liked Carlotta. She was my friend."

"What about Wang's? Was that also the new gang?"

"How should I know? I'm fed up with it all. Maybe the new gang were providing protection to Wang's and they didn't come up with the money. Or maybe it's a turf war, maybe Ava was still getting her stuff from the old gang, and the new gang were sending a message out to her supplier."

"You seem to know a lot about what's going on."

"It's all theory, Blake. I've been around for a long time. I'm not stupid. If it is a turf war, the new boys in town are probably from Europe."

"Why would you think that?"

"I read it in the paper – how Eastern Europeans have joined forces with gangs in England."

"You mean they joined up with people like Jasper?"

"Who's Jasper?" Luigi asked, his eyes full of hate.

"That couple at Pinky's mentioned his name."

"Let's cut the verbal ping-pong and get to the point. You're not one of Jasper's crooked cops, are you?"

"What crooked cops? I don't know what you're talking about."

"Don't bullshit a bullshitter."

"Fuck off," Blake said. He hadn't gone to Gigi's to be cross-examined. He stood up and left. He felt the young Italian eyes of Luigi's counter staff boring into his back as he went out the door.

Luigi sat at his desk until he was sure that Blake was gone. Then he picked up his phone.

Outside, Blake took a receiver out of his pocket so he could listen to Luigi's call. The Italian hadn't noticed the small button that Blake had tacked onto the underside of his desk – one of Locke's recording devices. Although he had difficulty hearing the recipient of the call, Blake could hear Luigi's voice, loud and clear:

"Okay Jasper, I get the message. I'm working for you now. You can stop with the hand grenades. But who's going to protect me from the old mob if I'm selling for you? Those guys are family, for God's sakes. We go way back. It's a matter of honour for them. It's not just the money."

Blake thought he heard Jasper mumble "Bullshit."

Luigi continued: "I'm an old man Jasper. Family is important to me. I can't take this anymore. The world is changing too much. What do you think the old mob is going to do when they hear I've started working for a bunch of Brits who are trying to take over their turf?"

Static as the button automatically searched for a clearer

frequency.

Luigi: "Okay, okay, it's a different world now. I just don't want a grenade thrown into my café by either side. You've won, okay? I'm with you guys from now on."

Jasper's muffled voice.

Luigi again: "Of course you can fucking trust me. Who am I going to report you to? The cops? You've got most of those idiots in your pockets anyway. But listen, we might have a problem. Blake's been around here a few times, fishing for information. Do you know why?"

"I'll take care of him."

The button found a better frequency that picked up both sides of the call.

"What do you mean, you'll take care of him?" Luigi asked.

"He survived Wang's, he survived Sebastian, he even survived Cameron's, the clever boy. In fact, he's so clever, he should work for us, don't you think?"

"Should I bring the subject up with him?"

"No. Don't bother. We'll let his mother do it. He'll listen to her."

"Good idea," Luigi said. "I'll leave it in your hands. But please, you've got to give me some protection – starting now! And no god-damned grenades!"

"Don't worry. You're safe. Trust me." The call ended.

Blake was furious. "*Let his mother do it!*" So, she was in on the act as well. Locke was right. You couldn't trust *anyone*, not even your own mother. He would show her. He knew exactly what he was going to do. There was a cab parked on the street near him – the driver was eating a sandwich.

Blake knocked on the widow - "Hey buddy, can you take me to the lower east side?"

The driver held up his sandwich and mouthed the words, "I'm eating!"

Blake took out his wallet and held up a fifty-dollar bill.

The driver rolled down the window, took the money and unlocked the passenger door.

"Get in."

"Thanks."

"Where to?"

Blake gave the driver his mother's address.

"A night out?" the driver asked.

"Sort of." Blake patted his jacket to make sure he still had his gun on him.

"Nice night tonight. Not too cold, at least for this time of the year…"

"Listen, buddy," Blake said. "Do you mind if we cut the small talk? I'm not in the mood."

"Yeah, sure. No problem. Just one thing."

"What?"

"Generic guru."

"Huh?"

The driver held his NYPD card up to the rear-view mirror so Blake could see it from the backseat.

"I'm your shadow."

'So,' Blake thought. 'I *am* being shadowed, after all.' The only problem was that he didn't want to be – not right now anyway.

"Why are you going to your mother's place?" the driver asked.

"I don't know how much you know. I need to talk to her about something. I just found out that she's part of Jasper's gang. Do you know about that?"

"Have you spoken to Lieutenant Warren?"

"No. I'm just so angry that she would lie to me."

"Speak to Warren before you do anything. Do you need a phone?

"No, I've got one."

Blake got out his phone and grudgingly called Warren. He told him about his trip to Luigi's and Luigi's conversation with Jasper – how Jasper was going to tell his mother to ask Blake to join his gang of corrupt cops. Warren told him to put the phone on speakerphone so he could talk to Mick, the driver. Blake did what he said and held the phone away from his ear so that the driver could hear.

"Mick, take him home." Warren said.

"Wait a second!" Blake protested. "I'm not going home!"

"Yes you are," Warren said through the phone's speaker. "You're going home and cooling off. Call me tomorrow when you get up." Click. The driver changed direction. Instead of going east toward the lower east side, he headed west toward Blake's place in the Village.

"For fuck's sake," Blake said, crossing his arms.

"Don't worry Blake." Mick said. "You're doing the right thing. I've worked on the force a long time. Warren's a good guy. Trust me."

24. Blanche's

While Blake did what his boss said to do – "go home" – Warren's boss, Captain Seligman was being given a foot massage by Blake's mother at her den of inequity. Seligman had only recently learned that Blanche's real name was Brooke and that she was Blake's mother, but it wasn't Warren who had told him initially. It was Jasper. Seligman was one of Jasper's corrupt cops. He, like Layton, had worked for the old mob, but when Jasper got to Layton, Seligman changed sides. After nearly forty years in the force, he had grown accustomed to the periodic change of gangs who ruled New York. You could either fight them or join them. Most cops did a little bit of both. The current turf war was almost over. And Jasper was winning.

Seligman sat in his favorite armchair in his favorite room at Blanche's while she massaged his shoeless feet through his sweaty black nylon cop socks. She didn't particularly enjoy what she was doing, but she'd got used to it. Seligman had been a regular client for so many years now that he felt like family. The foot massage generally led to a sexual act of some sort – nothing too energetic – with him still in his socks.

"What is it about men?" Blanche and the girls often asked each other. "They never take off their socks."

A bottle of Champagne was on the table next to him, with glasses for both him and Blanche. She drank slowly, as she did with most clients, while he gulped the stuff down like soda pop. At $150 a bottle, she encouraged him to drink as much as he wanted to, which had the added advantage that he might fall asleep before she had to do anything. She didn't have a lot of clients – they usually wanted the younger girls – but some of the older regulars liked her because they were used to her. They knew they could trust her, that they could tell her anything without her blabbing it all over New York.

"You still got them cigars, baby?" Seligman asked.

Blanche reached into the bottom drawer of an old filing cabinet leaning against the wall and pulled out a box of cigars that had "Product of Cuba" stamped all over it. (Nobody asked why the stamp was in English.) She set them on the table next to the Champagne. Although the exterior of the building looked impressive, the rooms were fairly basic. Apart from a double bed squeezed into a corner, the furniture in that particular room consisted of two raggedy armchairs, one metal filing cabinet, a Versace crystal ashtray and a plastic patio table on folding legs – the type of thing you might see on a campsite.

Seligman enjoyed preparing his cigar as much as he enjoyed smoking it. After removing one from the box, he rolled it gently between his fingers to make sure there weren't any lumps. Then he bit the end of it, spat it out, and took his thousand-dollar Dupont lighter from his pocket and lit it, blowing a thick cloud of smoke in the direction of Blanche who coughed and waved it away with one of her hands.

"Next time I'll make you go outside to smoke, bad boy,"

Seligman's rubbery jowls shook with laughter. After a few hits of tobacco, he set the cigar in the ashtray to simmer away while he looked at Blanche in a manner she recognized from previous visits. He wanted to get something off his chest – he was about to have a 'serious conversation.' She didn't want to get serious. She had enjoyed the dinner with her son – at least until they were interrupted by the news about Wang's - and she didn't want to ruin that mood with his bullshit.

"Now, Blanche," Seligman begun. "It's about your son."

He paused. Somehow, the words 'Blanche' and 'son' didn't seem right together. He had never imagined her with a son. Suddenly, she seemed as old as she was. A 'mother' rather than the glamorous, fun-loving fur-wearing Blanche that he had known in the past. Her blonde wig looked too much like a wig – the hair too thick for somebody pushing fifty. Her dark eyeliner accentuated her violet eyes, but it also drew attention to the crow's feet at the edges of her eyes and made the dark circles underneath them even darker. She looked tired, worn out, incongruous. He tapped his glass for a refill.

"What about my son?" she asked as she poured the Champagne.

Seligman tried to organize the drunken thoughts in his head.

"We want you to ask him to work for us," he said.

"I already have," she answered.

It was a lie, of course. The opposite had actually happened. She had told her son that she was on his side.

"You mean he already knows about Jasper?" the captain asked.

"Yep."

"Is he willing to become one of his crooked cops?"

"He's open to the idea. I told him I'd talk to Jasper," she lied again.

"As long as he doesn't mention anything to Warren."

"Don't worry, I told him not to mention anything to anyone until I got back to him. Are you going to try to enlist Warren in the crooked brigade too?"

"No. Too chancy. He still believes in good versus evil. And he's firmly on the side of 'good.' I'm fed up with it. He's a cop not a priest."

"What are you going to do about it?"

"I've been trying to get him to retire for a while now – for medical reasons. But he wanted one more case to prove himself, so he went to the Canaries to arrest your son. Except your son turned out to be innocent and the two of them broke up a drug ring that nobody thought would ever get busted. So, my boss, the Commissioner, said to bring Warren back to New York to bust the syndicate here.

"What gang in the Canaries?"

"Ginger's gang. She ran a club at the Yumbo. Provided most of the coke to the other clubs at the centre. It's a weird place. Mostly souvenir shops by day that turned into bars and clubs at night. There's a big gay community there."

He tapped his lap. She got on it. Each year she felt heavier, and he felt more flaccid.

"You like that baby?" he asked like he used to ask when they were both a lot younger.

"Actually," he said. "Maybe that's not such a good idea." She could tell he was in pain. She switched back to the chair she had been sitting on before.

"So, what happens now?" she asked.

"I'll convince my boss that Warren should retire – for his own good. Shit, if it was me, I'd retire in an instant. They'll still give him a full pension and a good severance package – he can spend the rest of his life whooping it up without worrying who's behind him."

"Except for his heart."

"I'm sure he'll be careful."

"So, what about my son? What happens to him?"

"I'm assuming he'll become one of Jasper's cops. At least if you ask him."

"I'll work on it."

"Thanks baby. I knew we could rely on you." He pointed to the floor. It was time for business. He expected her to get on her knees to service him. She kneeled down on the floor, knees aching.

'For God's sake,' she thought. 'He isn't even hard. What's he trying to prove…'

25. Busted

When Blake woke up the next morning, his conversation with Warren was still going through his head. When his phone techno-bleeped, he didn't need to look at the screen to know who it was.

"Feel better this morning?" Warren asked.

"Yeah. I guess coming home was the right thing to do."

"When are you going to see your mother?"

"I'm going to call her after this. Maybe I'll see her for dinner again tonight."

"If she asks you to join Jasper's gang, say yes."

"Huh?"

"You're undercover remember. You might be our way "in" to his gang. Did Locke give you an extra SD card when you gave you the button and the receiver?"

"I don't know. I think so. There were a few buttons and a few cards."

"Remove the SD card from last night so you can save the conversation you overheard, and put a new one in. I assume there's also extra buttons."

"Yeah, I definitely saw those. But what happens when Luigi discovers the button under his desk that I put there?"

"Don't worry too much about it for now. By the time he finds it, *if* he finds it, they won't know who put it there. The sooner you're accepted by Jasper's boys, the safer it will be for you. And don't worry, we'll have your back, as usual."

Blake wanted to say, 'like that night that Cameron and Carlotta got murdered,' but it was useless to argue. He would just have to trust Warren this time. He ended the call and rang his mother. No answer. He hung up when it went into message mode. Then he called again. She answered.

"What?" she asked groggily.

"What, what?"

"Huh? Oh, sorry, darling. It turned out to be a late-night last night. What time is it?"

"Almost noon."

"God, I'll have to open the place up soon for the lunchtime crowd. I hope all the girls are here."

"I have to see you."

"When?"

"Tonight."

"Where?"

"You choose."

"Do you know Hugo's? It's near you in the Village. It's a gay bar, but I know the manager. We'll be safe there."

'Safe from what?' he thought.

"I'll find it," he said. "What time?"

"Early. Six?"

"Okay, I'll see you at six. I need to tell you something."

"That sounds ominous. I've got something to tell you too."

"Really?"

"Really."

He hung up and turned on the TV to see if there was any news about Wang's. A few stations were broadcasting a story about a boat that was stuck somewhere full of passengers who might or might not have the Chinese virus, but the big story was a large bust that had occurred at Newark airport last night. There was a brief clip of a customs officer slicing open what looked like boxes of Panettone. When he cut through the cakes, plastic packages of cocaine fell out.

'So that's where he kept it,' Blake said to himself.

Other clips showed the cops arresting baggage handlers that were involved with the transport of the drug. Then there was a clip of cops in riot gear breaking into apartments in New York and arresting people. Strangely, in one clip the cop cars passed right by Luigi's without stopping. A broadcaster was saying that it was the end of the mafia in New York.

Then Seligman appeared on camera. He was outside the force's headquarters answering questions from the press. Blake called Warren, who answered his call immediately.

"What am I watching on the news?" Blake asked.

"Porky pig trying to sound important?" Warren answered.

Blake laughed. He had never heard Warren refer to his boss in such a derogatory way.

"What's up?" Blake asked.

"Fuck it. I might as well tell you. Remember when I said that I was with Seligman when Wang's got blasted? I tried to help. He didn't want to get involved. Told me not to ruin my cover. As far as he knew, you could have been having dinner there with your mother."

"Ruin what cover?"

"He didn't want the staff at Oscar's to know we were cops. He thought it might affect his style, that girls might not be so interested in going out with a cop."

"I don't get it. He's a cop. A good guy. I thought it was his job to help out people when they were in trouble."

"I could report him for how he acted. Yeah, he was off duty, but it still wouldn't look good."

"So, what's up with the press conference?" Blake asked.

"He's taking credit for the airport busts. Looks like the NYPD broke up the Mafia – again. Those guys were the ones that took over after the Mafia Committee trials in the late '80s."

"Did you know the bust was going to happen?"

"I heard that something was up – it's mostly a result of Carlotta's boyfriend singing in prison. Sorry that I didn't fill you in, but Seligman only wanted a few people to know."

"So, now that they're arrested, does it mean our job is

done? That was quick."

"I'm afraid it's just begun. There definitely is a turf war going on and it looks like the new guys just won. Jasper's boys are in charge now. If I was of a suspicious nature, I'd think that the cops helped them out – at least some of the cops – at least Seligman."

"Do you think Seligman was covering up for Jasper all this time?"

"Blake, do you remember when Lieutenant Locke said to suspect everyone?"

Blake paused and let what Warren said sink in.

"But if your boss is a crooked, where does that leave us?"

"We have to bust Jasper's operation. And my boss."

"How?"

"I'm not sure We need a plan. I've been discussing it with Locke – the one person I can trust. He doesn't think it's possible without the assistance of SIS."

"The MI6 in England?"

"Yeah."

"I don't get it. Why would they get involved with narcotics?"

"Dope isn't Jasper's only business. He's also into money laundering and supplying weapons to countries who shouldn't get them. The dope money is the oil that lubricates the operation."

"Warren, Is my mother safe?"

"No. Not while Jasper is still out there. None of us are. And getting Jasper is not going to be easy, but we'll get the bastard. And when we do, I can finally take that early retirement the force is always trying to get me to take."

"Really? What will you do?"

"Retire someplace nice. Someplace sunny."

"I know a good hotel in the Canaries" Blake joked. He was referring to the first place he stayed there last year – a crack den called the Nirvana Apartments.

"So, are you ready to go after Jasper's boys?" Warren asked.

"Yeah. Let's do it."

"Okay, but it won't be easy. We need a plan with people we can trust. You, me and Locke. Nobody else. Would you be up for a meeting of just the three of us?

"Yeah. Sure."

"I'll call Locke to arrange a time and place. Are you free tomorrow?"

"Yep."

"What are you going to do today?"

"I don't know. I have a lot to think about."

Blake didn't tell Warren he was going to meet his mother later. He was afraid Warren would warn him not to.

"Just one more question. Are you still 'clean,' Blake?"

"Of course, I am."

"Are you sure?"

"Yeah. Trust me."

26. Bear Night

When Blake arrived at Hugo's that night, it looked like there was already a party going on. Black balloons had been hung around the entrance; a different coloured Teddy Bear painted on each one. A female *maître d'* with bright red hair greeted him at the door and asked if he was Blanche's guest. When he answered in the affirmative, she motioned for him to follow her to "Blanche's favourite table."

Her favorite table? His mother had mentioned that she knew the place, but he didn't know she was that much of a regular. Why would she be a regular at a gay bar? He followed the *maître d'* through a crowd of mostly bearded, overweight men who were standing with big glasses of beer with handles – "pints" instead of glasses.

She sat him at a small table next to the hallway that led to the restrooms, threw a couple of plastic-coated menus down, and told him that Blanche was on her way – that she had rung from a taxi to say she was going to be late. Then, a group of men at a table across the room yelled "Maggie!" and off she went.

Blake looked over the large assortment of burgers listed on the menu and thought that maybe now was the time to start his vegetarian diet. They had three different types of bean burgers. As he tried to make a decision, his mother rushed into the restaurant like she was being followed. She went straight to his table and knelt down next to him.

"Listen baby, before anything happens, I need to reassure you that I'm on your side. Do you get that? *I'm on your side.* It may not seem like it sometimes – but that's just an act – I have to protect myself. Just go along with it. I'm sorry - it happened on the way over - I didn't have time to call you. Please, trust me."

He had no idea what she was talking about.

"Blanche!" someone shouted out from across the room.

It was Maggie.

"I'm so sorry, I must have missed you when you came in. Bear night is so busy. Have you ordered yet?"

"Magpie!" Blanche stood up and greeted her greeter. "Great to see you. I forgot about Bear Night. Hey, can you do something with this rag before somebody throws a milkshake at it?"

She was wearing an oversized fur coat of varying shades of dark brown mink that would have looked great on a red carpet in 1950s Hollywood but was distinctly out of place among all the checked shirts and jeans in the rest of the bar.

"Oh, Blanche, you're not still wearing that coat, are you? Those poor rabbits."

"Rabbits! It's mink darling," Blanche said as she handed over her coat for safekeeping.

"Uh-huh," Maggie said, holding the coat to her nose. "I'm from Wisconsin, and that doesn't smell like mink to me. It smells more like polyester."

"Even better. I got it in a thrift store about ten years ago…"

"And she's been wearing it ever since."

Blanche laughed. "It reminds me of Hollywood."

"Girl, the closest you ever got to Hollywood was watching reruns of Sunset Boulevard."

"I *love* that film."

"You *are* that film! Now what can I get you guys?"

"I haven't had a time to look at the menu yet," Blanche protested.

"You need to look at the menu? You must have seen it a thousand times – there's probably a tiny version of it imprinted permanently on its own brain cell by now."

"I was thinking more of my son."

"Your who?"

"Oh, sorry Mag, this is my son Blake. Blake, Maggie."

"No way. That gorgeous guy is your son?"

"He most certainly is. Can't you see the resemblance?"

"You look like sisters."

Blanche laughed. "He's straight."

"You still look like sisters. What'll it be, big boy?"

"I guess I'll just have a cheeseburger. Does it come with fries?"

"Does it come with fries! What sort of place do you think this is. Of course, it comes with fries. Ketchup is extra."

"Oh, okay, can I order some ketchup too?"

She laughed. "Only joking. It comes with ketchup."

"He's so sweet," she said to Blanche. To Blake: "Don't worry sweetie, I'm lez."

She took down their order and passed it to a waiter on his way to the kitchen. "And two pints of beer on the house," she added.

"Maggie's great," Blanche said to her son. "She used to work for me."

"But didn't she just say she was a lesbian?"

"Yeah, a lot of my girls are. Most of them hate men. That's why they're so good at their jobs."

Blake tried to process the information.

"I'm straight in case you were wondering," his mother said.

"Mind if I join you?" a male voice asked.

They looked up and saw a fair-haired man in his late twenties with bright green eyes and a gleaming white smile.

"Jasper!" Blanche stood up with a side-glance in her son's direction that meant 'remember what I said.'

"Hello, Luv," Jasper responded, nipping her on the neck.

"This is Blake, my son Blake," Blanche stuttered.

"My pleasure," Jasper said, holding out his hand.

Blake stood up and shook his hand. Then all three of them sat down. Blanche tried, unsuccessfully, not to look nervous. Blake couldn't help looking curious. Jasper looked like he was out for a good time. After a quick look at the menu that was still on the table, he called a waiter over like he was in the Ritz and ordered a salad and a double whiskey - straight.

"Any other orders?" Jasper asked. "It's on me."

Blanche ordered a diet burger with salad and Blake a cheeseburger with fries. Jasper got the Super-Duper Special – two thick patties with just about every extra on the menu. Blake liked Jasper. If he hadn't known he was a murderer, he would have thought he was a nice guy. When he excused himself to go to the "loo," Blake couldn't help but smile. Imagine a grown man using words like that? It sounded like baby talk.

"I'm sorry darling." Blanche said. "It's what I was warning you about when I came in. He called me while I was in the cab on the way here. He insisted on meeting us here. Nobody says 'no' to Jasper."

"But he seems like such a nice guy."

"He's not. He wants me to ask you to become one of his crooked cops."

"O.K."

"What do you mean, 'O.K.'?"

"I'll become one of his crooked cops."

"Blake. Are you nuts? I told you, I'm on your side. I'm trying to escape from that world."

"What I meant to say was that I'll *pretend* to become one of his crooked cops."

"O.K. I'll go along with it, but we have to be careful. Does Warren know about this?"

"He's the one who came up with the idea."

Jasper returned from the mens' room just as the food arrived. Blake noticed that as he passed Blanche's chair, he let his hand rest for a short moment on her shoulder – long enough for her to reach up and take what was in it – a wrap of cocaine. It wasn't long after that that she got up to go to the "loo" herself, singing a line from a Billie Holiday song as she left the table: *Please don't talk about me when I'm gone...*"

Blake and Jasper were alone now. They should have been looking at each other as enemies, but Blake felt like he had met a new friend.

"How long have you been in New York?" Jasper asked.

"Not long," Blake answered. "Where are you from in England?"

"Born and bred in Hackney, mate. Do you know it?"

"No."

Silence.

"Strange place, innit?" Jasper said, looking at the heavy-set men around him.

"It's bear night," Blake explained like he was an authority on the subject.

"You wot?"

"Bear night. I guess it means big and hairy men. Like real bears."

Jasper laughed. Then he stopped laughing. Then he looked around the room and started laughing again.

Blake shrugged. "To each his own."

"So, what do you think of the English accent, then?" Jasper asked, expecting him to say he "loved" it like most Americans seemed to.

Blake shrugged again. "I prefer French accents, to be honest."

Jasper scowled. "Ouch," he said.

Blanche reappeared with a smile on her face, practically skipping back to her seat,

"So, what have you two been talking about while I was gone? Not me, I hope!" she joked.

"Your son prefers the Frogs to the Brits," Jasper said.

"What kind of frogs?" Blanche asked, nervously, like she was afraid that Jasper was about to attack her son. Nobody insulted Jasper.

Jasper explained that "Frogs" was English slang for the "French."

Everyone relaxed.

"Hey Blake, do you want a line?" Jasper whispered.

"Jasper! For God's sake. He's a cop," his mother said.

"I know he's a cop. But I also know lots of cops who treat themselves once in a while. There's no harm in that."

Silence. Blake felt like he was being tested. He was. But he also wanted to see the color of the wrap that Jasper had passed to his mother. He could take the wrap into the restroom like they had - it didn't mean he had to do any.

"Sure. Why not?" he said.

"Go on then," Jasper said to Blanche. She handed the wrap that Jasper had given to her to her son under the table. Blake took it and went into the "loo."

He opened his hand in a cubicle. The wrap was gold - the same stuff that Sluggo had at the retirement centre and that Bobbie and Sarah had sold him. That's all he needed to know. It confirmed that Jasper was the supplier.

Blake opened the wrap and examined the powder, just to make sure it was coke. He better test it to make sure. Plus, Jasper might get suspicious if there wasn't some powder missing. He carefully laid the opened wrap on top of the toilet basin, scrapped off a thin line with his NYPD ID card, then added to it to make it a thicker line...

"What's he doing in there?" Jasper asked at the table. "Smoking the stuff?"

Blanche was too busy talking about how wonderful New York was to be concerned. Spring would be here in no time, and she *absolutely loved* New York in the Spring – when everything was so *new* – "how many days in February this year?" she asked.

Jasper couldn't tell if she wanted an answer or an audience.

"What comes after February?" she continued. "March! Isn't that when Spring starts, in March? March forward,

Spring backward, is that the expression?"

She didn't bother waiting for an answer. It was speech without thought. Her conversation flitted through a myriad of subjects, her eyes looking like they were about to burst out of their sockets.

"Do you think I should see if Blake is okay," she asked out of nowhere.

Jasper shrugged. He was getting bored.

"This shit is great!" she said.

"I know. Straight from the source. Let's order some more drinks."

"I'm still getting that numb feeling in the back of my throat. I love that feeling."

Jasper ordered another round of drinks from a passing waiter. Blake came out of the restroom dabbing his nostrils. He put the wrap under a napkin and gave it to Jasper.

"My go," Jasper said, as he left for the "loo."

They had hardly noticed that the waiter had delivered the food and booze to their table while all the shenanigans were going on. After they all made a few more trips to the "loo" they weren't interested in the food. The next time they ordered drinks, Blanche asked the waiter if he "could do something with the food."

"Is there something wrong, madam?"

"No, I, um, I just don't have much of an appetite. I ate before I came. We all did. Just take it away."

She continued to talk about how great the weather was going to be in the future.

"Don't you just love the Spring?"

The lights dimmed and a DJ in drag took their place at the mixing desk. Some of the bears started dancing with each other, first moving side to side and then eventually doing little twirls, but nothing too crazy. But when a techno mix of Loleatta Holloway's song from the 1970s came on - *The Greatest Performance of My Life* - nobody could resist whooping and moving and mouthing the words in the most exaggerated fashion imaginable. The bar turned into a room of dancing bears.

"This place is nuts!" Jasper said as he returned to the table from the loo, and a passing bear reached over and tousled his hair.

Maggie rushed up to their table and grabbed Blake's mother. "C'mon girl, let's have a dance. It's my break."

"Why not!" Blanche said. "Let's boogie." She let Maggie lead her to the dance floor, then went back to the table and grabbed Blake and Jasper.

"You too, boys!"

Blake and Jasper went along with it, but neither could dance like the bears. They were relieved when the song ended, and they could return to the table. Except, then a dance mix of a Lady Gaga song came on, and who could resist that...

27. The Hangover

Blake woke up with another hangover and out-of-control radiators. He hadn't turned them on last night when he got back from Hugo's, but they were still blazing away. He opened the bedroom window for a few minutes and wrapped himself up in a flannel robe he found in the closet. It was too short for his long legs, but it helped psychologically. The weather was starting to get milder – surprisingly mild for early February – so he just left the windows open.

He dragged a cup and coffee over to the couch and turned on the TV. Although the news stations were still making a big thing out of that Chinese virus, the President was reassuring everyone that it was like the regular flu and there was nothing to worry about. An agency at the UN had renamed it. Instead of calling it SARS, they were now calling it Covid-19. He wondered if he should be worried. Everybody who got it seemed to have a connection to China, but he had woken up with a runny nose, aching muscles and a headache. Then he remembered all the coke he snorted, the dancing and the whisky.

As planned, he had agreed become one of Jasper's "corrupt cops." In reality he would be working undercover and hoping to bust some of the real cops who had joined Jasper's operation. His mother still insisted that she was on her son's side, but he would keep an eye on her too. 'Suspect everyone,' Locke had said.

Blake's phone techno-bleeped.

"Hi mom."

"I'm not your mother," a man's voice responded. Blake had picked up the phone without looking at the screen.

"Warren?"

"Yes Warren. Good night last night?"

"I'm not sure. I'm still trying to put two and two together," Blake answered apprehensively, wondering how much his 'shadow' had observed, wherever he was.

"What did you think of Jasper?" Warren asked. You were seen walking out of Hugo's with him, with his arm around your shoulder, at about 2 am, with your mother limping behind you with a broken heel."

"He turned out to be surprisingly nice."

"Nice enough to convince you to work for him?"

"He asked."

"And you answered?"

"Yes. I answered 'yes'"

"Good. You're one of his crooked cops now. Except I assume you haven't changed sides, or you wouldn't be telling me about it."

"No, of course I haven't changed sides. I'm still a good guy."

"What about your mother?"

"According to her, she's still a good guy too."

"Do you trust her?"

"Yes. Maybe. Do you?"

"I don't know if I can trust you, let alone the two of you."

Blake laughed. "Don't worry about that – you can definitely trust me."

"Do you trust her enough to bring her to our meeting tonight?"

Blake suddenly remembered the meeting.

"Sure, but do you think that's a good idea?"

"We're going to need her help for our plan. Let me call Locke and I'll call you straight back."

Blake hung up and waited for the call. After a breakfast of coffee and toast, it came.

"Sorry about the delay," Warren said. "I spoke to Locke, and he had to call me back."

"Why?"

"He wanted to talk to your mother."

"Why?"

"He wanted to check her out. He has a device on his line that indicates when people are lying. Your mother's okay. She's coming to the meeting."

"Hold on, someone's trying to get in touch with me. It's mom. What should I do?"

"Take the call and ring me back."

He took the call.

"Are you as hungover as I am?" his mother asked.

"I'm on my second coffee, so I'm okay."

"Oh, the good old days – when hangovers only lasted a morning. Now they last until the next drink. Did you have a good time last night?"

"Sort of. If Jasper was someone else, I could even learn to like him."

"He's an asshole."

"You liked him last night."

"It was an act. I told you that. Remember how I always wanted to be an actress? My whole life is an act."

Blake wondered if she was acting now.

"Did you spend the night with him? He's not there now, is he?"

"Do you know what that asshole did?" she said. "After dropping me off, he said he was tired and was going home. Then he called me about an hour later at some broad's apartment, getting a blow job."

"Mom!"

"Sorry, darling, but we're a team now. I have to say it like it is."

"Anyway, then what happened – without getting too graphic, please. Why did he call?"

"He wanted me to provide the verbal."

"What do you mean, verbal?"

"Talk dirty to him while that other woman sucked him off."

"Do people do that? That's disgusting. Who was the other woman?"

"Who knows. He gets off on my voice – the things I say - but I'm too old for him, so sometimes he picks up on a younger girl and calls me."

"But where did he meet the other girl?"

"He's got loads of numbers on his phone. Or maybe it was just a street girl. At one point he asked her to make him a drink – I think he called her Jackie.

"Jackie?"

"I think that's what he said. Why?"

Blake's brain cells rewound. He remembered seeing Sebastian talking to Jackie before the class, and how he had never seen him before.

"So, what did you do when he asked for this verbal stuff?"

"I told him he was a fucking asshole and that the next time I saw him I was going to kick him in the face with my boots."

"What was his reaction to that!?"

"He gave me his credit card number. I don't do freebies. He's such an asshole, but $100 for ten minutes of insults isn't bad. He came really quick."

"Mom! Too much information - *again*!"

"Just bust the bastard before I have to do it again."

"We're trying. Did Locke ring you?"

"Yeah. I'm coming to the meeting tonight. Did the lawyer call you?"

"No, why?"

"There's a problem with your dad's money. They found a load of stolen goods in his house. They don't know if he stole them or just received them. Either way, they're not his. And it gets worse. He owed a lot of taxes. They've reconciled his bank accounts and there's a lot of money missing. The pluses don't add up to the minuses."

"How bad is it?"

He's being done for tax evasion. Or his estate is. When they're done confiscating everything and paying the fines and the interest on the fines, the lawyer's costs and the accountant's costs, the lawyer estimates that we'll getting about 500 grand."

Each?

"No. It will go to me, but don't worry, you'll get half."

"I knew it was too good to be true."

"Who gives a shit anyway? He was a creep. Who wants his money? We have our own."

"But didn't he have life insurance? What about that?"

"They're saying that he caused his own death. That he hung himself. They admit it was 'probably' auto-erotic asphyxiation, but we'd have to go to court to prove the death was accidental."

"How could we prove that?"

"Exactly. We'd probably have to spend most of the 500 grand on legal fees."

"Forget it."

"That's what I told him. Forget it. It's over. We'll get what we get. Now, about that bastard, Jasper…"

28. The Meeting

Organizing the meeting wasn't difficult. Warren and Locke decided that the safest place to hold it would be in Blake's apartment. He got out his expensive Marimekko cups and they – Blake, Locke and Warren - sat around his kitchen table drinking coffee, waiting for his mother to show up.

"I forgot how nice this apartment is," Warren said. "These cups cost more than $50 each."

"Really? I wish somebody had told me." Blake said. "I've already broken one. There used to be six of them. Now there's only five."

"Don't worry about it. Hospitality will take care of it. What day do the cleaners come?" Warren asked, looking at the empty pizza boxes on the counter.

"Cleaners? Nobody said anything about cleaners."

The buzzer went off downstairs and Blake jumped up to answer it. They could hear his mother's stilettos make their way up the stairwell.

"Oh, there you are!" she said when she saw her son leaning against the door.

"You know, mom, there is an elevator."

"I'm trying to lose weight, especially after last night. Those burgers at Hugo's just stick to your hips."

He was going to remind her that most of her burger went uneaten but thought it best not to mention that aspect of their evening, at least not in front of his colleagues.

Warren and Locke stood up when she entered the room. Warren helped her with her fur coat – the same one she wore last night – and introduced her to Locke who stood and shook her hand. After she sat down, he started on one of his history lessons.

"You know, in the old days, Hugo's was run by the mafia," he said. "A lot of those gay joints were. The Stonewall riots had as much to do with the mafia as gay rights. It was owned by Fat Tony of the Genovese family. The cops were after the mafia when they raided the place, but it turned into a gay liberation thing."

Blanche wasn't listening. She was too busy staring at Lieutenant Warren. She hadn't noticed how good-looking he was the last time she saw him.

"My god," she said, "You're almost as gorgeous as my son."

"Mom!"

Warren laughed.

"Are you…." she started to ask.

"Gay? No."

"Do you want a coffee, mom?" Blake asked.

"I don't care what it is, as long as there's a shot of whiskey in it."

Locke and Warren traded glances. Could they depend on somebody as colorful as her?

Blake made everyone coffees, put two shots of whiskey in hers and quickly downed a shot, himself.

"So, what's the plan?" Blanche asked when he delivered the drinks.

"Mrs. Webster…" Locke began.

"Westwood!" she corrected him. "I use Westwood now for a last name. But you can call me Blanche."

"Yes, well, um, Blanche, the main thing we need to know is your level of commitment. Can we trust you?"

"Don't worry about that. You can trust me." He wondered what the wink meant.

"Would you be willing to host a party at your premises that included city officials and undercover cops?"

Blanche looked at Blake with a question mark on her face.

"Nobody told me about that." Blake said. "I thought we were going to come up with a plan. I didn't know you already had one."

Locke asked Blanche again about the party, but the

downstairs buzzer went off before she could answer.

"What the hell?" Blake asked. Everyone who had been invited to the meeting was already there.

Locke quickly explained: "I'm sorry. I should have mentioned it before. Another officer is joining us."

"I don't like surprises," Blanche said. "I thought it was only going to be us four."

Blake answered the intercom: 'Who is it?"

"Generic guru," somebody said in a muffled voice with a foreign accent.

"Is this a police meeting or a meditation session?" Blanche asked.

Silence. Steps. A stranger came out of the elevator, singing to themselves, as though they were wearing headphones. A few friendly knocks on Blake's front door. He opened it.

"What the fuck is going on!"

Rider, who Blake had last seen in the Canaries, strolled into the apartment, singing in Spanish, like he owned the place.

"Hi Blake, *Qué pasa*, man?"

Blake looked at him, astonished, not knowing what to say. Then he slugged him.

"Blake!" Blanche yelled.

"You killed Candy," he said to Rider, emotionlessly, but ready for another punch.

Warren stood up to protect Rider. Locke stayed seated and told everyone to calm down. "Blake, Rider has a black belt in kickboxing. You could get hurt."

"I don't give a shit! I thought you said another *officer* was joining us?"

"Blake! He *is* an officer. Rider works for us. He always has. Well, not for us, exactly, but the Spanish version of us, or rather the Canarian version. He's our eyes and ears in the Canaries. A lot of criminals are based there – American and English – and the Canaries don't have an extradition treaty with the U.S., so we have to depend on local undercover agents, like Rider, to help us out. It wasn't an accident that Warren found you on the beach. Rider gave us that information."

"And I didn't kill Candy," Rider said, still rubbing his cheek where Blake had hit him. "Ginger killed Candy, *stupido*! It was as much as surprise to me as it was to Candy. Nobody in that room expected that. Ginger went crazy. She was in love with Candy, and she thought that Candy was in love with you. She thought Candy had ripped her off so the two of you could escape to that house in the suburbs with the white picket fence that Candy always talked about and live like normal people."

"What do you mean by normal?"

"Don't be a dope. You know Candy used to be a man."

Blake went for him again. Rider blocked it this time, shouted "KIAI," and flipped Blake over his shoulder.

"C'mon boys, for God's sake, we're in this together. You're not school children anymore, sit down and shut up."

Blake got up from the floor, rubbing his back, and he and Rider took their seats grudgingly.

"Are you okay?" Blanche asked her son.

"Yeah, of course I am. I knew Candy had the op, but she was 100% female."

"Don't worry about it," Blanche said. "It's not the 1950s, for crissakes. I don't blame Candy for wanting normality. I don't want to be a criminal anymore either. I'd prefer a penthouse with a doorman to a picket fence, but to each their own."

Rider held out is hand to Blake.

«¿*Amigos*?»

"No!"

"Blake!" his mother reprimanded.

He gave Rider the shortest possible handshake and the longest possible sneer.

"Does anybody mind if I smoke?" Blanche asked, riffling through her purse.

"At the table?" Locke asked, surprised that she would even ask.

"It's not your table," Blake sneered. "Of course, you can, mom. You can smoke wherever you want. I'll get an ashtray." He brought a saucer from the kitchen counter and set it on the table. "I'll have one too, if you don't mind."

Locke and Warren looked at each other with resignation as clouds of smoke floated past them. Blake rarely smoked, although he had been doing it a lot more since meeting his mother. It was more coughing than smoking, but he felt it necessary to make a point.

Locke tried to get the meeting back a starting point.

"So, Blanche, are you up for a party or not?"

Blanche did a double take.

"Party? Yes, I'm always up for a party. Who isn't. But what party? Where? When?"

"At your place in a few weeks. It depends on when the tech staff can have access."

"What tech staff?"

"We'll need to install small cameras and mics in the rooms we use for the party."

"I don't get it," Blake said. "How does that break up Jasper's gang?"

"Through blackmail."

"Blackmail? But that's not legal, is it?"

"Of course it's legal. We're the police."

"Have I missed something?" Blanche asked.

Locke explained.

"Have you ever heard the term 'honey-trap?' This will be a mega honey-trap. If we can get shots of city authorities that we know are involved with Jasper's boys doing drugs or paying prostitutes, we should be able to put them away with no problem. I'm not saying that if we get a shot of Seligman feeling up a prostitute that we would charge him – but we might be able to use the information to get him to play ball with us instead of Jasper. The more people we can get to testify against Jasper and his boys, the better."

"Who's on the guest list?" Blanche asked.

"That partially depends on who Jasper wants to invite or who you can convince him to invite. You'll know which city officials work with his syndicate. Don't you think he'll want to celebrate all his recent successes? Your venue would be a perfect place to do it. All those free girls."

"Free?"

"Don't worry, the force will foot the bill. The guests will have to bring their own drugs though."

Blanche loved the idea – she couldn't wait to get back at the assholes in city hall. She started adding up all the bigwigs.

"Now let's see, first there's the mayor…"

"The mayor!" Locke said in astonishment. He knew the mayor.

"Oh, sorry, no not the mayor, what's that other guy called – the head of the borough. He's a regular."

"I know who you mean." Locke answered. "He sounds more important than he is. He's just a figurehead but he still wouldn't want to be plastered all over *Page Six*. Who else?"

"I'll meet with Jasper." Blanche said. "He'll want to be careful because some of the city officials won't come if their bosses are going to be there."

"Seligman's the main one we want," Locke said. "I'll leave the list to you and Jasper. Then I'll meet with you to go over it. I have to warn you that I'll need to tell the Commissioner about this."

"Commissioner?" Blanche asked. "I'm not sure I want him to know about my establishment."

"He already does." Warren said. "The entire force

does."

She laughed. "Ah, the price of success! I suppose we do provide a good service."

"We can't do something like this without the Commissioner's knowledge," Locke continued. "He knows my reservations about Seligman, and he knows that Layton was corrupt. Seligman has been asking him to get Warren to resign for some time. Now we know why."

"I talked to the Commissioner after Wang's," Warren said. "I told him how Seligman reacted to the blasts. I was going to keep quiet, but it just kept going through my mind.'

"Now it looks like Seligman might be the one that will have to resign," Locke added.

"Resign?" Blake said. "He should go to jail."

"Lieutenants don't generally go to prison," Locke said. "They resign. It's only when there's a public outrage about brutality or some social issue that they are forced to go to court. In general, they leave the force with a good pension and disappear into the suburbs. Your friend, Candy, may have wanted a house in the suburbs with a white picket fence, but you'd be surprised what's lurking behind that fence in a lot of cases."

Locke turned to Blanche.

"Can you handle a semi-automatic weapon?"

"I have an old Colt 45 at the premises," she said. "Registered legally. I think some of the girls carry weapons, but I don't get involved with that. My place is pretty safe. Why do you ask?"

"You might need some protection on the night of the party. We'll make sure there are a couple of plainclothes officers there, but not too many. We don't want Jasper getting suspicious. You've already got a Beretta, Blake. Rider, we'll go over your weapons list later."

Rider gave him a thumbs up. Blake cringed - 'nobody uses a thumbs up anymore' he thought to himself.

"Will you be at the party? Blanche asked Locke.

"Warren and I will be in a separate room watching everything on monitors. We can always get stills from the video if we need to.

Blanche stood up and put her hand on Locke's shoulder. "You're my kind of guy," she said. They both laughed. "I'm sorry, but I need to get back to my premises," she continued. "I'm supposed to be hosting a party – a real party. Permission to leave?"

Locke patted her hand. "Of course, my dear." Turning to the others he suggested that they sort out the specifics at separate meetings. "Blanche, once you've worked out the guest list with Jasper, can you let me know?"

"No problem." she said, making her exit with a few waves to the group and a blown kiss to her son.

After she had gone, Locke told Blake to make sure that he kept in touch with his mother on a regular basis and to let Rider know about anything that came up.

"Rider! Why Rider?"

"You'll be living with him."

"What!"

"It's easier that way. You can keep tabs on each other."

"But there's only one bed!"

"And a couch."

"I didn't come all the way from the Playa Del Ingles to sleep on a couch," Rider said. "Blake can have the couch."

"It's my apartment! You're smaller than me. You can have the couch."

"Blake," Warren said, "it's the force's apartment."

Blake crossed his arms. "I'm not sleeping on that couch. It's too small for me."

Rider crossed his arms. "Me neither."

Locke intervened: "Okay boys, for God's sake, stop squabbling! You're supposed to be cops. Not kids. The bed is king-sized. You can both sleep on it."

"I'm not sleeping in the same bed with him!" Blake

protested.

«¡*Ni pensarlo*!» Rider said, crossing his arms. "Don't even think of it!"

"Boys, for God's sake, stop it," Warren said. "I'll get hospitality to deliver a portable bed. You can argue about it then."

"You know," Blake said, "if we bust Jasper and his gang, another gang will just replace him. Isn't that what you said before, Warren?"

Warren knew Blake was probably right, but his comment still made him angry – "so what do you suggest? That we never bust *anyone*? That we just let the criminals take over the city?"

Locke put his hand on Warren's right arm on to settle him down.

"Don't worry Blake," Locke said. "I'm talking to SIS about how we can get to Jasper's bosses in London as well – the ones who are really running the show."

"You are?" Warren seemed surprised.

"Yes. I am. I'll fill everyone in on the talks when I can. For now, let's just concentrate on the party."

The meeting broke up soon after that, leaving Rider and Blake on their own.

"What do we do now?" Rider asked.

"Fuck you," Blake said and went into the bedroom, slamming the door behind him. A few seconds later he threw out a blanket and a pillow.

Rider turned on the television, took the ashtray from the table and placed it on the floor next to the couch. He found a joint in the pocket of his jeans and lit it.

Blake opened the bedroom door.

"What the fuck are you doing?"

"I'm chillin,' man." «¿*El problemo?*»

"The 'problemo' is that you're doing illegal drugs. You're supposed to be a cop."

«*Es marihuana medicinal…*»

"Medicinal my ass. For what?"

"*Muchas* illnesses!"

"Oh, never mind. Anyway, you shouldn't be smoking in the apartment."

"Why not? Your mother smoked tobacco."

"Leave her out of this. I don't care what you do. I'm going to bed." He started to go back into the bedroom.

"Hey Blake…"

"What?"

"Do you want a hit?" Rider held out the joint.

Blake paused. "Oh, why not…"

They sat on the couch together passing the joint between them.

"Maybe it will help with my neck pain," Blake said, rubbing his neck unconvincingly.

29. Cancel the Nachos

The weeks that followed that meeting were quickly filled up with more meetings – small meetings between two or three people, so that Seligman wouldn't get suspicious. At one point, he held his own meeting with the Commissioner in order to get his boss' consent to retire Warren early because of his heart condition; but the Commissioner had already been alerted to what was going on by Locke and, although he had considered Seligman's suggestion in the past, this time he hesitated - he told Seligman to "put the retirement on hold" - that Warren was doing an admirable job and good policemen were difficult to find.

"But he can't even run," Seligman protested. "What if he needs to chase a pickpocket or drug dealer?"

The Commissioner looked at Seligman's stomach bulging over his belted slacks and asked him when the last time was that he had chased any criminals.

Seligman laughed good-naturedly at his boss's joke but wondered what was going on. Usually, his boss rubber-stamped anything he suggested. Had Warren told him about that night at Oscar's? 'Damn Warren,' he thought. He could ruin it for everybody if something wasn't done about him. He'd talk to Jasper about it the next time he saw him. Maybe there was another way of getting rid of him. Maybe they could discuss it before the party. He was looking forward to the party. When Blanche had invited him, he accepted immediately, and was looking forward to whooping it up in a group for once. Generally, he avoided parties. He just couldn't trust the other guests. They were usually too respectable. But Blanche's party was going to be a party for Jasper's gang. Seligman spent the weeks leading up to it fantasizing about all the fun he was going to have among the trustworthy crowd of criminals, drug addicts and prostitutes.

Blanche and Jasper compiled the list of party guests carefully – most were either part of Jasper's gang or had connections to it. When Blanche added a guest of her own, Jasper questioned it.

"Who's Rider?" he asked.

"You haven't heard of Rider? Don't worry, he's okay – the lead singer of a new band that's going to be big."

"I guess that's okay. Maybe he'll be a good source of customers in the future. I'll have a word with him."

The party was due to take place on the 22nd of March at 8 pm. All the cameras and microphones had been installed by the previous week, which was when Blanche started calling people on the guest list. She had originally planned to send out printed invitations, but Jasper decided that was a bad idea. It looked too much like evidence.

Blanche took the night off to begin calling people. The first person she called was someone she knew outside of Jasper's crowd – the rapper Toy Boy. Jasper had okayed him – he liked the name and the rapper loved cocaine – another potential customer in the music business.

"But what about the mayor's announcement?" Toy asked Blanche when she invited him.

"I'm not sending out announcements, just phone calls. Besides the Mayor isn't coming."

"No, I meant the announcement that Di Blasio made about the virus."

"What announcement?"

"The bars and restaurants have to close by midnight tonight – take-away only."

"You are joking?"

"No. It's all over the news."

She turned on the news. A reporter was interviewing two young women about the new regulations.

"It will never work," one said.

Her friend agreed: "How can you stop the city that never sleeps at night?"

"Besides, the President says people are over-reacting…"

Blanche returned to her phone call.

"I'll call you back," she said to Toy.

By the time she hung up and called Warren, one of the girls on the television was saying something about "Freedom!" and raising her fist to the camera. Warren told Blanche he would phone Locke and call her back. He called Locke and Locke called the Commissioner.

"The party is in five days. What do we do now?" Locke asked the Commissioner.

"Is Blanche's place a bar?"

"Well, not exactly. But they do serve Champagne."

"You call that Champagne?"

Warren laughed.

"Is Blanche's place a restaurant?" the Commissioner asked.

"No. Not exactly. They do serve nachos."

"Cancel the nachos. No food."

"That shouldn't be a problem."

"Be cautious anyway. Make it look like the place is closed. If any cops come wandering, tell them to call me. I'll be waiting for your call anyway."

Locke called Warren back and Warren called Blanche.

"The party's still on."

On March 20th, Blake got a call from Warren.

"Blake, we need to have one final meeting before the party. Just you, me, Locke and your mother. Tomorrow."

"But isn't a bit late? The party's the next night."

"It's just to make sure that everything is okay – that nobody's backing out at the last minute. Do you think your mother would go for it?"

"It's okay with me, but I'm not sure about mom."

"It's important. I promise that it's the final meeting. Can you call her and let me know? Sorry that it's so last minute."

"Okay, I'll call you back."

Blake rang his mother's private number. She sounded harassed. She didn't even say hello, just "are you okay?" Like he shouldn't be calling unless he wasn't.

"Yeah. Of course."

"Sorry. It's pretty busy right now. I'm at the front desk. What's up?"

"Warren just called me. He wants to have another meeting."

"What! Not another one. The party is the day after tomorrow."

"I know, but he said it was the final meeting."

"That sounds ominous. Are you sure it's not a set-up?"

"How could it be a set-up? It's just me, you and Warren and Locke."

"It's weird that they suddenly decide they need to have a final meeting the night before the party. What time tomorrow?"

"8 pm."

"I guess I can make it. Where? At your place again?"

"He didn't tell me. I'll find out and let you know."

"Wait Blake, did the lawyer call you?"

"No, what's happened now?"

"Now he thinks we won't even get the 500 grand. More likely it will be half that or less, after taxes."

"You can have the half you were going to give me."

"Don't be silly. Whatever it is, you'll get half. I'm too young to retire. I'd only get bored."

"Me too."

Blake called Warren.

"Okay, she's in. Where's the meeting?"

"Meet Locke and me at Pier 99 at 8 pm. We've booked a boat."

"A boat?"

"It was the most secure option. Once we're in the Hudson, it's extremely unlikely that anyone will interrupt the meeting to blast our brains out. And it's a way of avoiding the new regulations – not that we need to. We're cops, after all."

Where's pier 99?"

"Midtown. On the Hudson. Off Clinton Cove Park.

"Where is the boat going?"

"Nowhere. Up and down the river, until the meeting is over. Then we'll come back into port."

Blake liked the idea of the boat. He'd never been up the Hudson. His mother wasn't so eager though. It only added to her suspicions. Although it was true that they might be better protected from "invaders," it would also mean that they'd be at the mercy of whoever else was on the boat. Was he sure that it was only going to be the four of them at the meeting?

"Of course. I trust Warren."

"Okay. I'll meet you at the pier."

After Blanche hung up the phone, she reached into her desk drawer and took out her loaded Beretta. She made sure the safety catch was on and put it into the pocket of her fur coat that was hanging on a coat stand. She didn't want to forget to bring it to the meeting tomorrow, just in case.

30. Pier 99

At just before 8 pm on Saturday night, Blake Webster stood alone on the pavement in front of Pier 99, staring at the dark, undulating reflections of New York's skyscrapers in the water, the normally bright lights of the city dimmed by the new virus regulations which had shut down most of the restaurants and clubs. He could barely see New Jersey on the other side of the river because of a light fog that was drifting on the surface of the water. He had only been to New Jersey once – to visit Sluggo in that strange retirement home. He wondered what would happen to his friend after they busted Jasper, who was paying his bills at the home.

He heard a car approaching behind him, slowly coming to a halt, its headlights temporarily blinding him as he turned around to see his mother coming out of the back seat of a taxi. She stumbled out of the cab as best she could in what she was wearing – a short, tight black skirt and thigh-high patent leather boots – pulling on the bottom of her skirt to make it look longer in front of her son. Blake saw what she was doing and wished she wouldn't dress so much like a prostitute, even if she was one.

"This place looks deserted," she said, as she looked around at the deserted warehouses that surrounded them. Two of the buildings featured Department of Sanitation signage.

"What is going on?" Blanche asked, wrapping her coat around her. "Where is the boat?"

Blake shrugged. "Isn't that a boat?" he asked, pointing to a mooring.

"No, that's a mooring for a boot – a cargo boat. Blake, I don't feel safe here. Are you sure you can trust Warren? Anyone could just drive by and plug us full of holes. We're the only people here."

As if on cue, a small truck came barreling down the

road, catching Blanche's frightened face in its headlights. She screamed and hid behind a dumpster. Blake watched the truck pass and park near the warehouse.

"Would you call that fucking boss of yours and ask him where he is?" Blanche asked, peering out from behind the large bin.

Blake called Warren on his phone.

"Generic guru," the voice on the end of the line said.

Blake couldn't help but laugh at Warren's use of the password. He didn't generally use it for calls – Blake knowing his colleague's personal number was usually sufficient security.

"Yeah, yeah, yeah, generic guru," Blake said. "I'm with my mom on Pier 99, and she wants to know where the boat is. So do I."

"Pier 97."

"But you said it was Pier 99."

"I know. That was for security reasons. We couldn't risk anyone else knowing the real location before you got there. I'll meet you at Pier 97. Don't use your phones after this call. Sorry about that, but you know how it is with security."

"So how do we get to Pier 97?"

"Walk? It's not far."

"Mom's not going to like this," he warned. "She's not exactly dressed for walking. She's wearing these tight black boots with dangerously high, high heels."

"Just so long as she isn't," Warren answered.

"Isn't what?"

"High."

Blake said they'd be there. When he told his mother about the change of plan, he was right. She wasn't very happy.

"For fuck's sake," she said, trying not to get her heels stuck between the stones in the pavement as she walked down the pathway with Blake. "I could be in front of a glass of Champagne right now, making some money."

"I wish you wouldn't mention your other job," Blake said. "I'm supposed to be a cop."

"Whatever..."

They arrived at Pier 97 about fifteen minutes later. Warren was waiting for them, as promised.

"So, where's the boat? Blanche asked, looking at the empty river.

"The boat is actually on Pier 94." Warren said.

"What the hell is going on?" Blake's mother asked.

"I'm sorry Blanche," Warren said, "There was nothing I could do. I was under instructions not to tell you the actual pier until I was with you, to make sure you neither of you called anyone and told them where you were."

"Whose instructions?" Blake asked. "Detective Locke?"

"He's actually a Lieutenant like me, Blake, but never mind. No, not Locke. Don't worry about it. Wait until we get to the meeting. Everything will become clearer. Trust me."

"Now I really am getting suspicious,' Blanche mumbled mostly to herself, but loud enough for her son to hear.

As they approached Pier 94, civilization beckoned. Signs of human life included nighttime joggers taking advantage of a brightly lit path that surrounded Hudson River Park. Restaurants and bars may have been closed but jogging was still allowed.

"Here we are," Warren said. "And thar she blows!" he joked, pointing to a strange configuration of boat and meeting room docked to one of the moors. A long wooden room sat on top of the deck of an even longer speedboat. The round windows of the room were tinted so darkly that it was impossible to see the interior.

Warren and the others were met at the mooring by a

man in a mask.

"What's with the mask?" Blake asked, as they were led onto the boat. It was a light blue surgical-type mask – like the ones they wore in China to protect them from the virus.

"It's just a precautionary matter," Warren explained. "Maritime workers are getting nervous because of the outbreak on that British cruise ship, the Diamond Princess, last month. Two ships in Hawaii weren't allowed to disembark in Hawaii a couple of days ago even though nobody onboard had the virus."

Blanche looked at the boat they were about to get on.

"It's hardly a cruise ship," she commented as she cautiously stepped onto the deck.

She checked that the Beretta was still in her coat pocket once she was on board. They followed Warren to the meeting room where they were surprised to see two strangers, both dressed in conservative, black business suits standing on one side of a long meeting table bolted to the floor. Locke sat opposite them. He didn't stand up.

"Please, have a seat," one of strangers said in an English accent, motioning to three empty seats on the other side of the table. He introduced himself as Merrick as he reached out to shake their hands.

"English?" Blake asked.

"Yes. From London."

"And I'm Clinton," the other stranger said as he offered his hand. He was American – Brooklyn accent, black shiny hair, neatly cropped on the sides, longer on top. Merrick's hair was grey-blonde and balding. He was older than his American colleague. Both were wearing the same shiny black shoes that all cops seemed to wear.

Once everyone was seated, the boat was loosened from its mooring and began its way down the river. Blanche held on to her gun in her pocket. A crew member – not wearing a mask - appeared and asked if anyone would like a drink.

"Now we're talking," Blanche said as she crossed her booted legs while smiling flirtatiously at the American. She thought he was 'hot' - he looked like the gangsters who came to her club.

"I'll have a double whiskey. Straight," she said.

"Me too," Blake seconded.

The others ordered wine or beer.

"Is anyone a vegetarian?" the waiter asked.

Blake thought about saying yes, but then changed his mind. He could always become a vegetarian tomorrow. If the food was free, it might as well be meat.

"The first course will be salmon pate, followed by steak and fries and apple pie for dessert," the bored waiter explained. "Any other requests?"

"That will be fine. Thank you," Blanche said. She wondered why he didn't ask how they would like their steaks cooked. She hated raw meat.

"So, what's up?" Blake asked the English stranger. "Are you one of Jasper's boys?"

"Good God, no." the English stranger replied.

"Then who are you, and you?" Blanche asked pointing to the American stranger. We were told it was going to be a small meeting – to make sure everyone was still committed to the plan."

"It is," Merrick said. "Except there's another plan after that one."

"I knew it was too simple," Blanche said.

"Merrick is my contact in the S.I.S.," Warren said. "The Agency in the UK that used to be called the MI6. He's after Jasper's bosses in England."

"We're particularly interested in how they launder their drug cash to fund terrorist groups in Africa."

The other stranger identified himself as a member of the C.I.S. – the Criminal Intelligence Section – of the NYPD Intelligence Bureau.

"Mr. CIS and Mr. SIS - well, here's to the 'sistas',"

Blanche joked as she held up her glass for a toast. Blake kept quiet as he raised his glass with a sheepish look, embarrassed by his mother's joke.

"I'm sorry I wasn't able to tell you earlier about this meeting" Lieutenant Warren said, "but we couldn't risk anyone else knowing about it, even the other people on the force."

"Even Rider?" Blake asked.

"Even Rider." Warren said.

Blake sat back, satisfied.

"But *why* all the secrecy?" Blanche asked Warren. "Don't you trust *anyone*?"

Locke answered for him. "No, he doesn't." Then the bomb dropped. "Are you familiar with the witness protection program?" he asked Blake and Blanche.

"No way!" Blanche said, standing up. "Nobody mentioned that before." She turned to her son. "You know what they're going to do, don't you? They'll want us to testify. Then they'll hide us away in some rotten suburb in the mid-west. I didn't spend my life working my ass off to end up in fucking Idaho. Definitely not. I'm out of here. The party is over. So is the meeting."

She stood up to leave.

"Mom," Blake said, looking up at her. "You can't leave. We're on a boat."

"How fucking convenient," she growled, as she sat back down.

"We weren't thinking of Idaho," Mr. SIS responded calmly in his Oxbridge accent. "We were thinking of London."

"Huh?"

Warren explained: "Look Blanche. We're not going to end Jasper's operation just by busting his gang over here. We've got to go after the big boys in London. After we bust the party, we want to get you and Blake to London to work undercover there, like you've done here. We want to destroy the syndicate once and for all."

"But how are you going to do that?" Blake asked. "Jasper's bosses in London will know about the bust in New York. They'll know we were involved."

"Will they?" Warren asked.

Locke leaned forward with a serious look on his face. The lines that extended from the edges of his mouth to the beginning of his chin seemed deeper and harder than before, like a ventriloquist's mouthpiece. When he started to speak, it was like somebody else was behind him, pulling on a string.

"Here's the plan," he said...

31. The Party

On the night of March 22, 2020, Blanche stood behind the reception desk of her premises, nervously waiting for the party guests to arrive. The mayor's regulations turned out to be more of a help than a hindrance. It gave her an excuse to close down her place without her regulars becoming suspicious. Not every state had so many restrictions in place – the President was still saying that the Chinese flu would be as temporary as the ordinary flu.

Blanche wished that people would start arriving soon. One of the girls upstairs – a new girl who had arrived about a month ago from Syria - had given her three Captagon pills. She took two and saved one for later. She usually stayed away from the stuff, but she knew that some of the other girls took it too – she never objected to anything the girls took as long as they did their job. Apart from the new regulations, New York was a 24-hour city that needed 24-hour people to keep it going. Who was she to begrudge the girls a few pills if it kept them happy and, most importantly, awake?

Blanche waited for the first arrivals, bug-eyed and trying not to bite her nails. She asked herself if she was doing the right thing. Was Jasper really *that* bad? She had known worse. Leading a moral life didn't come naturally to Blanche. The gears of her brain were turning rapidly now, thanks to the Captagon. Maybe she had got carried away after finding out her son was a cop. God, how she had missed Blake over the years, but thinking about it now, did she really know him? How well can you ever know a memory?

At one point last night, when she was turning and tossing in bed, she had decided not to go through with the plan after all – there was still time to say 'no.' Did she really have the nerve to double-cross Jasper? How could double-crossing a friend be a virtuous act? Wasn't it the ultimate sin? Then she remembered that phone call – where he paid her to give him 'verbal' while someone named Jackie gave him oral. He wasn't a friend. He was a credit card. When she finally fell asleep, she was looking forward to tomorrow's party.

Blake was one of the first guests to arrive. He had promised to come early in case his mother needed help at the front desk. The minute he saw her, he knew she was as high as a kite.

"Mom, don't do any more drugs tonight, you need to have your head together for this. We're not supposed to be having fun."

'Who was he to tell her what to do?' his mom thought. The gears that were already spinning in her head, spun faster, angrier. Sometimes when she looked at Blake, she saw his father.

"Don't worry, darling. One of the girls gave me an upper. Just one. I had problems sleeping last night."

"How many?"

"Just one," she lied (again).

"Well, don't take anymore."

"Of course not, darling."

"I guess I should tell you now, in case anything happens…" He paused and looked at her with a worried expression on his face. "I love you mom."

"I love you too, son," she said, without emotion, like she was reading from a script. Blake went to the door and looked outside. The streets were so empty it was eerie – like the world was standing still. Blanche took advantage of her son's back being turned to pop the third pill that she had been given earlier. She had never been very good at saving her drugs.

The guests began to arrive. There weren't many, but there weren't meant to be - just enough to bust Jasper and his City Hall connections. Jasper arrived first, with two bodyguards, winked, and handed Blake a gold-colored wrap before going upstairs. Blanche pressed a button under the desk and a door to the right opened which led to a short hallway leading to an elevator and stairwell.

"See you guys later," she said as Jasper and his friends took the elevator to the party room on the second floor.

"One of us should go upstairs," Blake's mother said. "Some of the girls are up there to meet and greet, but it would be better to have one of us there as well."

"Don't worry, I'll go," Blake said.

"No, I should go," his mother said. "I know the room better."

Blake watched her suspiciously as she went through the door to the elevator, worried that she was going upstairs to party with Jasper. 'I hope she doesn't fuck this up,' he said to himself.

"Hey dude!"

Blake turned around to see Rider and rolled his eyes. Rider was dressed in full pop star mode – wearing a red velvet suit with a purple Versace scarf slung carelessly around his neck. His name on the guest list was 'Carlos Organza' – the gender-bending singer of a boy band called Frequency.

Under all the velvet was a veritable arsenal - a pistol in each of the two inside pockets of the jacket, a dagger in a leather holder slipped discretely under the cuff of one of his dark green tube socks, and large metal rings on each finger which doubled as knuckle dusters.

Blake buzzed his roommate in without saying anything. Rider barely had time to say, «¡Hola!» before going upstairs.

It wasn't difficult to notice Rider when he entered the party room.

"Excuse me mate, who are you?" Jasper asked. "It's a private party."

Blanche quickly intervened. "Jasper, I told you about Carlos when we were working out the guest list. He's the pop star – not the rapper, the pop star. Carlos Organza. I knew you weren't listening; you never listen to me. He's just signed to Island. He's going to be big."

"Really? What band?"

"Frequency."

"Actually, I think I do remember now. I've heard of you. Welcome to my party."

"Thanks." They bumped fists.

"You sound Spanish." Jasper observed.

"Puerto Rican," he lied. "Don't worry, amigo. I'm cool. Any Champagne around?"

"Of course," Blanche said, confused, trying to remember what she had told Jasper about Rider. She waived over one of the skimpily clad girls carrying trays of Champagne. As more guests arrived, Blanche tried to remember who they were. Had she really invited that many people? They all seemed to know Jasper which was the important thing.

Jasper asked Rider – or Carlos – if he'd like a line.

"Wow, thanks man,"

He rolled out three lines – one for him, one for Rider and one for Blanche.

"Thick New York style lines," Jasper said in his English accent.

"Are you from England?" Rider asked.

"Yeah, I'm from England. Been there?"

"Not yet, but I want to go. Any tips?"

Jasper gave him the low-down on London clubs and told him that if he was there at the same time, he'd be happy to take him on a tour of them. Then he introduced him to some of his "boys," and Rider started making the rounds. Everybody liked Rider. His personality was as innocently floppy as his hair. Nobody would ever suspect him of being a cop, or a martial arts expert, or a walking arsenal.

The room was filling up quickly. Locke and Warren were watching the activities from a locked room. So far, no city bigwigs had arrived. Where was Seligman? Where was the borough president that Blanche had promised? She looked confused, unsteady, overly enthusiastic. When she wasn't trying to talk to people who didn't want to talk to her, she stood on her own at the edge of the room, grinding her teeth.

Seligman finally arrived. Blake accompanied him upstairs, leaving some of Blanche's girls to take over the reception duties on the ground floor. Seligman looked around the party room and asked Blake if Warren was coming.

"I don't think he was invited. It's a private party for Jasper and his friends," Blake answered.

"I like you Blake," Seligman said. "I think we are going to get along just fine in the force. We should go out some night. Do you know Oscar's?"

"I've heard of it, but it's beyond my pay grade, I'm afraid."

"It'll be on me, of course."

Blanche walked over to Seligman from one side of the room and Jasper from the other. She led them to a private room filled with Champagne and a few of Blanche's girls. Jasper rolled out more lines. Seligman was reticent at first, but Jasper encouraged him. "C'mon old man. You're going to need some energy with these girls. We'll leave you alone with them." Jasper quickly did a line and then left the wrap for Seligman and the girls. Blanche followed Jasper into the main room.

Warren and Locke were finally getting the footage they needed. Small cameras hidden under the air conditioning grills in the ceiling were silently filming Seligman doing lines of coke with the prostitutes.

"You don't look old enough to be in a place like this"

he said to one of the girls, after patting his lap for her to come and sit on it. She held her finger to her nose and whispered, "I'm not, I'm only 16." The cameras continued to roll.

The borough president finally arrived, but the girls at reception were on Captagon and too busy talking amongst themselves to think of alerting Blanche. They buzzed him through with barely a look and he went upstairs to a room full of chaos - loud drunks spilling Champagne over each other, scantily clad prostitutes twerking to rap songs, and several opened wraps of cocaine on a table in the middle of the mêlée. When he saw Blanche rushing toward him, bug-eyed and biting her teeth, he quickly turned and left before she could get to him.

"Damn!" Warren said from the security room.

"Don't worry, at least we've got Seligman," Locke said, "but Blanche needs to settle down or she could ruin everything."

Blanche stood looking at the door through which the politician had just left and then turned around to face the room of partygoers. Most looked the other way. She was trying too hard to have fun.

By midnight, people were starting to leave. Blanche entreated them to stay, waving a half-empty bottle of Champagne at them like it was Aladdin's lamp.

"C'mon. It's early...." she pleaded, almost begged.

Someone asked if Pinky's was still open.

"Why wouldn't it be?" Jasper asked.

"Because of the virus restrictions," somebody answered.

"Don't be such a downer. Those were Di Blasio's restrictions, not Trump's!" Jasper said as if that made any difference. He put his arm around Blanche - Blanche, the party girl – who he knew would support him like she always did. 'Such a shame that's she's so old,' he thought to himself.

"New York is invincible!" she shouted cheerfully, backing up the 'gorgeous' man who had his arm around her. He turned and kissed her on the mouth. She wrapped her tongue around his and wouldn't let him go. She loved Jasper, she really did. Okay, maybe he could be a creep sometimes, but, if she was honest to herself, they always had a blast together – at least when she was on Captagon.

Blake watched with disgust. His mother was out of control. He looked away, only to have a flute of Champagne waved in front of his face like a hand puppet.

"I'll drink to that," the voice belonging to the Champagne waver said. It was Rider.

"Drink to WHAT?" Blake asked angrily, thinking he was referring to the sloppy kiss that had just taken place.

"To New York being invincible," Rider said. "Chill out, man."

Blake gave him a dirty look. He felt like slugging both of them - Rider and Jasper.

"Hey Blakey boy, what's the matter?" Jasper asked, his arm now tightly wound around the waist of Blake's mother. "Why don't you join in the fun?"

Blake scowled. "You call this fun?"

"Blake, please, no trouble." Blanche slurred.

"If you don't want trouble, tell him to shut his mouth," Blake answered.

"Easy, mate." Jasper motioned Blake over and offered him a line on the table.

"C'mon, lighten up. Have some fun. You're only young once. You're acting like an old man. Look at all the babes in the room. You haven't gone gay since your affair with Candy, have you?"

Blake pushed Jasper back by his neck.

"Who told you about Candy?" he asked.

"Your mom. Who else?"

Blake squeezed his neck harder. He had him up against the wall now, behind a filing cabinet.

"Listen you mother fucker," he said to Jasper. "If you don't leave my mother alone, you're dead."

"Blake, please!" his mother pleaded. "Leave him alone. I can take care of myself!"

Jasper laughed. "You're a mommy's boy, ain't ya?" he said to Blake.

The words "mommy's boy" went round and round in his head. It was what his father used to call him. He needed some air. He let go of Jasper's neck and headed toward the exit. Then he heard his mother ask Jasper if he was okay.

Jasper? She was asking if *Jasper* was okay? What about her son? Blake turned around, grabbed Jasper's neck again and hit his head against the wall – not enough to knock him out but enough for him to fall on the floor. Then he calmly walked to the other side of the room and poured himself a glass of Champagne as if nothing had happened. As far as everyone else in the room was concerned, nothing *had* happened. The action had all taken place behind a filing cabinet and Jasper had already started to stand up by the time Blake took his first sip of bubbly.

Blanche helped Jasper up. When she noticed his nose was bleeding, she got scared. Nobody gave Jasper a bloody nose, particularly a young upstart like Blake. She tried to wipe the blood off with her sleeve, telling him not to worry, that everything would be okay.

Jasper pushed her aside and went for Blake. Blake pulled out the gun he kept under his jacket.

"Blake, no! You don't know what you're doing! Put the gun away," his mother screamed from across the room.

Jasper stopped when he saw the gun. He wished he had his. He wondered where his bodyguards were – probably in a private room with some of Blanche's girls – dirty buggers.

"Blake, put the gun away!" his mother repeated. As she walked toward him, she grabbed her coat, which she had flung over a chair earlier, and reached into the pocket. Her gun was still there.

Jasper told Blake not to be so stupid. "You're supposed to be working for me, you idiot!"

Blake could see his mother out of the corner of his eye, getting her gun out of her coat and pointing it not at Jasper, but at him.

"Mom!" Blake yelled, surprised. "Whose side are you on?"

"I'm on your side baby. But you can't shoot Jasper. He's too powerful. Nobody will survive if he dies."

"I see how it is now" Blake said to his mother. "You were lying all the time."

"Drop the gun, Blake." Jasper said. "It's not worth it."

Seligman came out of his private room, looking for more Champagne. The scene that confronted him was Blake pointing his gun at Jasper and Blake's mother pointing her gun at her son. He immediately pointed his gun at Blanche whose eyes were rolling in their sockets like errant marbles.

"What fucking drug are you on?" he shouted at her. "He's your fucking son, for God's sake. Everyone, drop your weapons now!"

He knew that both mother and son were working for Jasper, but if he had to make a choice about who to shoot, he'd have to choose Blanche. Blake was a cop – a 'good guy.' There would be too many ramifications. Blanche was a criminal, a prostitute. A jury would think that she deserved what she got.

'Where were those fucking bodyguards,' Jasper asked himself.

Seligman took the first move, but not by shooting anyone. He swept the room with his gun, without firing, and quickly left, escaping while the going was good –

before anybody got shot and the real cops – the do-gooders on the force, arrived.

As Seligman ran down the stairs, Blake checked his aim in the rear sight of his Beretta. Blanche stared at her son like she didn't know who he was. Her pistol hand was starting to shake.

Blake cocked his pistol.

"I'm going to enjoy this," he said.

There was a loud bang as the pistol went off. But it wasn't from Blake's gun.

Blake slid to the floor, holding his chest. Hyped up on Champagne and Captagon, Blanche had shot her own son in order to protect Jasper. She knelt down, next to Blake's body, screaming "No!" She tried to 'will' him alive. "I love you!" she said. They were her last words to him. His parting words to her were "Fuck you bitch!" Then he was gone.

Blanche looked up at Jasper. "You killed him, you mother fucker, you killed my son!" But too many people in the room had seen what happened and had heard what was said. Jasper wasn't the person who pulled the trigger.

Then the sirens began. Some people managed to escape from the police who invaded the room, but most ended up in handcuffs. An ambulance took Blake's body away along with his sobbing mother. Officers quickly searched the other rooms, blasting locks open with their guns. They found Jasper's bodyguards with some prostitutes in one room and arrested all of them. They opened a second private door and found a person in a red velvet suit dabbing out a lit joint with his moistened fingers.

"Hey man, it's medical," Rider said. "I'm a cop."

When another group of officers opened the door to a third private room, they were surprised to be confronted by two men in suits, holding up NYPD ID cards. Guns drawn; the officers moved closer. They looked at the photographs on the ID cards and at the two men in front of them.

Lieutenants Warren and Locke raised their arms and said, almost at the same time, "don't shoot, we can explain everything."

32. The Phone Call

Perched on his usual bar stool at Oscar's, Captain Seligman let his phone ring without answering it. The bar should have been closed because of the new regulations, but like a lot of bars in New York, they managed to look closed, without being closed. As long as the staff knew you and you knew how many times to knock, you could get in. Only the bar was open though. The dining area was off-limits.

"Is that your phone?" Sal, the bartender, asked.

"Yeah. Don't worry about it," Seligman said.

The captain had stayed away from Oscar's for a few weeks after the incident at Wang's, not sure if he would still be welcome once the staff knew he was a cop. But Oscar's was such a good pick-up joint that he couldn't resist returning. When he did, the staff welcomed him with open arms. They didn't care if he was a cop. Given his apathetic response to what happened at Wang's, they assumed he was a crooked cop, and crooked cops came in handy in the hospitality business. So did his big tips.

Seligman sipped his whiskey and wondered how the stand-off at Blanche's had resolved itself. It was doubtful that Blanche would shoot her son or that Blake would shoot his new partner-in-crime. Arguments like that always seemed so dramatic to begin with, but usually simmered down fairly quickly. Blake and his mother had probably reached the soppy stage by now – saying how much they loved each other over spilt glasses of Champagne.

As far as Seligman was concerned, he was never at the party. Who would accept the testimony of prostitutes and drug addicts over a captain in the police force? When Big Sal, the barman, made small talk when Seligman arrived and asked him what he'd been up to that evening, he answered "nowhere, I've been here most of the night," Sal just winked and said "that's right, you're visiting a friend – me. Just two friends hanging out because we're closed."

"Sounds right to me," Seligman said as he slapped down a hundred-dollar tip on the bar.

Seligman's phone rang again. He looked at the screen. Warren. He had probably heard about the party. Seligman answered this time. He'd have to talk to Warren at some point and at least, this way, Warren would be able to hear the sound of his alibi in the background.

"Hey Warren. How's it hanging?" Seligman asked.

"We have to talk."

"I'm at Oscar's. Wanna join me for a drink?"

"It's open?"

"No, they're closed. I'm visiting a friend. You remember old Sal, don't you?"

"How long have you been there?"

"All night. Why? Has something happened?"

"We have a problem. Or, rather, you have a problem."

"Lay it on me. I love solving problems. What's up?"

"Well, the main problem is…"

"Yes?"

"You're a fucking asshole, Seligman."

He knew that Warren had resented him ever since Wang's, but he wasn't going to take that sort of abuse from an inferior rank.

"I could fire you for being so disrespectful, Warren."

"Disrespect this, bitch."

Seligman's phone bleeped. Warren had sent him a photograph - a picture of the captain doing a line of coke with Jasper.

"Where did you say you were tonight?" Warren asked again.

"Where did you get this?" Seligman asked, trying not to sound panicked. "It's been photoshopped. Who's the other person in it?"

Seligman tried to figure out who could have taken the

photograph. One of Jasper's boys? But then how did Warren get it? And why would one of Jasper's boys double cross him? One of the guests must have been undercover. That Puerto Rican guy seemed suspicious – Carlos whatever his name was. Who was he anyway?

"Are you saying you weren't at Blanche's tonight?" Warren asked.

"No. I was here. Sal, wasn't I here all night?" He held up the phone so Sal could vouch for him except Sal wasn't there anymore. He'd been replaced by a different bartender.

"I'm Mike," the new bartender said.

"What happened to Sal?"

He shrugged - "His shift ended. Why? What do you need? That looks like whiskey to me. Double or single?"

"Fuck off," he said to Mike. "What do you want?" he asked Warren.

"An ambulance plane to London. Blake is in a medically induced coma. He needs a heart transplant. He might not even survive with that. A contact in SIS found one on ice in London – but we need to get him there within 24 hours."

"What the fuck happened at the party?"

"Blanche shot her son to protect Jasper. But don't worry, the place was raided, and Jasper was arrested too."

Warren seemed to know a lot about the party for someone who wasn't there.

"That Carlos guy was undercover, wasn't he, Warren?" Seligman said.

"Carlos Organza? He's a pop star, you idiot."

"Why do you have to go all the way to England for a heart, Warren? What's wrong with an American heart?"

"There aren't any."

"What? How can an entire country not have a single fucking heart?" Seligman screamed over the phone. "There must be a heart somewhere. What about the

Midwest? There must be tons of hearts in the Midwest. It's huge."

"There are too many regulations over here. Blake would have to be put on a waiting list."

"But he's a cop! It's an emergency!"

"Yes, it is an emergency. You're right. That's why we have to get him to London, NOW. You know there's a plane sitting at JFK for emergencies like this, it just needs your authority."

"No, it needs the Commissioner's authority. Why don't you bug him about it?"

"Good idea."

Another bleep. Warren had sent him a short film. Seligman pressed 'play' and watched himself snorting cocaine with a 16-year-old prostitute on his lap.

"I should have forced you to resign after your cardiac arrest," Seligman said.

"Seligman, call the Commissioner, get permission for us to use that plane and you'll remain a cop. Nobody's going to say anything about you being at that party. I'm the only person with the footage."

"But how…"

"Never mind. Just get the fucking plane."

"Okay, okay, I need to make a call. How soon can you get to the airport?"

"We're in an ambulance now. Less than an hour."

"Okay, just get to the airport. And make sure everyone has their passports."

"They do."

Seligman had a direct line to the Commissioner. He explained Blake's situation without mentioning the party – "he was running after some guy who had grabbed a woman's purse and the guy turned around and shot him."

"Were there any witnesses?"

"I think Blake's mother was there. Right now, we just need the plane. Can you approve it?"

"Yes, of course, I'll make the call right now…"

After Seligman ended his call to the Commissioner, he searched for "Carlos Organza" on his phone's browser. The only thing that came up were listings for fabric suppliers. He rang one of Jasper's flunkies.

"Don't talk," Seligman said when the guy picked up. "And get rid of the phone after the call."

"Okay. Go ahead."

"I know what happened at the party. There was somebody named Carlos there – he was supposed to be a pop star, but it looks like he was undercover. He's got films. Kill him and his phone."

"No problem. I'll get one of the boys on it immediately."

"Tell Jasper we need to do something about Warren too."

"Jasper's in jail."

"I know. But he'll probably be out soon. Tell him I want to see him."

"Will do."

"But, for now, just get Carlos, as soon as you possibly can."

"Consider it done."

33. The End

When Warren made his call to Seligman, he was already sitting in the force's ambulance plane at JFK. Mr. SIS, the representative of England's security force who had participated in the meeting on the boat, was seated next to him, listening in on the call; as soon as it ended, the jet's engines started up and the flight to England began.

The passenger seats were arranged in a column of six two-seated rows on the right-hand side of the plane's interior. Behind Warren and Mr. SIS was Blanche, who had a row to herself, then Locke and Amanda, the nurse who had helped Blake to detox in the Canaries the previous year and finally, Rider, aka 'Carlos Organza' who also had his own row. Although Seligman had issued the order to "get Carlos," it was unlikely that anyone would be able to reach him in mid-air.

Blake was in a hospital bed on a trolley locked to the floor on the left-hand side of the plane, his face covered by an oxygen mask, and cannulas attached to both of his forearms with bandages. Narrow tubes led from the cannulas to two separate bottles of liquid that hung on tripod-like stands that were also locked into place. Three thick straps held his body firmly to the trolley bed.

The passengers were silent while Warren was on the phone to Seligman, but as soon as he hung up, he turned to Mr. SIS and said, "Looks like he fell for it." Everyone cheered. The plan had worked.

"Can I get up now?" a muffled voice asked. It was Blake speaking from his oxygen mask.

"Hold on, darling," Amanda said. She unlocked her seat belt, went to the side of his trolley, and removed his mask.

"Thank god," Blake said. "I felt like I was suffocating."

"Sorry about that," Amanda said. "Here, let me undo these straps." She took off the tape that held the fake cannulas in place and undid the straps holding him to the bed. "There's an empty seat next to your mother."

"Sorry mate," Mr. SIS said. "We had to make it look convincing, although I doubt if anyone even saw us. Better safe than sorry."

"What a night!" Blake said, as he sat down next to his mother. "Thank god the vest worked."

"It was only a blank, darling," Blanche reassured him.

"Still, it's kind of weird being shot by your own mother!"

Everyone laughed. An outsider would have seen a happy group of people, possibly embarking on a holiday together. A male steward with an English accent asked if anyone was a vegetarian. Blake decided that now was not the time to begin his vegetarian diet – maybe once he got to London.

"Dinner or breakfast or lunch, depending on what time zone your brain is operating in," the steward continued "will be an old English specialty – fish and chips. Okay with everyone?"

Blanche waved her hand. "Could I have something other than potato chips?"

"No luv," the steward said. "Chips are French fries in England. Are fries, okay?"

"Oh yes, perfect. Thank you so much."

The steward gave her a camp curtsy in return and Blanche almost applauded. Blake cringed.

"What about booze?" Blanche asked, too loudly.

The steward smiled and asked if Champagne was okay.

"Champagne is always okay, darling."

'It's like they're old friends,' Blake thought.

"We thought you'd like to toast to your success" the steward said to the group in general, without knowing what their success had been. They looked like they had enjoyed their adventure and wished that he could have an adventure someday. Sometimes it seemed like the only excitement he ever got from life was popping other people's corks and eavesdropping on their conversations. He wondered who Seligman was and what the film footage was that Warren had sent to him.

When everyone had a glass of Champagne in their hand (Locke didn't drink, so his glass was filled with carbonated water - or "sparkling water" as it was called in England), Mr. SIS stood up at the front of the plane and offered a toast "to success!"

"To success!" the passengers said as they raised their glasses. Blanche slurred her toast noticeably, not having fully recovered from last night's party. It would be night again by the time they arrived in London.

Mr. SIS's toast turned into a speech: "First of all, I'd like to thank everyone, particularly you Blake and Blanche, for carrying through with the plan so perfectly. I hope the rest of it is as successful. Blake, I'm sorry we had to transport you in an ambulance, but it was the only way to make it seem like your mother really had shot you. And we need both of you for our plan in London."

Locke added: "That's why I had to keep the Commissioner updated. He knew that Seligman was going to call him for permission to use the plane."

"You mean he knew we were going to London from the beginning?" Blake asked.

"Not exactly. When I first told him about the party, it was because I had to. We couldn't do something like the party without his permission. But as things got moving, the plan broadened. He knew about London by the time of the meeting on the boat."

"I still don't understand why we had to take the drastic measure of me shooting my son!" Blanche said.

"Shooting Blake might have seemed like a drastic move," Mr. SIS said, "but at least it showed the length you would go to in order to save your friend, Jasper. With that sort of credential, we should have no problem introducing you into the upper echelon of Jasper's gang in London. You'll keep low for a couple of weeks after you arrive – it will give us time to fill you in on everything – and then reappear. Blake will disappear for a period, as well, before he is also introduced to the gang."

"How does that work?" Blanche asked. "I can understand why Jasper's boss would trust me – I tried to save the life of his No. 1 man – but why would he trust Blake?"

"It will partially be up to you Blanche, to convince him," Locke said.

"But Blake would be too ill to join a gang if he had a heart transplant!" Blanche said.

"Don't worry about that, Blanche," Mr. SIS interjected, "Once Blake gets to London, it will turn out that his condition is not as bad as we thought. After a few stents, he'll be as good as new. He won't really have the stents implanted, of course, because he won't need them. His heart is perfectly fine, but Jasper's boss doesn't need to know that."

"But Jasper's boss will talk to Jasper in prison. Jasper will give Blake away!" Blanche said.

"That's exactly why we did things the way we did," Mr. SIS said. "Blake only got angry at Jasper because of how he was treating you. He certainly didn't turn him into the cops. As far as Jasper's gang is concerned Blake is still a crooked cop."

"And what about Seligman?" Blanche asked.

"What about him?" Warren said. "He thinks I'm the bad guy – or the good guy – depending on your view. And that Rider aka Carlos was acting undercover."

"The whole syndicate will be after me," Rider said.

"Well, you are clearly *suspected* of being undercover and that information will be passed on to Jasper's boss, no doubt," Mr. SIS said. "But Seligman has no proof that you were undercover, and besides, by the time the gang in

England meets you, you'll be somebody else. Remember, there was no Carlos Organza."

"But where will I live? What will happen to me when we land?"

"For now, we've arranged for you to have a flat in the Ladbroke Grove section of London. You'll have protection – a shadow – which has already been arranged. Lay low for a while to give our English connections time to spread the rumour that Seligman was the double-crosser. Not exactly difficult to believe."

Blanche leaned forward in her seat to get the attention of SIS.

"Okay, so Rider gets a house in some orange grove, but what about Blake and me? Where do we live?"

"Ladbroke Grove isn't exactly an orange grove," Mr. SIS explained. "It's an area in West London. Blake and you will get a two-bedroom apartment in Central London. We have access to some flats in a small cul-de-sac named Grimm Street. They look like offices, but they're actually residential."

"Grim Street?" Blanche asked.

"With two 'm's' - named after the fairy tale writers – the Brothers Grimm." Locke explained.

"The building is already under surveillance because of the other residents," SIS continued. "Ex-cons, retired dealers, that type of person. The perfect place for two 'criminals' like yourself. Try to make friends with your neighbors. We might be able to arrest them."

The food arrived. Mr. SIS told everyone to "tuck in."

"We need some music," Blanche said and asked if the radios on the back of the seats worked. Rider tried the one in front of him and was able to tune into some stations. He scrolled through them, but they were mostly news.

"Hold on," Blanche said. "I want to hear if there's anything about the bust."

Rider tried to find something about the bust, but most

of the stations were broadcasting stories about the Chinese virus. As he continued to search for some music, Blake's phone rang.

'It's Sluggo!" Blake said after looking at his screen. He pressed the phone icon to answer it. "Sluggo?"

"Blake! I finally got through."

Where are you?"

"Well, I'm standing at the Port Authority terminal with about five shopping bags full of crap from the retirement home. Jasper got busted and they kicked me out. They stuffed a roll of bills in my hand, told me not to talk to anyone and called me a cab. I guess my contract is cancelled."

"Sluggo, hold on a second. No, actually, let me call you back in a second. I'm on a plane."

"A plane! You can use your phone on a plane? Are you going on a holiday? I thought I might be able to crash at yours."

"Well, not exactly a holiday, but yeah, phones work in planes. I'll call you back in about ten minutes."

Blake had a conversation with Warren and Locke. As soon as they were all in agreement, he called Sluggo back. Meanwhile Warren called a friend at headquarters.

"Sluggo, can you get back to your bar?"

"What good would that do? It's not my bar anymore."

"Don't worry about that. There'll be a policeman waiting for you with the keys. It's yours again. They'll be busting those losers who took it over soon, if they haven't done so already. They won't be back."

"Wow, Blake, that would be great. Are you sure?"

"I'm sure alright. And email me your bank details. I'll make sure you're taken care of."

"My god Blake, I didn't know you were so important. Who are you?"

"Don't worry about that. Just get back to your place."

"Yeah, sure. Thanks."

He could hear Sluggo running, then stopping, out of breath. "Hello?" he said.

"It's me Blake."

"Oh, sorry about that I forgot to hang up," Sluggo said. "One other thing Blake. I just wanted to say thanks. Thanks a lot. Nothing interesting ever happened to me until you came along. Now my life is really exciting!"

Blake's heart was warmed. He would have hugged Sluggo if he could.

"Everything will be fine in the future, my friend. Just like the old days," Blake said.

"Gotta go, Blake. I'm here now. Thanks again for everything."

Sluggo hung up. He had reached his old bar. He looked up at the Pinky's sign and was determined to get rid of it as soon as possible. A cop was standing in front of the building.

"Are you Sluggo?" he asked.

"Yeah. Are you a friend of Blake's?"

"Yeah. Sort of."

The officer had the keys to the front door with him and he helped Sluggo inside with his bags. Sluggo stood there, looking at all the changes. Even though there was a weird clock on the wall behind the bar and an even weirder juke box by the door, it still felt like the same place. The walls were a brighter colour but 'nothing that a lick of black paint couldn't fix,' he told himself.

Sluggo felt like he had come home. He wondered if Johnny was still a regular at the bar. He looked forward to seeing him again when the regulations ended. It would probably only be a couple of weeks or so before they got this virus thing under control. Who would have thought that he would miss the bar so much, that the days he had spent listening to alcoholics telling him their problems would later become the "good old days," like Blake had referred to them. But they really were the good old days.

He really had come home. He felt like he was going to cry. He couldn't wait to see Johnny to tell him about that crazy retirement home.

"Hey," Rider shouted out from the back of the plane. Do they have medical marijuana in England?"

Blake groaned.

"Don't worry. You'll be fine in Ladbroke Grove," Mr. SIS reassured him.

"Cool."

Rider finally found a station playing music – a slow rap called *Super Real*: "Take off your shoes and chill, that's how the music feel, we should just smoke and chill, just keep it super real…"

"Tune!" Rider exclaimed excitedly.

"Can't you find something we can dance to?" Blanche asked. "Like old-fashion disco?"

The music suddenly stopped, and the DJ came on to announce that the Prime Minister was about to make a speech.

"What's a Prime Minister?" Blanche asked.

Mr. SIS hushed everyone and explained that the Prime Minister was the President of Great Britain. Boris Johnson began to speak:

"Good evening. The coronavirus is the biggest threat this country has faced for decades – and this country is not alone. All over the world we are seeing the devastating impact of this invisible killer..."

"Invisible killer?" Blanche interrupted, drunkenly. "Sounds like the Invisible Man. Ha, ha. Do you remember the Invisible Man, Blake? We watched it on TV when you were a kid…"

"Mom, please, this is serious."

She shook her empty glass at a steward and gave him a wink. "Can I have a top up please?"

Warren gave Blake a 'can you please do something about your mother' look as the steward poured her another glass of Champagne.

Boris Johnson continued with his speech:

"...So, it's vital to slow the spread of the disease. And that's why we have been asking people to stay at home during this pandemic. And though huge numbers are complying - and I thank you all - the time has now come for us all to do more. From this evening I must give the British people a very simple instruction - you must stay at home..."

"Huh?" Blanche said to nobody in particular. "Stay at home where?"

Johnson continued: "... the critical thing we must do is stop the disease spreading between households. You should not be meeting friends. If your friends ask you to meet, you should say no. You should not be meeting family members who do not live in your home. You should not be going shopping except for essentials like food and medicine - and you should do this as little as you can. And use food delivery services where you can. If you don't follow the rules the police will have the powers to enforce them, including through fines and dispersing gatherings."

Rider turned the volume up.

"To ensure compliance with the Government's instruction to stay at home, we will immediately close all shops selling non-essential goods and other premises including places of worship; we will stop all gatherings of more than two people in public – excluding people you live with; and we'll stop all social events, including weddings, baptisms and other ceremonies..."

"Is this a joke?" Blanche asked.

The Prime Minister continued, "We will beat the coronavirus and we will beat it together. And therefore, I urge you at this moment of national emergency to stay at home, protect our NHS and save lives. Thank you."

"What's the NHS?" Blanche asked.

"The English medical system," Mr. SIS explained.

The radio DJ came back on: "And that was a message from the Prime Minister..."

The D.J.'s voice faded away and instead of music, there was only static. Mr. SIS stood up, excused himself, and went into the cockpit. The rest of the passengers reached out to the steward with their empty glasses.

When SIS returned, he reassured everyone that there was nothing to worry about, that he had spoken to the pilot who was in touch with Heathrow, and that the plane would land as planned. Cars would be ready to take them to their destinations in the city, and he would have more information for them later.

The passengers looked at each other, not knowing whether to be worried or not. Their own President had said there was nothing to worry about in regard to the virus, that it was just another version of the ordinary flu. The English "president" seemed to think otherwise.

"Fuck Boris Johnson," Blanche said, as she held up her glass defiantly. "Here's to the future!"

"To the future..." everyone repeated, dutifully holding up their newly filled glasses of Champagne, more confused than defiant. They sat in their seats sipping quietly to the sound of static, not realizing that the future to which they had just toasted was about to land them into a pandemic that would change at least some of their lives forever.

Finally, somebody spoke. Leaning over her son's armrest, Blanche slurred, "What happened to the fucking music..."

[end]

Printed in Great Britain
by Amazon

84845278R00150